AFTER THE BALL

by

NEIVE DENIS

Book seven in the Sonoma Whittington series

Copyright

First published in 2020
Copyright © Neive Denis 2020

Cataloguing-in-publication data
Creator: Denis, Neive, author

Cataloguing-in-Publication details are available from the National Library of Australia
www.trove.nla.gov.au

ISBN: 978-0-6483950-5-8 (paperback)
ISBN: 978-0-6483950-6-5 (digital edition)

Contents

Other Books by the Author

An Ancient Solution
A public Service
Missing!
Connections
A Different Obsession
Shattered Illusions

Chapter 1

It's not good news when the phone rings in the middle of the night. I stumbled out of bed, fumbled for the phone and croaked, "Whittington Investigations…"

"Sonny, it's me, Emily. Callum is missing. I don't know what to do. I don't know what's happened, but I think it's something terrible."

"Emily, what part of the world are you in at the moment? And, have you any idea what the time is here in Millhaven?"

"Yes, I know it's a ridiculous hour to call anyone, but I'm a long way from home. I know something bad, very bad, has happened to Callum. The police aren't interested. We were at a B&S ball. They, the Police that is, are treating his disappearance as just another drunk who wandered away and collapsed somewhere to sleep it off. That's not the case. He wasn't drunk before he disappeared. There is no sign of him, and I have looked everywhere."

"Are you sure it's not because your *very special Callum* isn't by your side that you think something terrible has happened to him. What sort of 'terrible' might it be, and what makes you think that's case? Tell me what happened."

"We were at a B&S ball. I still am. It was held in very noisy old tin hall. Callum wasn't enjoying the night much; nor was I. He said he was going out to the bar for a drink and to give his ears a rest. Someone got me up for a dance, so I said I would join him outside as soon as the dance finished. The band played a couple of encores… the dance lasted longer than expected. When I went outside, I couldn't find Callum. I looked everywhere. *I did look for him.* I even went inside again to search for him in case he had gone back in there without my noticing him. *A*fter about half an hour inside, and still with no sign of him,

I went outside and searched everywhere again. He isn't here."

"You don't suppose he decided enough was enough and went home? Perhaps he thought you were enjoying yourself and didn't want to spoil your night by dragging you away with him."

"I've tried calling him several times and left messages. He wouldn't go home without me; not without telling me first he was going. He knew I wasn't enjoying myself. Just as we decided to leave, this other bloke asked me to dance. Callum told me to have the dance, and then we would leave straight afterwards. I said I would meet him outside to find our vehicle and leave."

"It's not hard to understand why the police weren't interested, but there are a few things I'm having trouble understanding. Here's the list: where are you, why did you call me, and what do you expect me to do when you're where ever you are and I'm here in Millhaven?"

"Sonny, I need your help. Look, we could spend the next hour discussing this, but I really would like you here to help me work out what's happened. And … I have a funny feeling, when we do find out, I might need a friend. He was – is someone special. I think he might be the one to figure in my future. Maybe that helps you understand why I'm frantic about his disappearance. It is not like him to just go off and leave me. When I was asking some of the blokes if they had seen him, they made vague references to an incident in town earlier tonight. A couple of them thought Callum might have been with the group involved. God knows why he would do that, or if they are right. Please, Sonny, I need your help. I know the outcome is going to be bad."

Wide-awake now, I could see no point in going back to bed. Instead, I took myself off to the office via the kitchen to grab a cup of coffee. Then, with the computer also awake, it was time to document the key points of Emily's call. First, I asked Google Maps to show me where Emily and Callum were spending the weekend. For a few years, Emily's employment with the mining company's operations kept her based in the mine's town of Moxton.

Two years ago, that mine, along with several others in the region, was taken over by a major international company. Around twelve months ago, the company centralised those operations common to all of its mines in this region. Millhaven's central location made it the place to locate those common functions. Planning, HR, testing and analysis, and several other administrative departments relocated to a new set-up here. As part of the relocation, Emily, a chemical engineer, moved to live and work here too. Callum worked in the planning department and moved to Millhaven when his department moved from Brisbane to their new central complex.

"Okay Google, show me where *Winyard* grazing property is." It took a moment or two for Google to respond. The map it produced wasn't much use until I looked at it in much finer detail. "Ah hah, so that's where you're spending the long weekend." Winyard wasn't too far west of Moxton. The area's central town appeared to be Cranvale rather than Moxton. It was a four- to five-hour drive from Millhaven to Moxton. I figured from Moxton to Winyard would add about another two hours to the trip. From Emily's information, I understood the ball was being held in some sort of shed type building on the periphery of Cranvale.

With all the key points of Emily's conversation recorded, I sat back to reflect on her situation. Perhaps she was entitled to feel concerned about Callum's disappearance. It was out of keeping with what I knew of him. My gut told me whatever lured him away from that ball was nothing good. Although I wasn't aware of making a conscious decision, I knew I was about to spend seven or more hours on the road.

After packing, I called Emily to tell her I was coming, woofed a quick breakfast, and was on the road as dawn streaked the sky pink and gold. My original intention was to drive to Cranvale to organise accommodation before doing anything else. Emily insisted I make Winyard my base. Spending tonight at Wynyard made sense. Cranvale was another two hours beyond Winyard, making it a long day's drive. Claire, Emily's friend and daughter of the property owners, already had prepared a room for me.

Claire Darnell and Emily became friends at university. Their friendship continued through Claire's years overseas. After she came home to help run Winyard, the two women managed to meet up at least two or three times a year. As far as I knew, this was Emily's first visit to the property to see her friend since Claire came home. Maybe it was the first time ever. I don't recall ever hearing Emily speak of visiting the place.

By mid-afternoon, it was ridiculously warm for a spring day. After driving into the blazing sun since early morning, I was pleased to be going only as far as Winyard. I turned off the highway onto a dusty track running through the property. The big old homestead sat amidst a green oasis perched on top a slight rise. A few big old trees and just about every imaginable type of shrub shaded and cooled the house.

Emily bounded down the steps to meet me. She flung open my car door and reached in to hug me. "Thank you. Thank you for coming, Sonny. When the police weren't interested, I didn't know what else to do except to call you. I think whatever you discover out here will not be good news. But, I want to be involved. I want to help." She hurried me through to my room. It was spacious, had a high ceiling and, as with every other room in the building, opened onto the wide veranda running around all sides of the homestead. That was all I had time to notice about the room before being called to join Claire and Emily on the veranda for iced tea.

As soon as the usual requisite pleasantries were over, I began what proved to be a tortuous process of extracting information from the two women. I needed to know everything that happened from when they left Winyard for the B&S ball until this morning. We barely began when Claire left to answer a phone call. It provided an opportunity to gather some background information from Emily. "Tell me how this weekend came about."

"Since she came back, Claire's been nagging me to come out here for the festival. Well, more to the point, to attend the B&S ball. Her long-held ambition seems to be for me to come out here and meet the man of my dreams. She probably was a little disappointed when I brought Callum with me. Anyway, it sounded like it should be a good weekend. Callum and I took a flex day off to make a long weekend of it."

"Callum fitted right in with Claire and me. We both helped Claire with setting up for the ball. Then, we came back here late in the afternoon to dress for the ball before being back in Cranvale by seven o'clock."

"That was an early start. I would expect a ball to kick off a bit later than that."

"You're right. The official start time was eight o'clock. A few arrived as it started, but there weren't many people until about 8.30pm. We needed to be there early to see to a few last-minute things."

Although I didn't want to pre-empt what I might find, I couldn't help feeling whatever happened to Callum would wreck the weekend for everyone involved. As I expected, nothing happened before the ball got underway. So, it was time to find out what happened after that. "Okay, so the crowd arrived and were enjoying themselves. Tell me about the set up at the hall."

"Let me think. The band started playing around 8.30 p.m. There was quite a good crowd by then. Everyone began dancing – and being rowdy – as soon as they arrived. The hall is big, but it wouldn't have coped with the crowd if everything was set up inside. That's why the bar tent and the food marquee were outside. Oh, and the toilet block is a separate brick building to the rear of the hall."

"I assume, at some point during the night, everyone ventured outside for one reason or another – even just to escape the noise."

"Yes, that's true. I don't know whether it was because we didn't know people, or because it wasn't our sort of thing, but neither Callum nor I was enjoying it. A bit before eleven o'clock, Callum came over and shouted to me that he was going out to the bar to get a drink, and to give his ears a break from the noise for a while. With band so loud, everyone inside the hall tried to speak above it. That resulted in nobody hearing anything anyone said."

"You said you didn't go outside with Callum…"

"No. As Callum finished telling me he was going outside, Claire's current heartthrob came over and asked me for a dance. The bloke – his name is Terry – is manager of a property close to Winyard. He and Claire have had a thing going for a few months now, but I don't know if either of them is about to commit to anything serious. They do get on well together though."

"Did you go outside as soon as your dance with Terry finished?"

"I did, but by then, Callum had been outside for quite a while. I thought the dance would never end. When the music finished the first time, everyone on the floor shouted for more. The band obliged. They played the same set of tunes again, so our dance ended up lasting twice as long. As soon as it finished, I raced outside to find Callum… and to avoid being asked to dance by anyone else."

"What was it like outside the hall?"

"A lot were outside; mainly men. Most were standing around talking in groups. A few sat on the hay bales provided for that purpose. All had a drink in their hand; many were smoking. The main crowd milled around the bar. There were so many blokes out there, looking for Callum wasn't easy. I walked around every group and wandered through the throng at the bar."

"You didn't find any sign of him outside?"

"No. after spending about half an hour out there, it occurred to me that, when the dance went on for so long, he might have gone back into the hall to wait for it to finish. I went inside again and wove my way through the space around the dance floor. After three circuits, checking out everyone standing around or on the dance floor, I decided he hadn't come back into the hall."

Emily struggled with her emotions. Both of us needed a rest from the question and answer routine. We drank our iced tea, exchanged comments on how long Claire's phone call was taking, and shared a few moments of silence while staring at the landscape. I expected, the moment I started asking Emily questions again, Claire would materialise and put an end to it. But, Emily seemed relaxed again. I decided to push on while the opportunity existed.

"Do you feel okay to continue?" Emily nodded and I picked up from where we left off. "What did you do after you realised he wasn't in the hall?"

"I went back outside and repeated my earlier search; still no sign of him."

"About what time was that?"

"Supper was supposed to be in the food marquee at midnight. I must have checked my watch because I remember thinking, 'Claire will be anxious. Supper is fifteen minutes late already'. About then, people began streaming out of the hall towards the marquee. I stood a short distance away and watched everyone go in for supper. No Callum. Supper proved a drawn-out affair. After the food, there were speeches and awards of some sort were handed out. It was gone one o'clock when the first of the guests exited the tent."

"Did the dancing continue after supper?"

"Sort of; not many went back into the hall. The majority stayed outside to have one last drink and to say goodnight to friends before heading to their campsite or wherever they spent what was left of the night. A few diehards were on the dance floor when I went back into the hall. They had a couple of dances before Claire and her helpers started stacking chairs and generally giving them the message the ball was over. Terry wasn't staying. He starts early every morning, and wanted some sleep before his working day began. I must have looked frantic. Claire and Terry on their way to the door, stopped to ask what was wrong."

"They were unaware Callum was missing…?"

"They knew I was looking for him earlier, but thought I found him. I don't know how many times I called Callum's phone during the night and left messages, but he didn't answer. Terry suggested Callum might have hitched a ride back to Winyard with someone going that way. My car remained where I parked it and I still had the key. Terry said he would call at Winyard to check if Callum was there. I was sure he wasn't, but I didn't argue."

"It sounds as though not many people were around by then."

"No, hardly any; four or five blokes perched on the hay bales were finishing off a bottle of rum, and Claire and some of her committee finished cleaning the hall. As soon as Claire went back inside after seeing Terry off, I went to check my car. It had been a boring night for Callum and me. I thought he might have escaped to the car to sleep rather than endure any more of the ball. When I tried opening one of the doors, I realised he couldn't be in the car. I had locked it, and I still had the key."

"Nobody remembers seeing Callum after he left the hall earlier in the night?"

"When I came outside again just before supper, I asked a few of the blokes standing around if they had seen him. They would remember him. The hunky blue-eyed blonde stood out amongst the locals. Although none remembered seeing him, one suggested he might have gone off with a few others for a look at the incident happening in town."

"What incident…?"

"I don't know. I understand a fight, or something similar, broke out between a few locals from the ball and a number of strangers who arrived in town earlier that day. From all accounts, the strangers – I think they mentioned three or four of them – were a rough-looking mob. Someone suggested they might be members of a motorcycle gang. No one had details of what or where the incident happened, so I asked one of the police officers about it. He was rude and refused to answer my questions; wasn't even civil to me."

"Okay, this sounds like two people missing each other because they were both moving about all the time. Can you see what I'm suggesting? When you came outside to look for Callum, he might have slipped back inside, or he might have been in the toilet block. Then, when you went back inside, he looked for you outside because that was where he expected you to meet him."

"I understand what you are saying. You're suggesting our paths crossed without us seeing one another. When I first went out to look for him, I thought about the toilet and wandered out there. Then I realised how ridiculous I was. What was I going to do, stand outside checking everyone going in or coming out?"

"Yeah, you might look a bit conspicuous – not to mention suspicious."

"Later, when only a handful of people remained, I did

walk around the toilet block to check it out. Don't know what I thought I might find, but I didn't find anything."

"What time did you return to Winyard? How did Claire come home, was she with you?"

"Terry collected Claire and took her to the ball but, because he left early, she came home with me. We didn't return here until around midday." My eyebrows hiked up towards my hairline. Emily noticed and answered the implied question. "Breakfast the morning after the ball is a big deal. We set up the food marquee and organised everything for breakfast after they finished cleaning the hall. Diners started arriving for breakfast from about six o'clock. The 'kitchen' stays open until ten o'clock. Diners have until eleven o'clock to eat and be gone. Once the kitchen closed, Claire and I left. Some of the local committee members dealt with the food marquee after breakfast."

Claire returned to join us on the verandah. I spent a few minutes with her going over much the same territory as I did with Emily. She had nothing new to add, and nor did Terry she assured me. After the call she went to answer, she called Terry to check whether he knew anything or had heard anything useful. Although the afternoon slipped away while we occupied the verandah, I was restless. I wanted to be poking around at Cranvale, not stuck at Winyard for the night, but courtesy demanded I be pleasant and polite while availing myself of the hospitality.

I didn't unpack. I was leaving early next morning, and assured Claire I did not want breakfast before I left. Emily made a fuss, insisting she should come to Cranvale to help me investigate. Sometime before I fell asleep, a strange thought came to me. Although I tried brushing it aside, its ghost lingered in the back of my mind. Would Callum deliberately stage his disappearance to escape a weekend not to his liking? While Emily seemed besotted with him, I harboured some misgivings about the bloke, not the least of which stemmed from his continued interest in other *younger* females.

Such feelings and thoughts were best not shared with Emily, and definitely not while she was in her current frame of mind. If my thoughts about Callum staging his disappearance proved to have substance, it would be difficult enough sharing it with Emily when the time came. Apart from anything else, I couldn't handle the thought of her following me around looking over my shoulder while I established the facts surrounding his disappearance.

Chapter 2

Monday mornings in Cranvale are not a hive of activity … well, not this Monday morning anyway. My first priority was organising accommodation for the next couple of days. I wasn't planning to stay in town long. Didn't think I would need to, but needed to be able to extend my stay if necessary. The options were a small motel towards one end of the main street or an historic-looking hotel in the centre of town. Not a difficult choice. I pulled in at the motel. It was too early to book in. Rooms were not available before midday … but I could leave my bags if I wished and come back later. I filled out the form, declined to leave my bag, and told the receptionist I'd return late afternoon.

Cranvale was a typical small rural town attempting to appear something more. The main street was bitumen and red dirt. Struggling to survive along its centre were a few trees surrounded by patches of dead grass. Shopping in Cranvale was simple. Every business was to be found lining the short main street. The pub dominated the landscape and stood out from the dusty and tired looking shop frontages. Signage once featuring bright paint now fought to show through a film of red dust.

The hall and surrounding area where the B&S ball happened was at the other end of town from my motel. Like the pub, the hall looked as though it had been around since the town began. A huge shed-like structure with corrugated iron roof and wall cladding, the hall was incongruous with my mental picture of young things in glamorous ball gowns and tuxedos. Of more recent vintage than the hall itself, were the blue and white sign occupying the whole of the front fascia, and a set of concrete steps leading to a narrow landing

12

at the front door. The sign told me the hall belonged to the local branch of the Country Women's Association. I had no doubt it had been the venue for Cranvale social events for many decades.

After parking in the shade of a big old tree, I began a tour of inspection. The locations of the tents and hay bales remained clear on the ground. Little else about the place indicated anything happened here in recent times. Another newish addition to the place greeted me when I reached the rear of the hall. Constructed of concrete blocks, a substantial toilet block stood about five metres from the rear of the hall. Apart from one small floodlight mounted on the hall's rear fascia, no other exterior lighting was evident at the rear of the hall. The area out to the toilet block would be poorly lit at night.

Between the hall and the toilet block, herds of feet had compacted the ground to a hard red surface scattered here and there with blades of dead grass and a tumbleweed blown in from elsewhere. When close inspection of the area produced nothing of interest, I switched my attention to the toilet block. As expected, I found the doors locked. With no way of looking inside, I decided to check the area beyond the building. I was about to turn the corner at the 'gents' end of the block, when there was a sound.

Probably nothing more than a soft footfall but, in the stillness of the place, it sounded deafening. As I spun around to face the direction of the sound, I dropped into a crouch position. A familiar voice prevented me embarrassing myself further. "Can I help?"

"What the hell are you doing here?" I bellowed. The owner of the voice halted midstride. The stunned look on Emily's face silenced me as she stammered a response.

"Sorry, I … I didn't mean to startle you. I couldn't stay out on the property and not know what was happening here. Isn't there something I can do to help? Please let me be involved in trying to find him."

Again, I barked at her. "I don't know how you can help. I haven't found anything to investigate yet – not even something to initiate an investigation. You're here now, so I suppose you can tag along."

The moment I said it, I felt bad. I knew how concerned she was about Callum's disappearance. It was my own frustration at not having found any evidence so far making me so bad-tempered. A hasty apology helped smooth some of the ruffled feathers before I continued. "So far, there is nothing to indicate Callum was ever here. I was about to check around the back when you arrived. Come on, let's see what's behind here. If nothing else, we should establish what lies beyond."

"Well, this isn't telling us anything more than the rest of the place did. There is nothing helpful to see here. It's as though he disappeared into thin air; just vaporised." Standing with her back almost against the rear wall of the toilet block and her hands on her hips, Emily swivelled her head from side to side as she scanned the area in front of her. Although I had no idea what we might find, Emily was right. There was nothing. But, in her current frame of mind, agreeing with her observation wasn't going to help in any way.

"Hmm… Yeah, there isn't anything obvious," I murmured. "To satisfy my curiosity, I might take a bit of a wander through that scrub to see what's on the other side of it."

A patch of scrub began a short distance from the toilet block. I didn't think it would tell us anything, but it intrigued me. It was a green oasis in an otherwise dry, red environment. As I started towards the scrub, Emily trotted along. It occurred to me there were better things she could be doing than traipsing about in a patch of scrub unlikely to produce anything useful in terms of our investigation. "Were you planning on returning to Winyard this evening?"

"No, I said my goodbyes, packed up and left. They expected me to leave today as I'm due back at work tomorrow."

"What are you planning to do? If you're heading back to Millhaven today, you should hit the road soon or you'll be driving well into the night. On the other hand, you will need somewhere for tonight if you plan to stay in Cranvale."

"I contacted work this morning to tell them I wouldn't be back for a day or two. Perhaps I should look for some accommodation before too much later."

"Okay, while I have a bit of a tramp around in the scrub, you go back to that motel at the other end of town and book yourself a room. By the way, when you called your workplace this morning, did you tell them about Callum's disappearance?"

"Uhmm… No, I didn't mention it. What could I tell them? I don't know what happened to him, and I'd look stupid telling them he disappeared into thin air if he were sitting at his desk in his office."

Ahh … I detected doubt in that statement. If I read her correctly, Emily didn't appear any more convinced about Callum's 'disappearing act' than I am. It might be a good thing in the end, particularly if it turns out he abandoned her. The big problem with that line of thinking is, I don't know how he would travel from Cranvale to Millhaven without a vehicle, and with no buses or trains running over the weekend. Emily broke into my train of thought.

"I suppose I should go try my luck at booking a room at the motel. I'll come back here after I do that."

"There is something else you might do. Call your mate Claire and ask if she can suggest someone we might talk to about the supposed 'incident' in town on the night of the ball."

"I asked first thing this morning. She gave me two names, but she didn't know if either of them would prove helpful. One of them is a leading light in their anti-fracking campaign, and the other is some sort of journalist. I think he is a part-time freelance writer who supplies the metropolitan newspapers with occasional articles about what's happening on the rural scene out this way."

"What's this about 'fracking'…? What's has it to do with anything?"

"Don't you read the papers? The CSG mining companies are trying to move into this area to tap the gas using the fracking method of extraction. The community is mounting a strenuous opposition because of the likely damage it will cause to prime agricultural land and the associated under-ground water supply. Some of the mining company bigwigs were in town on Friday. The locals mounted a demonstration outside the council chambers, but they didn't have enough time to rally many participants, as the visit by the mining mob was hush-hush. Nobody knew they were coming. As a result, there is now suggestion in some quarters of the community that the Shire Council Chairman is involved with the CSG mining companies. People are questioning whether he is receiving backhanders for helping smooth the companies' way into the area."

"It has the potential to become messy before it goes away. From what I've seen happen in other areas, the community stands little chance against the might of the big mining companies. How could the community fund a campaign which could end up a legal challenge in the High Court?"

"Most of the landowners contributed to a 'fighting fund' and they've run a number of social and other fundraising events. The festival and ball were part of that. Every year the funds raised over the festival weekend go towards some charity or community project. This year all monies were to go to the CSG fighting fund. Claire is committed because of Winyard. The mining company has identified at least a hundred sites on Winyard where they want to drill wells. She and her father believe the fracking will ruin the property and contaminate both its natural springs and underground water supply."

"If I remember correctly, Callum now works in the planning department of your mining company. And, he is a geologist. I don't suppose his visit to Winyard had anything to do with the CSG fracking extraction process planned for the area." My tongue occupied my cheek, and my eyebrows reached skyward in question as I made the comment.

"No… well, not really. It's not the only reason we came out here for the weekend. Of course, we were interested in what was happening around the area. The company we work for has an interest in natural gas extraction operations in other countries. It's not beyond the realm of possibilities they might become interested in being involved here too. It makes sense for us to be aware of the implications if the company decided to do that."

My teeth somehow clamped down on my tongue in time to prevent the escape of the thought uppermost in my mind. While I don't dispute their desire for information in case their mining company chooses to join the current CSG market rush, I saw another strong motivation for Callum's eagerness to visit the area. Cynical as I am by nature, I couldn't help thinking his moonlighting as a freelance writer who supplies articles under a pseudonym to the major tabloids might have something to do with it.

At last I could begin exploring the area of scrubland. I felt sure Emily would have no difficulty getting a room at the motel now the weekend's festivities were over. I wanted to continue my search for evidence relating to Callum's disappearance without the distraction of having someone along – or having someone yapping to me while I was about it.

After she booked her room, Emily was to try to interview the two people Claire suggested might know something about the incident in town on the night of the ball. I still harboured some doubts about Callum's supposed 'disappearance', but thinking about his sideline as a freelance writer raised new questions. What if, while he was outside the hall, he caught a whiff of something worthy of a potential article? I didn't doubt the temptation to observe the incident would outweigh any concern about abandoning Emily, if he bothered to give Emily a thought at all in such a situation. Did Emily know about his freelance writing? I made a mental note to try introducing the subject into conversation over dinner.

With all thoughts of Callum corralled deep in the back of my mind, and with my eyes glued to the ground, I wandered along the edge of the patch of scrub. It looked as though, at some time in the past, they cleared the scrub back in a straight line some distance from the road to provide an area to accommodate development of the town's commercial centre. An additional area cleared at some later stage provided for the erection of the hall. A possible further extension of the clearing occurred to accommodate the new toilet block. These later clearings had not followed the earlier straight-line approach. Their ragged edges suggested they mimicked the footprint of the new construction site. This left the untidy edge to the scrubland I now scrutinised in the hope of finding evidence of any traffic in out of it.

Such evidence didn't take long to find. On any number of occasions in the recent past, people – and dogs – entered the scrub from behind the hall. Some of the tracks probably dated from the weekend; made by blokes deciding it was quicker and easier to go behind a tree than wait in the queue for the toilet. With nothing useful gained so far, it was time to go for a wander through the scrub. I didn't feel optimistic about what I might find.

From outside, the area looked a mixture of tall old trees dotted through typical low scrub. While the vegetation looked dense, it didn't strike me as impenetrable. My survey of the edge of the scrub focused on the area immediately behind the hall. Something suggested I should check further along the edge before charging into the interior. I heeded the suggestion. Anything to delay entering the bush had a certain appeal. It likely was home to hordes of mosquitoes and biting midges, all of which found me irresistible. Their attacks brought me out in enormous lumps that itched for an eternity.

About three metres further along, a set of very different tracks caught my attention. I could make out men's footprints entering the scrub, but there were other more sinister marks amongst them. Allowing them a wide berth, I walked around the area where those tracks entered the scrub. From every available angle, they tended to confirm my initial assessment. My stomach tightened. A wave of nausea swept over me. Those tracks clearly marked the place where a group of men dragged someone into the scrub. The person was conscious at the time. His marks indicated he struggled, sometimes managing to plant his feet in a bid to prevent being dragged further.

As I stood staring at the marks, an important question came to me. Why did I think it was a man they dragged along? Could it be a woman they dragged into the bushes for some unthinkable pleasure – like gang rape? I took a closer look at the where the victim managed to leave clear prints. Definitely a man's footprints. Even if a woman had such big feet, she would not have worn flat-heeled brogues to a ball.

I did not like the way things were shaping up, nor the prospect of what I might find in the scrub. Trying to convince myself it might not be Callum was pointless. My gut argued against it. After adding more photos to those from along the scrub line, it was time to face the biting and stinging things, and whatever else lay hidden in the bush. In an effort to preserve the tracks, I stayed about a metre away as I followed them into the undergrowth. It wasn't an easy task.

Although it proved not as dense as it appeared from the outside, the low scrubby growth made it difficult to see the ground in some places. If there were something good about being in the there, it was that the leaf litter kept the ground moist. While it obliterated the footprints in places, the drag marks disturbed enough of it for them to remain clear. After a minute or so of crashing through the undergrowth, another sound drifted to me above my own noise. I froze. Was someone else thrashing about in here? It took me a few moments to reassure myself all I heard were the sounds of Nature… and Nature could be noisy in her own way. Birds twittered and crows added a raucous chorus. High up in the treetops a light breeze rustled the leaves to release a shower of fluffy petals and pollen from the iron barks. A goanna scuttled through the undergrowth and scrambled up the nearest tree trunk. The smell of eucalypts combined with that of mouldy leaf litter. With nothing threatening discovered, I pressed on.

A few steps further on, I lost the tracks. They couldn't just vanish. Some alien spaceship didn't beam up those responsible for them… and they didn't suddenly take to swinging from the branches to fool anyone who might want to follow them. Their trail had to continue somewhere around here. The next few minutes of searching a wide area from the end of the tracks failed to find any trace of them. Stop rushing about like a mad thing, I told myself. Stand still for a minute and think about this. The idea had a lot to recommend it.

While the sun didn't penetrate the canopy, no breeze entered the scrub either. The moist leaf litter helped create a high level of humidity. Combined with the other elements, this made for a close, energy-sapping environment. I wandered over to a rock and perched a part of my backside on its edge. Strange there should be such a conveniently placed rock. I hadn't seen any rocks since entering the scrub until this one. As I sat cursing losing the tracks, the sound I heard earlier drifted into my consciousness again. This time, no other thoughts distracted me as I listened.

"That's water! There must be a creek close by," I told the

trees, before levering myself up off my rock and striding off in the direction of the sound. Rocks littered the ground, sparsely at first but becoming more prevalent as I neared the sound. I burst through the last of the undergrowth and stepped into a cleared corridor running along both side of a small creek. Close to the water's edge, the moss-covered rocks were slippery and nearly had me on my backside as I picked my way to the edge of the stream. A dead branch lay among the rocks. About two metres long, three centimetres in diameter for most of its length, and almost straight, it provided an ideal 'walking stick'.

The source of the water must be a nearby spring. While it would be nice to locate that spring, it was not why I was wandering around in the scrub. "Keep moving," I told myself aloud as I felt my frustration deepening. I picked my way through the slippery rocks back to clear ground before following the creek deeper into the scrub. While this seemed a good move at the time, a little voice kept reminding me I was supposed to be looking for the tracks I had lost 'way back there somewhere'.

Up ahead, the creek curled around a large rock. After crashing my way through the undergrowth to circumvent the rock, I discovered the next part of the creek ran through a particularly rocky area. Rocks dotted in the stream caused small cataracts as the water foamed and tumbled over them. Then I saw it. About two metres ahead of me, the ground on the creek bank was disturbed … and it looked recent. On closer inspection, I could see footprints and a furrow from something – or someone – being dragged through the soft earth. I had found my tracks again.

I went down on my haunches for a closer look. The soft earth here made the prints more distinct than they were through the scrub. Here were three clear sets of footprints. Between two of those were two long furrows made by either the feet or knees of someone dragged along by the footprints' owners. The furrows sent a chill through me. Although I told myself anything – or anyone – might be responsible for the drag marks, I didn't believe it. Instinct told me Callum made the furrows.

Almost at the water's edge, a large area of disturbed ground caught my attention. It was about a metre and a half square and was a quagmire. A mass of indistinct indents and marks covered the whole area. Then I saw the rocks. Two rocks about forty centimetres back from the edge of the stream bore clear evidence of their involvement in whatever happened here. Their surfaces now sported thick streaks of mud instead of their once lush covering of moss. Interpreting the scene before me wasn't too difficult. Someone slipped on those moss-covered rocks. It forced the owners of the foot-prints into a frantic two-step as they tried to maintain their balance while retaining a hold on their victim, and thereby ploughing up the area in the process.

Something more sinister caught my eye. It was on another rock much taller than the others and standing beyond the ones bearing evidence of someone having slipped on them. A dark brown stain spread over it and down onto the ground. Taking care not to disturb the scene too much, I moved closer to the stained rock. Yep, there was no mistaking that stain: blood… dried blood and plenty of it. I must be objective; control the emotions and be professional. That's what I told myself as I felt my stomach tighten at the thought of what the blood meant.

From the tracks they left, it was clear this group of people intended crossing the creek. The water didn't appear deep enough to be a problem for them but, right now, it was a dilemma for me. I wore good shoes today and not my ragged old hiking boots. I didn't plan on tramping through scrub or crossing a creek. Apart from that, I figured rolling up my skinny-leg jeans was nigh on impossible.

A distant voice startled me. In my haste to stand and move away from the site, I almost slipped. My recently acquired sturdy walking stick prevented my falling face first in the mud – or onto the rocks. The mud sucked at my shoes as I ran from the scene and, as quietly as possible, endeavoured to lose myself in the undergrowth.

Chapter 3

"For goodness sake, Emily, do you have to make so much fuss?" I barked. While I regretted my outburst, it somehow felt justified. My only consolation was the thought that, had I slipped and fallen in the mud, I would be twice as cranky and Emily might be on the receiving end of something worse. Bellowing my name, she had come blundering through the scrub like a runaway draught horse.

"Sorry; I panicked when I couldn't find you. I thought you disappeared as well."

She looked so upset. I rushed to alleviate the situation before she burst into tears. "How did you know I was in the scrub? You might have found yourself in a dangerous situation charging in here as you did. What if it weren't me in here, but something worse?"

"I know, I know. I saw your footprints leading into the scrub. I worked out you were following other tracks. Then I panicked when I couldn't see or hear you. What about those tracks anyway, did they lead anywhere or tell you anything?"

"Uhmm… no, not really; when you came thundering in, I was about ready to give up and deny the mosquitoes and midges anything more to feed on." It was a long way from the truth, but I didn't want to share my suspicions yet. Emily's performance when she thought I was missing was clear indication she was not up to handling potentially devastating news about Callum. My dilemma was that I hadn't quite finished searching along the creek. I wanted to pursue a couple of ideas – but without Emily tagging along. Thank God for the arrival of inspiration. A possible solution popped into my mind.

"Emily, did you happen to see a coffee shop anywhere in town while you were out and about? After my early start this morning, I could murder a cappuccino about now."

"Yeah, there was a sort of diner place. A sign outside advertised coffee."

"Great; if you fetch a couple of coffees, I'll have a bit more of a look around in here and then meet you under the big tree out front of the hall."

I expected an argument. It didn't happen. As soon as Emily went for the coffees, I retraced my steps to where I was when she interrupted. Still not inclined to cross the creek, I opted instead to work my way further along the bank to see if the group crossed back to this side. With eyes glued to the ground for any sign of tracks, I continued along the creek for about another hundred metres to where it narrowed to nothing more than a trickle about four centimetres wide. After another ten metres, it dried up altogether. Damn! Now I could cross to the other side of the creek without getting wet, but I didn't have time before Emily came back.

After making a mental note of my surroundings, I took the most direct route back to the hall to arrive at the big tree mere seconds before Emily returned. What a nice surprise; the coffee was excellent, and the apricot Danish she couldn't resist was warm and flaky. Nothing else mattered until I'd dispatched the Danish. Then it was time to ask Emily what her morning's enquiries yielded – if anything. She confirmed she had no problem booking a room at the motel. I couldn't decide whether it was a good thing or not, but decided it was best to look pleased about it.

"That's good. I didn't think there would be a problem. Now, how did you get on with those two names Claire gave you? Did you manage to catch up with either of them?"

"Yeah, I spoke to both of them, but I'm not sure I gained anything worthwhile from the exercise. I started with the journalist bloke because he was easiest to find. He produces a local newspaper – more of a newsletter than a newspaper – once a week. You know the sort of thing; it's only of interest if you're a local. One of the large tabloids stationed Lance, the journalist, here as their rural reporter. When readership declined in the area, they cut him adrift and he was left here married to a local girl, but without a job. Her family bought him a bit of equipment, and the local newsletter thing began. The locals seem to hold him in high regard."

"Did he have anything useful to say about the supposed incident in town on the night of the ball?"

"Well, 'useful' might be an exaggeration. He knew there was an incident, but didn't witness it himself. A couple of the mining company executives were meeting with the mayor in the hotel restaurant. Our journalist got wind of the meeting and booked a table at the same restaurant for himself and a colleague from Moxton. They spent the evening trying to eavesdrop. It wasn't until afterwards he heard about the incident, and only has second-hand information about it. By the way, his dining companion from Moxton is a reporter for a major Central Queensland newspaper."

"Good of Lance to think of his mates. What about the other person Claire mentioned? Doesn't he have something to do with the anti-fracking committee?"

"They are not an actual committee or organisation as such. Almost the whole place is against fracking, so there isn't a need for a formal structure. A couple of people have emerged as leaders and become their representatives. Chris is one of them. I think Chris is a mate of Claire's Terry, but I suppose, out here everyone knows everyone anyway."

"So, did you catch up with this Chris?"

"I did. He was still in town after the weekend. We had a long chat… and very pleasant it was too. You should see the gorgeous hunk of a bloke. Well-educated, well-spoken … extreme eye-candy. I don't understand how he is still single."

"Ye-es, but did he have anything worthwhile to tell you?"

"He said some of the local blokes who had a few too many at the ball decided to make a nuisance of themselves in town. It was in front of the council chambers. Apart from the mining executives who were dining with the mayor, a few other mining company people were in town as well. They might be senior staff, like mining engineers or geologists, but Chris earmarked them as 'bully boys'. There are only two police officers stationed in Cranvale. The local blokes, expecting the usual drunken behaviour to erupt over the weekend, brought in other officers from out-of-town. It was a good move. It took all of them to break up the ruckus once it got going."

"When he calls them 'bully boys', does he think they were in town for just this purpose? I suppose the big question is: what happened after the police broke up the ruckus? Were there any arrests? Oh, and here's the *really* big question: was Chris a part of the action?"

Emily inspected her nails for a moment before answering. "He says he wasn't. He heard about it at the ball and rushed down town. By then, the police had it under control."

There was nothing odd about anything Emily said, but something about the way she said it made me think there might be more to the story. When in doubt, ask questions, has always been a sound approach for me.

"So, what else did he say that you haven't told me?"

"Nothing... Truly...! He didn't say anything else. Nevertheless, he looked as though he might have gone a few rounds in the welter weight division recently. He didn't have a black eye or anything so definitive, but his cheekbone was grazed and I noticed the knuckles on his right hand looked as though they made recent contact with something solid." She shrugged and looked a bit embarrassed. Oh dear, might the missing Callum be losing the fair Emily to the hunky Chris?

"I don't suppose you know how much longer Chris might remain in town. If he were still here tonight, we might feel obliged to invite him to dine with us. What do you think?"

"Well, since you ask … I know he plans to be in Cranvale for at least a couple more days. I believe our motel – where he also happens to be staying – has a good restaurant."

"Excellent; your next mission is to see if you can locate him somewhere in town and issue an invitation to dine with us tonight. Don't waste too much time looking for him. If you can't 'happen to run into him' in the street, leave a message for him with the motel's reception. I'll poke around here a bit longer before I meet you back at the motel. You might pick up something for lunch while you are roaming around town."

Not wanting to alarm Emily again, while I waited for her drive off in search of Chris, I wrote up my notes from this morning and checked the images I took. As soon as she left, I headed back to the place along the creek where I was when she interrupted me, and walked a short distance beyond the end of the water to where the ground was dry and hard. After a moment listening for any intrusive sounds, I bolted across the dry creek bed and into the undergrowth on the other side. Another few moments were invested in listening for any unwanted attention I might have attracted. My racing pulse almost drowned out the sounds of the scrub, but I seemed to be alone.

The terrain on this side of the creek was different. Here, the land was a little higher. The bank ended in an abrupt drop to the creek bed about fifty centimetres below. There were more tall trees and the undergrowth was thinner. It allowed what little breeze there was to filter through. One other difference on that side of the creek didn't fill me with joy. The ground there was dry and hard. My survey of the area found no tracks.

In the hope the ground might be damp and softer in the creek bed, I clambered down from the bank and began picking my way back towards the hall. By the time I emerged from the scrub directly behind the hall, all I had to show for my efforts was a heightened level of frustration and a myriad of insect bites. My watch indicated it was lunchtime and I should be heading to the motel to meet Emily. Not quite ready for her yet, I allowed myself a few minutes of solitude before heading back. Anyway, I was sweaty and every uncovered part of me itched from all the bites I'd collected during the morning. Right now, a shower held more appeal than food.

It was time to review my morning's efforts and work out how to proceed.

I sat writing up the rest of my notes in my car with all the windows open to catch whatever breeze drifted by. An idea came at me from left field. "They weren't locals!" I told the empty car. It's good nobody else was around or they might have called the men in the white coats to come for me. The idea they weren't locals opened up a truckload of new thoughts. I needed someone else to help me analyse those thoughts. I drove to the motel for a shower, Emily and lunch, not necessarily in that order.

After a shower, I felt more civilised, and hunger made its presence felt. Our first priority was to dispatch lunch. While Emily cleared wrappers and containers from the small table in my room, I retrieved my morning's notes and mentally rehearsed the conversation I was about to have with her. As soon as Emily sat down again, her questions opened the door for the conversation I wanted to have. "So, how did your morning end up? Did you manage to pick up anything useful from around the hall and the scrub?"

For a couple of heartbeats, I wrestled with the hard question: should I risk upsetting Emily needlessly by mentioning the tracks I followed and finding what I believed was blood on those rocks – potentially Callum's? If I didn't mention those things, the conversation I wanted with her would be impossible. Deep breath and plunge in, I decided.

I watched her closely as I delivered the first instalment of what I hoped would be a solid think-tank session. "Emily, please don't jump to any conclusions yet, but this morning I followed a set of tracks some distance through the scrub to the bank of a small creek running through it. I lost the tracks at the edge of the water. There were no corresponding tracks on the other side of the creek or anywhere else around that creek. They just stopped at the water's edge. That's where I think one of the members of the group making those tracks slipped on the moss-covered rocks and injured himself. There is what looks like dried blood in the area."

Emily's reaction was much as I expected. Shock hit hard. The colour drained from her face and her breathing became shallow and fast. She fought hard to retain composure, and found sufficient voice to ask, "Was it Callum? Do you think what you found has something to do with his disappearance?"

"I don't know. Honestly, Emily, I don't know. There was nothing to indicate Callum was involved, nor were there any clues to suggest anything else. It's why I would appreciate our spending some time throwing ideas around."

After biting her lip as she paced around the room a few times, she nodded resolutely and sat down at the table. I got on with things before her resolve cracked.

"Right, we need to put all thoughts of Callum to one side for the moment. It won't be easy I know, but it's about being objective. Here's the situation: I need to talk about those tracks I found. After all, that's all we have so far. And, I need a sounding board to help me make sense of it all. Are you up for it?"

She nodded and took a deep breath before replying. "Yes, I am. I want to help. So, can we get on with it please?"

"Okay, here's how it goes so far. A group of people made those tracks, not one person. I don't think they were locals."

My supposition and its relevance brought a flurry of questions and comments. "My guess is at least half the people at the ball weren't what you might call 'locals', but some were more local than others. Some came from somewhere in this district and weren't complete strangers to the area, not like we were. Anyway, on what do you base your assumption?"

"If they were local, they wouldn't have crossed the creek where it had water in it. They would continue to beyond the end of the stream to cross over on dry land as I did. I know what your next question is: did they cross to the other side or is that another of my assumptions? Before you ask, I'll admit I found nothing on the other side of the creek to indicate they crossed it."

"What about if they travelled along in the creek for some distance rather than going straight across from where they entered the water?"

"I searched the length of both sides of the creek. There were no other tracks after they appeared to enter the stream. The hard, dry ground I found on the other side might result in no tracks being left behind anyway."

"Apart from the ones you followed, were there any other tracks through the scrub?"

"Not really; immediately behind the toilet block, a few went in a short distance but they didn't carry on through the scrub."

"How far back does the scrub stretch? If you walked right through it, where would you come out?"

"I don't know the answer to either of those questions. I only went as far as the end of the creek."

"I assume those tracks are fresh or you wouldn't be interested in them. It would be handy to have some local knowledge – even a map of the area – to give us an idea of what the scrub and the area beyond it is like. I wonder if there ever was anything in that area … you know, old buildings, mines, or the likes. As I see it, for people to slog their way through that scrub, they must be going somewhere specific, and not just going for a hike in the bush."

"Good thinking … and it's exactly what we need to find out. We need a map, or someone with appropriate local history knowledge. If we can't identify any likely locations, we will have to explore the area ourselves. Do you think the journalist you spoke to would know some-one who might be able to help?"

"Possibly; for want of any better idea, he seems a logical place to start. I have his number. I'll try calling him. Is there anything else we should discuss?"

"No, nothing else I can think of at the moment. Are you okay?"

"I'm okay. I'm thinking I might have a nap before dinner." At the door, she turned back and said, "I almost forgot to tell you, Chris Tremaine is delighted to be joining us for dinner at seven. See you later."

Something tells me needing a nap wasn't the reason for Emily's hasty departure. At the end of our discussions, I noticed she again became agitated. I suppose thoughts of Callum and the possibility it was his blood down by the creek came back to haunt her. It would be a good thing if she did sleep for a while. It might help her develop some resilience for whatever lies ahead.

The time alone allowed me to take care of a couple of things before dinner. The first was to make a phone call. A mature female voice answered. This was not the usual receptionist at Emily's workplace, but she seemed to know what she was doing. "I wonder if I might speak to Callum Farquhar please."

"I'm sorry; Mr Farquhar is not in today. Could someone else help you?"

"No thanks, I just wanted to give Callum a message about a private matter. Is he likely to be away for a while?"

"He is due back tomorrow."

Well, that eliminated any thoughts I had about Callum abandoning Emily and staging his 'disappearance' to return to Millhaven early and alone. I sent Emily a mental apology for not having shared her level of concern for Callum's well-being. Perhaps it was time for me to accept the possibility he had met with some form of foul play. After making notes about the phone call, I strode out to the reception area.

A neglected-looking rack in a corner of the motel's reception area held tourist information. There was a range of tired and dusty brochures advertised interesting things to do in Cranvale. Among them was one promoting a heritage walk along the main street. As the buildings along the street were not so old, not so great, and there were not many of them, the agony of such a walk should be over quickly.

I rummaged through the contents of the rack until I found a brochure about Cranvale's historic sites. Its centre pages contained a sketch map identifying 'places of interest' for tourists. With the brochure tucked under my arm, I continued my search for a more formal map of the area, and found one produced by the Government Printer ten years ago. Thinking it was out of date, I was about to put it back when I realised it remained current. Nothing in Cranvale looked as though it had changed in over a decade. Armed with the brochure and the map, I went back to my room to familiarise myself with the surrounding area.

The jangling of my phone brought me crashing back to reality from imagined scenarios generated by my research. "I wanted to make sure you remembered Chris was joining us for dinner in the restaurant at seven o'clock. Are you still okay with the arrangement?" Emily asked.

"Yes, of course – and no, I hadn't forgotten about it." It was close to a white lie. I hadn't forgotten, but neither had I given it another thought after Emily left my room. "I'll be there at seven o'clock."

"Well, I thought we might be at the restaurant a little earlier. We could have a drink while we waited for Chris to arrive. It would be good if we were there to meet him when he came in. Perhaps if we were there, say, ten minutes beforehand..."

"Okay, it makes sense and would be polite. Let's plan to be at the restaurant by 6.50pm."

There was no mistaking the undercurrent of excitement in Emily's voice. It was clear, for Emily, dinner tonight was about more than Callum's disappearance. Getting ready for dinner was not a major undertaking for me. The clean shirt and jeans I put on after my shower at lunchtime was as good as anything my current wardrobe had to offer. With nothing more to do than wash my face and comb my hair, I had about half an hour before worrying about dinner. Good news! It gave me a valuable half hour to formulate a few well-worded questions to put to our dinner guest.

About five minutes before I expected Emily to stop by on her way to the restaurant, I began my preparations for dinner. Face and hair were the least of these. Although I usually didn't feel the need to take a handbag to dinner, tonight was different. After replacing the batteries in my digital recorder and plugging in my phone to ensure it was fully charged, I made a note of the questions I wanted to ask and then slipped the notebook, recorder and phone into my bag.

By the time Emily knocked on my door, I felt well prepared for what I hoped would be an informative evening. The reality was, we were desperate for something – anything – to help with our investigation into Callum's disappearance. While I pinned a lot of hope on what Chris Tremaine might tell us, my gut told me not to count on getting too much out of dinner tonight.

Chapter 4

"So, what's our game plan?" Emily asked over the top of her glass of Merlot.

"Game plan…? What are you on about?"

"What's our approach… how do we handle our meeting with Chris?"

"Why do we need a game plan? I thought this was to be a friendly dinner with a fellow motel guest."

"You did not think that, Sonny. Stop buggering about and tell me how you want to handle this evening."

"You should make like the interested tourist and ask all sorts of question about the area and what goes on here. I will chime in at appropriate times with questions and comments I hope might extract information useful to our investigation. By the way, aren't you supposed to be back at work tomorrow?"

"I called and told them I wouldn't be back until next week."

"What about Callum? He is supposed to return to work tomorrow as well. Won't they think it odd when he doesn't request extra days off too?"

"N-o-o, why would they? No, they won't connect the two things. Nobody at work knows about Callum and me. I'm not sure they approve of relationships between employees. Anyway, we didn't want us being the current topic for water-cooler discussions."

I kept my face deadpan as I nodded in response. If she believed that, I didn't want to ruin her delusion, but I felt sure it was more a case of Callum wanting to keep their relationship quiet. He would not want office gossip ruining his other relationships around town.

As I thought about it, I saw someone. "Hmmm… *v-e-r-y n-i-c-e…,*" I murmured.

"What…?" Emily squeaked.

"Don't turn around, but I think Chris entered the restaurant. Fetch him and introduce me."

In no more than a few heartbeats, Emily was off her bar stool and striding towards Chris. Introductions over, and with drinks in hand, we settled at a table in a back corner of the restaurant. Emily's 'eye candy' assessment of Chris wasn't an exaggeration, and he proved as intelligent and well educated as she claimed. Conversation was light until our meals arrived, and then came in stilted snatches while we dispatched our main courses. While she and Chris waited for their desserts to arrive, Emily went into 'tourist' mode. She was perfect. Her questions provided opportunities for me to ask mine too.

As we all still would be at the motel the following night, we agreed to have dinner together again. While sipping our coffees, I became aware of pointed looks from the staff. It was time to make a move. "I think we've outstayed our welcome. Perhaps we should retire to our rooms before being thrown out."

"It has been so pleasant, none of us noticed the time slipping by. Based on tonight's behaviour, I hope they won't refuse to feed us tomorrow night," Emily giggled.

We said goodnight to Chris at his door before Emily and I continued to my room. "Do you want a debrief session?" Emily asked.

"If you're not too tired, I would like to review what we learned and plan what we might do tomorrow." With maps and notebooks spread out before us on the table, we began.

"Ah, now I see why the questions about minerals in the area, and if mining occurred here in the past. You knew about the old mine site marked on this map."

"Yes, but those questions about mining and minerals extracted interesting information from Chris. They led onto discussions about the company planning to undertake fracking extraction of natural gas here, and the community's opposition to it."

"I suppose they were worthwhile. Was tonight a successful information gathering exercise?"

"Yes and no. I think Chris sidestepped telling us anything about the incident in town on the night of the ball. Why would he do that? For the record, I agree he looks as though he went a round or two with someone recently."

"Some of what he told us was interesting – like the history of that old mine."

"Yeah, interesting… and edited. I think we received an abridged version of 'facts'. I can't help wondering why. Tomorrow, I will verify Chris' information or confirm my suspicions. If it's the latter, it will make for interesting conversation when we dine with him again."

I saw Emily's face drop and realised my comments disappointed her. She appears quite taken with Chris. A second later, she recovered and returned to professional mode. "Okay, so what's tomorrow's plan? We aren't any closer to finding Callum."

Emily's hysteria when I first arrived in town had abated somewhat. Concern remains – understandably – but it has changed. Maybe Emily isn't sharing all her thoughts with me. Maybe they have changed from something having happened to Callum, to his having engineered his disappearance. It's a possible line of enquiry for another day. Tonight is for remaining calm and establishing plans for tomorrow. My plans didn't inspire Emily.

"The old mine site begs me to investigate it. I don't know how long it might take, what is there, or what it might produce to assist with finding Callum. Nevertheless, I'll head there in the morning, while you try to round up the journalist bloke again. See if he knows more than he's already told you. Hint at there being a story in it for him if he helps, but don't be too specific about it."

"I don't think the journo knows any more than he told me, but it's possible he's dug up a bit more since then. Talking to him won't take up much of the morning. What else do I do?"

"Go to coffee shop. It won't be busy I shouldn't think. Try chatting up the staff about the festival, the ball and the incident in town you heard a whisper about. If all else fails, ask about why everyone is talking about, and being so uptight about this fracking thing. Be an interested tourist who is confused by what's going on in the area."

Alone after Emily left, I tried making sense of what Chris said over dinner – and tried guessing what he didn't say. I needed everything we knew to date in one solid block of information on which to base a strategic plan for tomorrow morning – and maybe beyond that. Tomorrow's investigations were unlikely to have an auspicious beginning. First, I planned to visit the police station to try convincing them something untoward happened on their patch on the night of the ball. But, I still lacked anything concrete to convince them to become interested in Callum's disappearance. I didn't mention visiting the police station to Emily to avoid raising her hopes or having her demand to come with me.

*****

The visit to the police station was a bummer. No one was there. An old and tatty notice taped to the door advised the station would be unattended until after lunch. I pondered what major crime dragged the two officers away this morning. An elderly woman walking her shaggy lapdog startled me when she spoke. I almost barrelled into her as I strode down the steps onto the footpath.

"They're always closed one morning every week when they go to visit outlying areas. They're supposed to open up again after lunch."

While I hadn't expected today to start well, I didn't fore-see this situation. It wasn't too bad though. I could explore the old mine site, and maybe somewhere else, before talking to the police later. With luck, I might find evidence to help interest them in a possible missing person. I tried convincing myself accordingly as I drove to the best place from which to begin my trek to the mine site.

Much had changed since my map was printed. The map showed a road leading to the edge of bush. The road now sported an industrial area which cut off my planned route. My alternative was to enter the bush from behind the hall as I did yesterday. It made sense to find the place where I emerged from the scrub yesterday, and to enter the scrub from there.

The swarms of biting insects waited just inside under the trees where I left them yesterday. They wasted no time in attacking me. Somehow, the day seemed hotter and, the deeper into the bush I went, the steamier it became. Yester-day, the thinner undergrowth here seemed to allow more air to circulate ... but not today. My shirt plastered itself to my back. The mine was located in further than the map gave me to believe.

By the time I had the first indications I was approach-ing the site, my hair hung in lank damp tendrils. After only a few metres into the scrub, I had pulled my hair up into a half-arsed ponytail to keep it off my neck. Some strands escaped and now plastered themselves to my face. I was thirsty and breathing heavily, but determined not to stop until I reached the mine site.

After yesterday's brief experience in this part of the place, I expected today to be a similar relatively easy trek. How wrong could I be? Today's trail was over rough, rocky ground, and up a steep incline for much of the way. The first of the identifiable buildings and infrastructure were a further hundred metres from where I first saw evidence of the site. A large concrete block a few metres from the entrance to the mine provided a welcome seat. Having planted my backside on the block, I took the opportunity to attend to my thirst. As I had expected an easier trek, I only brought one small bottle of water. I would have to make it last. I still had the walk out of the scrub ahead of me.

While I sat there drying off and regaining control of my breathing, I devoted my thoughts to how difficult it would be to drag an uncooperative body all the way to this site. Finding Callum here seemed unlikely. Nevertheless, I was here, and needed to get on with the task in hand. As I sat surveying the place, I felt the cold hand of dread tightening its grip on me. You would not hold a live and conscious person here if you intended he should remain alive.

Quite a few boards had either rotted away or been deliberately removed from the boarded up entrance to the mine shaft. Of the two buildings still standing, the smaller of the two once housed offices and facilities. Built on a concrete slab, only the floor remained sound. Areas of the walls were missing and large holes peppered the roof.

I entered through what I presumed was the front door, its remains hanging at a drunken angle from broken hinges. The remnant part of the door wedged itself against the floor, leaving only a narrow opening to squeeze through. Discretion warned against applying a too concerted effort to open the entrance wider for fear something would collapse on me. Regardless, I put my shoulder to it and shoved. Apart from its creaking in protest, nothing happened. I didn't try again. It was too heavy to shift and I could sidle through the existing narrow opening.

The area immediately inside the door once served as office space. Remnants of office fittings and what was once a reception counter suggested it had been a basic admin area. A passageway led through to the rear section of the building. Behind the front office area was another small office, probably for the mine manager or someone similar. Its walls were lined with fake wood panelling. Time, the weather, and possibly termites had destroyed most of the panelling, including the front of a large built-in cupboard. Installed in the lower half of the cupboard was a good-sized safe. Its door presented a temptation I couldn't resist. Whether due to a lack of use for so long, or because it was locked, I couldn't open the safe.

With nothing else of interest in the office, and with time slipping away, I picked my way through fallen timbers along the passageway to enter the back section of the building. This had been a lunchroom. Tables and benches remained bolted to the floor. Further exploration confirmed toilets and showers occupied the far end of this section. Beyond the facilities area, the back door overlooked the other remaining building.

Outside, I stood for a few moments breathing in fresh air to clear my lungs and lose the musty smell of rotting wood and dust. I recalled that, as I had wandered around in the building, I stirred up clouds of dust and dislodged cobwebs. I must be the first to enter the building in years. The group of people who left their mark where they crossed the creek certainly had not been in here. This place was not where I would find Callum.

As I walked the same path between the two buildings as miner staff trod years before, the silence was eerie. The occasional birdcall was faint and distant, so unlike how they were in the rest of the bush. No breeze intruded here. Nothing flapped or rattled in the still air. Time slipped away, and the day warmed up noticeably. I felt a sudden desire to finish poking about and be away from there. After a quick look at the area around the two structures, I strode to the entrance of the second building.

Nothing barred entry here, the door having disappeared long ago. This once imposing two-storey edifice appeared to be where processing occurred; a crushing house of sorts maybe. It was obvious this building had deteriorated more than the other. Much of the roof was gone and large areas of the corrugated iron walls were missing. Vines were reclaiming the site. They entwined themselves around rusting hulks of machinery and hung from bits of the building wherever its walls were substantial enough to bear the vines' weight. Large concrete blocks set in the floor bore evidence of large pieces of machinery having been bolted to them in the past. With the machinery long since removed, the place was a gaping cavern.

No need to explore this building. There was little to see and nowhere to hide anything or anyone. A quick scan of the floor area immediately inside the doorway showed nothing disturbed here for some time before my arrival. Outside again, I took a moment to note the few pieces of rusted and tangled machinery and foundation blocks dotting the area between the crushing house and the mine entrance.

Then, the time had come. With nowhere else on the site to investigate other than the mine itself, I wondered how safe the shaft was after all this time. The thought made me hesitate for a moment or two. "For God's sake, Sonny, get it over and done with," I admonished myself aloud.

Again, there was no evidence of anyone venturing into the shaft in a long time. It was dank and dusty. I felt my nose wrinkle up at the prevailing smell. A few metres in from the opening, all trace of daylight disappeared. My powerful torch seemed swallowed by the impenetrable blackness stretching out before me. "This is not one of my most favourite places," I said aloud. The sound of my own voice somehow eased the tension building in me. But, that other small voice, the one in my head, did not help matters by continually reminding me this was a foolhardy endeavour and one where I should have backup. In the interest of doing a thorough job, I picked my way over rubble and other debris for about 30 metres along the shaft to where a rockfall blocked it.

It was an old fall, not a recent incident. For a moment I wondered if it was what closed the mine. Were workers trapped by the fall? Was the place now a tomb? Such thoughts were not helpful in my current situation. Having determined I couldn't go any further, I retraced my steps to emerge into clean air and dappled sunlight again. I checked the rest of the site for any other possible places to hide a person – or body – before heading back.

Recollection of something said at dinner last night flashed to the front of my thinking. When I asked Chris about early mining in the area, he mentioned the abandoned mine site and said it was a gold mine. The fact I had never heard about gold in this area didn't mean much, but I now doubted the accuracy of his statement. I don't know much about mining, but I do know something about prospecting for gold. Those on the look-out for gold looked those parts of the place with sizable quartz areas, the quartz serving as indicator of possible gold deposits. There is no quartz in this area. It's mainly sandstone with some granite. It's more likely this was a coalmine. The few lumps of 'black stuff' scattered in and around the crushing house tended to support my assumption.

The whole exercise, while a disappointing, confirmed Callum was not on the mine site. Time to face the return trek through the scrub. My instincts are not usually so far off target as they were about this site. Evidence found in the bush yesterday strongly underpinned today's investigation. While the morning was not a waste, I am no closer to finding Callum, and I still have nothing substantive to use to persuade the police to investigate a missing person.

My time at the mine site allowed my shirt and hair to dry. By the time I emerged from the scrub and headed for my car, they were both soaked again. A few minutes sitting under the big shady tree in today's whisper of a breeze helped dry my shirt a bit before I climbed into my vehicle and drove to the police station. The sinking feeling I had as I marched into the station proved justified.

Sergeant McClelland, the officer in charge, arrived at the station only a few minutes earlier and still looked hot and bothered from his trip. He made no secret of the fact he wasn't keen to waste time listening to my story, but I persisted.

"An acquaintance, who is a work colleague of a friend of mine, went missing some time during the evening of the festival ball. He seems to have vanished without explanation before midnight. No one has seen him since and he has not returned to work at Millhaven. As unlikely as it seems, given what we know of the man in question, his continued disappearance is worrying. Our concern is tending towards his having met with foul play. Under the circumstances, we feel compelled to report him as a missing person and ask your assistance in locating him."

To say I was summarily dismissed would be polite. The good Sergeant was rude, and generous with insulting comments. Before showing me the door, he told me the man, if he were missing, probably felt disappearing was the only way to escape two demanding females. Not normally prone to speechlessness, McClelland's parting comment brought it on. I stormed out to my car and fumed all the way back to the motel.

"I haven't had lunch," I told the universe as I approached the motel's parking area. A quick U-turn had me parked a few moments later in front of the only food place I knew of on the street. Armed with a chicken and salad roll and a bottle of orange juice, my intention was to eat in my room, until I saw Emily sitting under the pergola attached to the rear of the motel. She seemed engrossed in whatever she was reading and didn't look up. The frown creating deep furrows across her forehead was not a good sign. She jumped when I spoke.

"What's with the face? Whatever you're reading can't be good news. Perhaps you should tell me about it so we can share the concern."

"You startled me. I was reading my notes from this morning. The notes I made after my meeting with the journalist. I don't think he had much happening today, so he gave me quite a bit of time and we ended up having lunch together."

"Sounds promising… Did he have anything enlightening to offer? I'm guessing, by the frown on your face, he didn't have good news."

"It's a bit intriguing. He says he's confirmed there was an incident – 'brawl' is a better description, he says – between a group of locals and some mining company heavyweights. No one seems to know anything, or is prepared to talk about it. He has hit a brick wall with trying to put together a story. There are snippets of news about the mining company's big wigs' visit, and he heard whispers of a major anti-fracking rally to take place the day after tomorrow. It's part of the 'Lock the Gate' campaign encouraging landowners to make a stand against the mining company. The campaign is happening in all areas of the state where fracking is planned."

"I wonder why there is a blanket of silence over the incident and who is behind it. My suspicion is there is covert collusion between the mining company and some renegade local element. It would be interesting to know whether all of the landowners with properties earmarked as fracking sites are opposed to the proposal, or if there is a splinter group more interested in the dollars they might receive. Perhaps it's something to ask Chris over dinner tonight. I wonder if the reason Chris' spending a few days in town has something to do with the forthcoming rally. It won't be easy asking him about it, if no outsiders are supposed to know."

"Yeah, I agree, and I wouldn't want locals to know the source of our information. My friend, the journo, has to work in this town afterwards."

"Apart from his being so good looking, what's your opinion of Chris?"

"While I agree about his looks, I also think he is friendly and good company. He seems happy enough to answer questions and provide information about the area … and I suspect you are about to tell me you think otherwise."

"Hmm, the jury is still out on that one. However, I do have some reservations about how much of what he tells us is the truth. I have the feeling there is a certain degree of bullshit amongst it." I explained about his goldmine being more likely a coalmine.

"So, he didn't remember all the details correctly. It doesn't mean he was careless with the truth. Maybe over dinner tonight he will be able to convince 'the jury' he is the real deal." Emily tried to make her response sound light hearted, but I know her well enough to detect an edge when I hear it.

For Emily's sake, as much as to convince me to trust him, I would like to believe Chris is the 'real deal', as Emily puts it.

Chapter 5

With Emily doing her own thing for the rest of the afternoon, I was free to sit and think. To think about what the hell I might do next to find Callum. In spite of again poring over the map and tourist brochures, no new thoughts emerged. There was nowhere in Cranvale environs to hold someone without the locals noticing. Maybe Callum was spirited away to somewhere outside Cranvale… but where?

Any of the large surrounding pastoral or agricultural properties could be ideal for holding someone captive. "Would it be possible without the landowner's knowledge or involvement? Suppose one of the landowners who supports the fracking initiative is involved. A remote building on his property might be available. Nah, the idea is too far-fetched," I murmured, continuing my conversation with myself as I further examined the map.

"Is it too far-fetched?" I yelped, startling myself. "It *is* possible, but it wouldn't happen unless Callum did something to cause it."

This new line of thinking had possibilities. It's the only plausible explanation for his disappearance. Callum is not a local and, as far as I know, had nothing to do with CSG in this area before coming here for the weekend. He needed to threaten the mining company's plans in some way to necessitate his removal from the scene. What could he do that was so serious? I don't know what Callum thinks about fracking. Was he for or against it, and what were his thoughts about drilling on prime agricultural land? I should have asked Emily about it. It might prove wise to know before dinner with Chris tonight.

Emily didn't answer her room phone. I tried her mobile; no answer there either. Five minutes later, she called back. "Sorry, I was having a swim."

"You might have been getting wet, but you weren't swimming." The motel's postage-stamp-sized pool would allow no more than one stroke in any direction. "If you you're not doing anything else, come to my room once you've dried off. I've a couple of things to run past you before we go to dinner."

I got straight down to business when she arrived. "I have a vague idea. It needs more information to develop it. Time is slipping away and we aren't any closer to finding out why or how Callum disappeared."

She nodded. Then, near to tears, she shook her head as if to rid herself of bad memories. "I know. I've been trying not to think about it. What information do you need? I don't know if I can help. Maybe between us…"

No point tiptoeing around the subject. Get on with it. "I'm not convinced Chris is familiar with the truth. Maybe I'll feel differently after dinner. Tonight, I'll ask direct questions about the mining company, CSG, fracking, and Chris' involvement in any or all of it. Feel free to jump in if you think of something to strengthen the questioning or clarify an issue. I don't want you trying to soften or water down my approach because of your soft spot for Chris."

"Thank you, Sonny; as if I would. I'm quite capable of playing the game. My feelings for Chris won't get in the way because there aren't any. In case you've forgotten, it's Callum's disappearance we are investigating, and that's my focus."

More ruffled feathers. Nevertheless, Emily is behaving unlike herself. I might be wrong, maybe it's not feelings for Chris, but her concern for Callum influencing her behaviour. I spent the time until dinner trying to make amends. Emily remained tense when we entered the restaurant, but I felt things between us were safe enough not to create a problem.

Chris was at the bar. We ordered drinks and moved to the same table we occupied last night. Until someone came to take our meal orders, we could proceed with tonight's conversations. I opened in neutral territory. "How was your day, Chris? I assume you had business to deal with, and these few days in town are not rest and recreation for you."

"Yeah, I am waiting for parts for one of our pumps. I think they're coming from Brisbane by camel. Meetings occupied most of the day, so I'm not hanging around just for the parts."

Emily put on a grave face. "You must be feeling drained after a day of meetings. I would rather run a marathon than endure that. I find most meetings exhausting even if I haven't had to do any more than look intelligent and stick my hand up to vote when necessary."

"Meetings can be like that. Today's were interesting and lively. So, for a change, I don't feel exhausted so much as hyped up by positive outcomes."

I sensed he was itching to share, to crow about those 'positive outcomes'. I decided to oblige. "Well, since your day was exciting, can you share anything to help brighten our day?"

He laughed. "They all dealt with local issues; important but uninteresting to outsiders."

As she leant in closer, Emily donned an excited expression. "Try us. So far, we haven't anything to skite about when we return home. How little it would take to stir our interest might surprise you. So, try us; brighten our day."

Chris, mimicking her actions, leant over towards Emily. "Well…" he whispered in a conspiratorial way, "the meetings were all about fracking." He laughed and sat back in his chair. "See, I said it wouldn't interest you."

With their eyes locked, Chris and Emily were grinning like the proverbial Cheshire cats. Time to put this evening back on an even keel. "I would like to know more about this fracking thing everyone in town is talking about. I want to understand how it works and why it's causing so much fuss. What can you tell us?"

It worked; the two pairs of big blue eyes unlocked and both parties looked embarrassed as they straightened their cutlery. God, spare me from love struck thirty-something-year olds, I mentally pleaded. Best to pretend nothing happened. I continued my quest for information. "I remember hearing about fracking causing serious community upheaval in some parts of New South Wales, and I think in Queensland too. How does it work? What is this CSG I keep hearing about, and what's the problem with it?"

"Coal Seam Gas… it's a big money earner for the mining companies who export it overseas. They export so much, domestic supply is scarce and, therefore, expensive. The government is applying pressure on mining companies to make more available within Australia, and thereby lower the domestic price. If there is a better domestic supply and the price comes down, the end consumer – everyday Australian households and businesses – get cheaper electricity and the environment benefits from clean electricity production."

So far, Chris hadn't told me anything I didn't know but I tried looking fascinated. Then I tried looking perplexed. "Okay … sounds reasonable. So, what is the problem?"

"The mining companies don't want to reduce overseas exports and lose revenue. A solution is to make more gas available. That involves more drilling. A favourite extraction method is fracking."

"S-o-o, fracking is the problem, and not the use of CSG?" Emily asked.

"Yes. Concern is about the possible impact fracking might have on underground water supplies in Australia where so much relies on our huge artesian basin for water. In addition, some overseas researchers suggest fracking might increase the likelihood of earthquakes. They identified a substantial increase in earthquakes in non-traditional earthquake prone areas where fracking occurred."

"They seem good reasons for concern," I commented. Chris continued with our education.

"In this area, the mining company wants to extract CSG from prime pastoral and agricultural lands. This involves dozens – sometimes even hundreds – of drill sites on an individual property. The landowner ends up with much of his land thrown out of production, either because his water supply is affected, or by the fencing around each well occupying so much area. Australia needs cheaper electricity, but it also needs its agricultural and pastoral industries. Many Australians, apart from landowners, rely on those for their livelihood."

"Lost production could affect all of us. I like plenty of reasonably priced fruit, vegetables and meats to choose from when I go shopping." I looked at Emily as I finished speaking. She added her comments.

"Even bread could become expensive if availability of flour is impacted by prime grain growing land being thrown out of production."

Our meals arrived causing the usual interruption to conversation. The hiatus allowed me to mentally frame my next questions for Chris.

After allowing a few minutes to savour the food – mediocre at best – I reignited the conversation. "How do you stop a mining company coming onto your land and destroying your livelihood? As the landowner, can't you refuse them permission to drill on your land? When a whole community is against it, surely the mining company wouldn't stand a chance."

"It's a bit like David and Goliath, with the community as David and the mining companies as Goliath. An individual landowner has no chance. Even a whole community stands little chance against the multi-million dollar mining companies, especially when the government is encouraging the companies to extract the gas."

"So it's a hopeless cause," Emily murmured. "I saw bits on TV about people chaining themselves to pieces of equipment and barricading their gates. Some went to jail for their efforts. I think one old bloke shot someone to keep them off his land."

"Yeah, we've recourse to fairly futile means of preventing intrusion on our properties. The problem is, a landowner owns only the land. He doesn't own anything under the land, including any minerals and water. They remain the property of the government. Our only hope is to be as disruptive and to make as much noise as possible about our plight in a bid to garner support from outside our community, including from politicians and environmental groups."

Chris went on to outline Cranvale's attempts so far to block the mining company. They were the usual measures employed in the past by every other community confronted with the same situation … and which suffered the same lack of success. Emily persisted with her questioning. "Isn't there something else – something more effective or powerful – to try?"

"This mining company has sunk to a new level. They brought in their own bullyboys to deal with any trouble. In the past, the police and sometimes the army kept things under control. There aren't many police officers out here, although every one of them was in town over the weekend."

"Why…? Was trouble expected?" I demanded. This was what I wanted to know about.

"Some of the mining company's top executives were in town for a meeting with the Mayor, Council CEO and a couple of the town's other 'leading lights'. It was all hush-hush. Most people didn't know it was happening. The executives came in by light plane early Saturday morning. Their pack of goons arrived by road during the day. The way their visit was orchestrated told us something rotten was afoot. The goons' arrival in town confirmed our concerns."

After discussing the community's past efforts at resisting the mining giant, I was about to ask a major question when my companions' desserts arrived. I waited while the other two moaned in pleasure over their sweets. While they ate, I signalled a waiter for coffee all round. Then, I pushed on with exploring the community's stand against fracking.

"You indicated your campaign has had little effect against fracking. What's your next move? I don't see many other options open to you."

"You're right. There are not a lot, and none of them is likely to make a difference. Nevertheless, we can't sit on our backsides and do nothing. It's why a major rally is planned for tomorrow. Quite a few people from outside the district indicated they will slip quietly into town to participate. The rally starts at ten o'clock. Even if it achieves nothing else, it will make life difficult for the mayor and his cronies for a few hours."

"Why hold it tomorrow?"

"Tomorrow is the first 'official' meeting between the mining company and the community about their plans for the district. Some company executives will arrive between now and then. Their advance vanguard has been here since the end of last week. There's word of rough looking blokes arrived in a neighbouring town today. We suspect they are the mining company's heavyweights who probably will be in Cranvale in time for the planned meeting tomorrow morning."

It's surprising such info filtered through to the residents. Locally, there is strong suspicion the mayor and possibly a couple of his close mates on the council are in bed with the mining company. I wondered how much 'backhander' they received for their 'assistance'. I needed to be an interested bystander at the rally tomorrow.

Coffee arrived. While I waited for everything to settle again, I thought about how to use Chris' comments to move the conversation to where I wanted it to go. I decided to jump straight in with my BIG question.

"I've heard whispers about an incident in town the night of the B&S ball. Given all you said about the mining company bringing in its own heavyweights, do you think such an incident would involve locals as well as the imported muscle? Do you know about any incident?"

There; I had asked the question I wanted to ask for the last two days. I hoped my wording made it difficult for Chris to avoid a straight answer. His answer might help sort out what happened to Callum… and it might indicate whether we can trust anything Chris tells us. Chris took a while to consider my question. When he began, he avoided eye contact – not an encouraging sign – before again stirring what remained of his coffee, and clearing his throat a couple of times. After a quick scan of the restaurant, he answered in a voice not much above a whisper.

"Yeah, I believe there was a ruckus in town over the weekend. I wonder if I might interest you two ladies in a nightcap. We could retire to somewhere more comfortable perhaps."

I thought about the state of my room. The map and tourist brochures were scattered over the table, but I could fix that. "Sounds like an excellent idea. Let's take something from the bar back to my room." I'm sure this is not what Chris had in mind, but I wanted to take charge of the situation, to hold the position of power perhaps.

When halfway to the bar, I turned to Emily and Chris, trailing in my wake. "I'll let you two choose our nightcap. Have them bring it and a pot of coffee to my room." I headed out of the restaurant. Emily and Chris continued to the bar to arrange our fortification for the next phase of our evening.

In my room, I gathered up all the paper strewn on the table and shoved it into the bottom of the wardrobe. I plonked two bottles of water and glasses from the bar fridge on the table as the other two arrived. Our coffee and nightcap arrived shortly after. There were the usual few moments of fussing about until we settled. I wasted no time restarting the dialogue.

"Okay, Chris, what is so confidential you couldn't share it with us in an empty restaurant? What's going on… or perhaps I should ask why mentioning the incident from the other night makes you so nervous."

"I can confirm the incident in town. It was an all-in brawl. Look, I'm not trying to avoid the question, or be devious in any way, but I have to ask why you're interested in what happened. In fact, I feel all our conversations have amounted to a gentle but definite interrogation. Now it's my turn to ask. What's going on?"

I tried looking surprised, but I'm not good at pretence. Emily's eyes were focused on her hands on the table. Perhaps coming clean with Chris, is the only way to get any information from him. "Right, cards on the table; Emily was a visitor invited here for the festival weekend. I'm her friend and a private investigator. I came to Cranvale in response to Emily's call after something disturbing happened on the night of the ball. Emily was due to go back to work, but stayed on to assist with my investigation. Did I answer some of your questions?"

"Thank you. Yes, but you posed another one. Was the 'disturbing happening' the incident in town, or something else?"

"Without wanting to appear obtuse or to avoid the question, I don't know. It's why I wanted details of the incident. With so little information about it, it's hard to know where to begin, or what assumptions it's safe to make. If you tell me about the brawl, I might make more sense when I try to explain our situation."

For a few moments, I withered under his hard gaze as he weighed up his options. Then, having made his decision, he began his story.

"A couple of local lads from one of the stations came into town for the festival weekend but didn't go to the ball. After too much to drink, and having seen the mining company executives go into the council chambers, they made a nuisance of themselves in the street outside the chambers. An older brother of one of the boys was at the ball. Someone called him about the situation in town. He rushed to try to sort things out before his brother got into trouble, but was too late. By the time he reached the council chambers, his brother and the other lad were lying in the gutter. They suffered serious injuries from the beating they received. He noticed a few rough-looking blokes prowling outside the council chambers, and called a mate at the ball about what he found."

"I suppose they had drunk enough by then to feel bullet-proof, and charged into town to make heroes of themselves." I could imagine how everything escalated from there.

"Yeah; the bloke who got the call rounded up a few of his mates and they headed into town. Word spread around others at the ball. A few of them decided to join in. When we arrived at the council chambers, the second brother – the one who called to rally his mates – was lying unconscious in the middle of the street. The goons parading outside the council chambers moved down to form a line along the edge of the footpath. We couldn't get to the two boys lying in the gutter, but we could see they were badly injured. Buoyed up by alcohol and the fact we outnumbered the goons, we rushed the blokes on the footpath. An almighty brawl broke out."

"It sounds like you were lucky to escape with just the marks on your face and your knuckles. What happened to the injured lads?"

"Even with extra police brought in for the weekend, there still weren't many of them. They expected any trouble on the night to happen at the ball, and stationed themselves around the hall. Someone must've tipped them off about the brawl, but they were a while arriving. As if by some miracle, the brawl broke up the moment they arrived. The council chambers' door partially opened and the goons disappeared inside. The police called the paramedics. They carted those with serious injuries off to hospital. The rest of us either returned to the ball, or went home to lick our wounds. Does that help with whatever you're investigating?"

"Possibly… It might have some bearing on our situation, but I can't see how or why." I looked at Emily. She was silent since the conversation began, and remained focused on her hands now clasped tightly on the table. Some comment from her would be good, but it wasn't likely. Perhaps gentle persuasion is required.

"Emily, do you think it's possible Callum went to see what was going on in town? From what people said, I think the timing is about right."

Emily shook her head. "I wouldn't think so. I can't see why he would want to. He's not local and isn't involved with what's going on here. Why would he be interested?"

Her logic was right, but she overlooked another aspect of Callum. I realised she might not know about the other side to her recent romantic interest. Go gently with this one, I told myself as I tried formulating an answer.

"As a geologist, I understand Callum's interest in the community's thoughts about fracking, but something else might underpin Callum's interest." I saw Emily frown and shake her head in confusion.

"What else? Apart from spending the weekend at the festival with me, I mean."

I let the comment about 'with her' slip by unanswered. "I thought he might see the situation here as a potential story, the basis of a feature article perhaps."

"What are you talking about, Sonny? We are talking about Callum, not the journalist I had lunch with."

So, Emily is unaware of Callum's freelance writing career. Since he writes under a pseudonym, she wouldn't know unless someone told her about it – and it's obvious Callum didn't. I did. She struggled with the information.

"Why wouldn't he tell me? You'd think he'd be proud to tell those close to him about it. I'd be interested in reading his articles." All I could do was shrug. While I hated the thought, sometime soon I would have to tell Emily about his other 'interests' besides her. But, that was not now.

Chris knocked gently on the table for our attention. "Hello, I'm still here. Thought I should remind you in case you had forgotten about me. Would someone care to tell me about this 'Callum thing'? Who is he, and why do I sense you both are worried about him?"

"He's disappeared," Emily blurted out.

Chris spun around to face me. His eyebrows were heading for the ceiling. "A little more information would be handy, like when he disappeared, and from where."

It took only a few moments to tell him as succinctly as possible what we knew about Callum's disappearance. It didn't take long because we didn't know anything other than he was missing. Chris directed a couple of questions to Emily: did you have a row? Was he bored with the festival? Emily gave him the same one-word answer to both questions: NO. With no success there, Chris turned to me.

"He might have gone home and has returned to work."

Out of the corner of my eye, I saw Emily straighten as she prepared to argue. I jumped in first. "No, he is not back at work. I checked. It suggests he hasn't gone home; hasn't left this area."

In my peripheral vision, Emily aimed a hostile look my way. The reality of the situation spread across Chris' face.

"You think he tagged along to the ruckus happening in front of the council chambers, and things went bad for him. If any of the mining mob recognised him as a reporter, they might single him out for 'special' treatment … more special than they dished out to the locals, I mean."

Damn; I knew what Chris meant, but did he have to spell it out in front of Emily? Not wanting to encourage further such talk, I gave him only a slight nod in response.

"What about the police? Have you...?"

I cut him off. "Yes, I have spoken to them. They were no more interested today than when Emily spoke to them at the time Callum disappeared. There seems to be an 'information embargo' over that ruckus. Even the journalist Emily spoke to has managed to glean only sketchy details about what happened."

I glanced at Emily. Tears welled in her eyes and were about to cascade down her cheeks. Chris correctly interpreted the meaningful look I shot him.

"It's late, and I don't think there is much we can do tonight. Leave it with me. I'll have a bit of a nose around tomorrow to see if I can find out anything."

I could have kissed him for the way he responded to the situation. Instead, I restricted myself to thanking him and handing over my mobile number so he could contact me if he discovered anything.

After Chris left, it took me a few minutes to settle Emily sufficiently before letting her go back to her own room. Tomorrow would arrive soon enough. Another day since Callum's disappearance and still no leads on his likely whereabouts.

Chapter 6

What a night…! I feel as though I haven't slept at all. Thoughts about what I might do today to progress finding Callum kept me company all night, and have me no wiser than when I went to bed. I ordered breakfast in my room for six o'clock. When I ordered it last evening, I told myself I needed time alone to develop an action plan for today. Now, I think I was being a coward. It was about not wanting to face people when I didn't have a clue what to do next.

As a clear indication of how desperate I felt, and how totally out of ideas I was after so many days, Ben Richards' name came to mind. Ben, top cop at the Millhaven precinct, was out of town at some conference all of last week. While dawdling over my coffee, I realised he was due back on the job this week. Ben and I go back a long way as friends. At one time, it looked like we might become something more than that, but the timing wasn't right, and then life intervened to separate us for a few years. Since re-establishing our friendship, Ben has saved my skin a few times when cases I was working turned sour and, on occasion, became life threatening. On the other hand, some of my investigations helped with his cases, and balanced the ledger a bit.

After dithering for too long about whether to ring Ben or not, my coffee was cold. I abandoned pride and ego, and opted for asking for his suggestions on what I might do next. It was early, but I knew he would be up and possibly even at work by now.

"Sonny, how nice of you to welcome me home – finally, and at such an early hour too. No, don't tell me… you have a problem with the case you're working on." Then a more serious note entered his voice. "Is it an emergency? Do you need rescuing? What's happened?"

"Yes, welcome back and all that. Now, if you stop asking questions long enough for me to get a word in, I'll tell you about my case."

"If it's not urgent, why not tell me about it over dinner tonight? I'll bring something. We can catch up on what happened while I was away, and look at sorting out your case while we are about it."

"Nice idea …but, unless you're planning to be in Cranvale by this evening, it ain't going to happen." Detailing Callum's disappearance took up the next few minutes. I ended by telling him the Cranvale police were not interested and dismissed the whole incident as some sort of domestic situation. After checking a few details with me, Ben went quiet. I assumed he was analysing my information, so I waited with as much patience as I could muster until he spoke again.

"Some unsavoury whispers about the mining company in question circulated at the conference I attended. It amounted to plenty of suspicion but no evidence. Cranvale eh…? As top cop in the Ralston district police area, Cranvale falls under Pete Messell's jurisdiction."

"Should I call to discuss Callum's disappearance with him?"

"No, don't do that. I'll give him a call. He also needs to be aware of what I heard while at the conference. Some major ongoing incident in Ralston at the time prevented Pete from attending the first couple of days of the conference. By the time he was free to attend, he decided it wasn't worth it. Let me talk to him first. He'll probably contact you afterwards. Stay in touch. I need to know you are safe and haven't done anything stupid – like disappearing the same way this Callum bloke has."

Ben's parting comment sounded sweet until rational thinking kicked in. He wasn't being sweet; he was being concerned. For him to be concerned about my safety while investigating this case, those 'whispers' he heard at the conference must be bad – really bad. The fact he didn't share them with me tends to back up my assumption. If I'm right, I now have concerns about Emily's safety. She should return to Millhaven where she would be safe, but I know convincing her to leave Cranvale would be impossible.

After breakfast, I spent the next few hours in my room updating my case notes, and yet again poring over the map and tourist brochures. They hadn't changed and failed to produce any new clues for me. It was just after ten o'clock when Pete Messell called.

Early in their careers, Ben Richards and Pete Messell served at Millhaven. Their careers seemed to progress in unison. Where one went, the other followed. Although they climbed the rankings ladder at much the same pace, Ben always was one rung above Pete wherever they ended up together. The tie binding them was broken after Ben's promotion to Officer in Charge at Millhaven. When Ben left the Ralston precinct, Pete inherited Ben's previously position as OIC at Ralston. The three of us shared a strong friendship from those early days when both men were at Millhaven, a friendship which extends to the current day.

I expected to repeat the story of Callum's disappearance for Pete, but was surprised. Ben did a thorough job of passing on the information. Pete's call was brief. He asked few questions and provided little information other than to say he would be having dinner with me tonight. Not too difficult to interpret his comment: Pete Messell would arrive in Cranvale some-time today.

Later, I wondered whether this was a lone senior ranking officer coming to Cranvale, or if he were bringing his 'cavalry' with him. Ah well, maybe I'll find out at dinner tonight. In the meantime, I still had to work out what to do with myself today. Time is slipping away too fast to be in Callum's best interest … if I continue to believe he is still alive. My priority this morning might be to avoid Emily. Whatever I choose to do today, her involvement has the potential to be a hindrance rather than helpful. She is too close to the situation and, understandably, too emotionally invested in it.

With nothing scheduled until the rally supposed to begin at ten o'clock, I wondered how to fill in my time. Then I remembered the last thing Emily said before she left my room last night. Today she intended hanging around town to covertly observe the rally and to see who might be involved. If she followed through on her plan, it wouldn't matter if I wasn't there. Having settled that issue for myself, I decided again to explore the scrub behind the hall. So far, I had examined only the area along both sides of the creek. There was plenty more scrub to tramp through.

As I threw my backpack in the car in readiness for my morning's bushwalk, a thought hit me. Leaving my car near the hall for all to see while I wandered around in the scrub might not be in my best interest. Perhaps it would be wiser if my activities in that area remained unknown. With my back-pack slung over one shoulder, I took a slow and nonchalant amble through town before detouring down a laneway almost at the other end of town.

The laneway led to a service road running along behind commercial premises at this end of the street. After following the service road along to the last building, I peeled off at right angles and dashed across about five metres of open ground to the edge of the scrub. After a short distance into it, I turned and made my way towards the rear of the hall. I was almost at the hall before I realised how quiet the town was this morning.

Given it wasn't too long before the rally was due to start, I expected there to be a build-up of activity; more vehicles entering town, more people on the street. I was wrong. In fact, it seemed quieter than in previous days. Perhaps part of the rally strategy was for nothing different to be obvious to give the game away to any interested observers. Maybe the rally participants were gathering at some designated place out of sight and away from the main street. Sometime later today, it will be interesting to hear Emily's account of this morning's events but, for now, my focus was on exploring more of the scrub.

Today's route took me off at an acute angle away from the area explored previously. The undergrowth here was thicker than I encountered yesterday. I applauded my decision to forego shorts and summer shirt in favour of a long-sleeved shirt and jeans today. With my shirt buttoned up to the collar, the hordes of mosquitoes and other biting insects disturbed as I ploughed my way through the undergrowth took their revenge on any unprotected part of me, such as head and hands.

This part of the scrub proved hard going while yielding nothing in the way of clues about Callum's disappearance. I was about to give up and turn back when I noticed the undergrowth appeared to thin out a little up ahead. After telling myself I'd come this far and I might as well see what's up ahead, I pushed on. After another few minutes, I almost stumbled out of the scrub into a clearing.

Not a natural clearing, it looked as though it was created for use as a laydown area for a construction firm. The large area, bounded on all sides by thick scrub, was accessed via a now clearly defined track only a few metres away from where I stood. A number of shipping containers, and a small demountable building such as construction firms often use as a site office, occupied the area closest to me. Stacked in various piles along one side of the clearing were lengths of piping and what I guessed to be large valves of some type. A number of pieces of heavy equipment were parked at the far end of the area.

The place looked deserted. What better opportunity for a look around…? While there was no fencing to keep intruders out, somehow I felt visitors were not welcome. I hesitated for a few moments at the edge of the scrub. I could claim I was being cautious but, in reality, I was plucking up courage to overcome my foreboding about venturing into the clearing. No courage required in the end … the decision was taken out of my hands.

As I was about to step out into the open, I caught the sound of a vehicle approaching … fast. Careering further back into the undergrowth, I found myself a position with a good view of the first half of the clearing. I barely had stopped thrashing about in the bushes when two large black four-wheel drive vehicles sped into view and came to an abrupt stop almost in front of me.

Six blokes in total spewed out of them as soon as they stopped. The drivers remained in the vehicles. A couple of minutes of frenzied activity followed as blokes rushed in and out of various shipping containers. Somewhere out of sight, a number of engines sprang into life. One of the SUVs moved forward and disappeared into one of the larger shipping containers. I heard the heavy doors of the container slam shut, and saw the driver rush to another container.

Within moments, a procession of bikes came towards where the second vehicle remained parked and idling. I counted four trail bikes and two quad bikes. After exchanging a few words with one of the blokes, the driver of the SUV turned his vehicle around and headed out of the clearing. At about the same time, another engine started and a third quad bike came to join the rest of the contingent waiting patiently in front of me. The rider of this last bike was the driver of the car now stashed in one of the containers. Something of a last minute conflab between the riders occurred before, in a neat single file, all seven bikes roared out.

Indecision kept me anchored amongst the undergrowth. Should I take the opportunity for a good look around, or should I leave the area while it appeared safe to do so. One question nagged me. What if I miscounted the number of people who arrived, and one of them remained somewhere on the site? I almost convinced myself to seize the opportunity when the sound of another engine put paid to the notion. The deep throb of the motor approached at speed. It seemed to arrive before I had time to do much more than sink down onto my knees again.

This new arrival was a powerful motorbike ridden by a huge bloke with a flowing red beard. Dressed in black leathers and wearing a vest decorated with many colour patches, he was an imposing sight. After dismounting, he stood hands on hips surveying the clearing for a while before beginning a patrol of the site. He strode off to the far end before making his way back towards me, checking on each of the containers as he went. At one of the nearest ones, he stopped and tried to shine a small torch through a window set high up in the side wall. This was a departure from his method of checking on the other containers.

He tried various angles for a better view of the interior of the container before abandoning his efforts and marching into the small demountable building. After a few moments inside, he returned to the container he had shone his torch into. This time, he unlocked and opened the doors wide enough to shine his torch inside. Satisfied with whatever he found there, he locked it again before slowly ambling back towards his bike, his earlier urgency now disappeared.

My legs ached and began to cramp. I needed to stretch them to start circulation flowing again. Just a bit longer, I told myself. I felt sure the bloke's intention was to return to his bike and depart the scene like the others before him. But, it seems my assessment of the situation was wrong. The rider now carried his helmet. His mop of springy red curls matched his beard. Instead of going directly to his bike, the bloke seemed happy to just wander around stroking his beard while making several phone calls.

Perhaps his mission was to remain at the clearing until the others returned. Maybe he was a sort of security guard and would patrol the area until relieved by someone else. Such thoughts were no comfort. I knew I couldn't move without drawing attention to myself, but I also knew I couldn't maintain my present position for too much longer. A glimmer of hope came when, with his phone still clamped to his ear, he marched into the demountable.

After allowing a few moments to be sure he wasn't going reappear, I judged it safe to try moving further back into the scrub. My legs had other ideas. They didn't want to co-operate and didn't seem capable of supporting me. Not quite upright, I managed to hobble a short distance before a sound made me freeze. I covered only a couple of metres before the sound of Black Leathers exiting the demountable brought my escape to an end. My pulse escalated and I think I stopped breathing. Had I alerted him to my presence? Further observation eliminated that concern.

The bloke worked his mobile phone with obvious increasing anger. No one seemed to answer his calls. Then I heard him yelling into his phone. I couldn't make out what was said, but someone received an unpleasant voice message. After that, he gave up on phone calls and took to stomping about without going anywhere. Perhaps it was his way of dealing with his anger, but frequent checking of his phone didn't help. Finally, his phone rang. By then, his stomping about had taken him further across the clearing from me. While I couldn't make out what was said, it was a heated call.

When it ended, the bloke resumed patrolling the area. It was obvious his anger had not abated. As he neared the far end of the clearing again, I prepared to make another attempt at moving deeper into the bush. The sound of an approaching vehicle foiled my plan. Within moments, an expensive looking black 4x4 growled into view. It halted a short distance into the clearing. Black Leathers stormed over to the driver's window.

A serious argument erupted through the partially lowered driver's window. Then, the driver slammed open his door, almost knocking Black Leathers off his feet. The well-dressed new-comer climbed out of the car. Wow, that driver was one ballsy bloke! Black Leathers was huge and mean looking. Not deterred by the look of his opponent, the driver continued the argument out in the open, and the situation escalated. Within a few moments, the argument became one-sided – with the driver in control.

It appeared the driver laid down the law and Black Leathers took it in silence. While I ached to know what was being said, what happened next was self-explanatory. With the battle apparently conceded in his favour, the driver gave Black Leathers a clear 'piss off' order. Without argument, Black Leathers, stormed over to his bike and roared off out of the clearing. The driver, smoothed down his jacket, straightened his tie, shot his cuffs, and climbed back into the car, slamming the door. I expected his immediate exit. He had other ideas.

While sitting in the car with the engine idling and the window up, the driver made a long phone call. His angry gesticulations suggested the call was not for a friendly chat. When it ended, he remained in the car drumming his fingers on the steering wheel for a few moments before climbing out of the vehicle again and heading for the demountable. He emerged only a couple of seconds later and went to one of the containers. The same container Black Leathers partially opened earlier.

He spent about a minute inside the container before locking its doors, and returning to his vehicle. Still he wasn't in a hurry to leave, instead taking a slow drive around and through the whole area before exiting via the track. While spending the next twenty minutes encouraging my legs to return to fully operational, I decided what to do next. No one else was around, and there was no indication of anyone's impending return. This was my opportunity. Having decided it was safe to enter the clearing for a poke around, I left my cover and started for the clearing. It was not meant to be.

The sound of bikes – several bikes – halted my progress. They were coming in my direction. Discretion demanded I get away from there before their arrival. I turned and picked my way carefully – but fast – back through the scrub to emerge behind the hall. My return to the motel was less covert than this morning's effort, and took quite a bit longer. This time, I wandered through town, stopping here and there to admire an old building, or to look in shop windows.

Evidence of a rally or any other major activity in town was just as scarce as it was this morning. My stomach rumbled reminding me it was now afternoon and I had missed lunch. I called in at the coffee shop in the hope a sandwich might be available. The owner emerged from out the back when she heard the floor boards creaking under my footsteps. I embarked on a fact finding conversation while she toasted my sandwich and made me a coffee. "The town seems quiet today," I suggested.

"No. This is about normal for a weekday here in town. Most weekends there is a bit more life in the place when the young ones off the surrounding properties come into town to let their hair down."

Well, that didn't go anywhere. Her comments didn't sound evasive, just honest. Have protest rallies become so common-place here they don't rate mention anymore? I hurried back to the motel in the hope of eliciting more information on today's rally from Emily. Thoughts of her brought something else to mind: how to avoid having dinner with her and Chris, if he is still in town, so Pete Messell and I could dine alone. When I caught up with Emily later, the dinner issue turned out not to be a problem.

Chapter 7

Late afternoon, Emily rang to see if I was in my room. Over another coffee, she confirmed Chris was still in town, and she apologised for not dining with me tonight.

"Chris is having dinner with friends on their nearby property and asked me to accompany him. The invitation extends to you as well."

I begged off going with them, telling her some work matters needing attention probably would keep me in my room this evening. While she didn't exactly jump for joy, it was obvious she wasn't disappointed.

It was about six o'clock when Pete Messell called to say he was booked into the motel and to enquire about dinner arrangements for tonight. We agreed to eat in my room. I ordered dinner for two from room service for about 7.30pm. Dinner taken care of, I wrote up my notes from my day in the scrub. That's when it hit me. "Damn! I forgot to ask Emily about the rally," I said as I reached for the phone.

"Sonny, I'm standing here dripping water all over the floor. I just got out of the shower. Was there something urgent you wanted?"

"No. I was going to ask you about today's protest rally but, perhaps it can wait until you dry off and put some clothes on."

"Ah well, that won't take long. There is nothing to tell. It didn't happen. I spent the morning with my friend, the local journo, in the hope being with him might give me more insight into who was involved and what was happening. When the appointed hour came and went and nothing seemed to be happening, he made a few phone calls. Didn't find out much, but there were indications the mining company big

70

boys, who were supposed to be in town today, didn't arrive. So, the locals agreed there was no point in holding the rally. I might discover more at dinner tonight. I'll let you know what I find out, but right now I am running late. Chris will be banging on my door any minute now … and I can hardly open the door to him in a bath towel."

The saucy giggle she gave after her last comment suggested it might be what she would like to do. While I'm sure her concern for Callum is as deep as ever, I think Chris is now the romantic frontrunner with Emily. With barely enough time to shower and change before Pete arrived, there wasn't time to dwell on anything she had told me.

In the last few minutes before Pete Messell knocked on my door, I decided to try identifying on the map where the clearing in the scrub might be and from where vehicles might access it. It only took a few moments to realise the rough map I had was of no use. It didn't give wide enough coverage or provide sufficient detail. A proper touring map would be better. The local service station might have one, but finding out if they do will have to wait until tomorrow. In the mean-time, Google might have something to offer. As I started my search, Pete arrived.

Over drinks before dinner, Pete told me what he knew of today's aborted protest rally, but emphasising his information was second hand. "It seems information about the Cranvale rally leaked to the mining executives. They promptly cancelled plans to fly in today. Not all their contingent of bully-boys waiting in nearby towns received word of the changed plans. About seven or eight of them arrived in Cranvale and, strange as it might seem, they knew exactly where the protestors were gathering prior to the rally. Quite a skirmish occurred before the intruders left town with their tails between their legs."

"That does tend to confirm someone 'in the know' is the Cranvale leak. I don't like their chances if the locals find out their identity. Is there any word on what happens now? Is a protest rally still likely sometime soon?"

"There is a whisper the mining executives will arrive in town either late tonight or early tomorrow morning. It seems the locals have heard the rumour too, and have postponed today's event until tomorrow. I suppose my main challenge while I'm here is to root out the local renegade who is leaking information to the mining company. My only interest is in making sure he stays alive and intact. As you said, I don't like his chances if the locals identify who it is."

Dinner arrived and, as we ate, I went over the details of Callum's disappearance. Then we arrived at the difficult bit. Pete wanted details of my investigation to date. The big question for me was whether to tell him about today's discovery or to withhold those details until I knew more about that clearing. It was something of a relief when Pete's interest focused on the trail along the creek and the blood I found there.

"I can understand it creating excitement when you found the blood but, as you pointed out, there is nothing to link it to Callum. Some bushwalker might have slipped and been injured on the rocks. What did you find on the other side of the creek? Was there any evidence of anyone having been there recently?"

"No; no indications of any visitors to the area in recent times. I don't think anyone's been near the place in a long while. It was disappointing. I thought the old mine shaft might be an ideal place to hold someone captive."

After dinner, we spent the next hour or two examining every aspect of Callum's disappearance and my investigation to date. When we exhausted this process Pete asked, "What have you done with Emily tonight? I'm surprised you managed to organise for us to have dinner alone. How is she holding up under the stress, and how serious is this thing between her and Callum?"

"It goes without saying she is concerned about what might have happened to him. Things seem to have changed a little since the night of the ball. When she rang me, she was close to hysteria. I'm not suggesting she is no longer concerned, but I sense her feelings for the man have changed. While I might describe her as being besotted with him before this happened, I think her romantic interest at the moment is more focused on Chris Tremaine."

"Chris Tremaine…? He is one of the leading lights in this anti-fracking mob isn't he? Does he show any sign of reciprocating Emily's interest?"

"You're right about his involvement in the anti-fracking mob. He has been booked into this motel since last weekend, and claims to be hanging around town waiting for some part for one of his pumps to arrive from down south. It was Chris who told us about the protest rally scheduled for today. So far, he has been a perfect gentleman, but there are signs he is interested in Emily. She is with him tonight… Oh, I don't mean like that… She went to dinner with him at his friend's place. Make what you will of it, but I think there is something developing there."

"Not enough to take her mind off finding Callum…?"

"No. As I said, she remains concerned for him. I think she just sees him in a different way now. I can't say I'm unhappy about it."

It was about ten o'clock when I surprised myself by deciding to tell Pete about what I found today. By the time I shared everything I knew and answered Pete's barrage of questions, it was quite late. Rather than looking to end the night, Pete seemed reinvigorated by my information.

"Where exactly is this clearing? Show me on a map so I can see its relation to the town." I explained my lack of a decent map and how I was about to interrogate Google when he arrived this evening. "Let's not bother Google at this hour of the night. Give me a minute while I slip back to my room.

I brought a couple of maps with me. We should be able to locate the clearing on at least one of them."

Tempting as Pete's offer to retrieve his maps was, it was late. My concern was, Emily might call in to chat to me after she and Chris returned to the motel tonight. Right now, I didn't want her to know Pete was here. In spite of my trust in Emily, she appears too close to Chris. I think it wise to keep her in the dark regarding the presence of Pete and his cavalry. After I explained my thinking to him, Pete agreed with me and returned to his own room. His hasty departure proved unnecessary. I waited until after midnight for Emily to contact me.

As time slipped by I became worried something might have happened to her. Against my better judgement, soon after one o'clock, I phoned her room. She didn't answer. Part of me was pleased, while a part of me was concerned. At least I wasn't embarrassed by intruding on her personal life, but I still didn't know if she was all right. I don't know what time she returned to the motel. I do know worrying about her caused me a restless night.

*****

Over breakfast, I pondered where to focus my investigation. What I wouldn't do is hang around town to witness the rally. While having some sympathy for the locals' fight against fracking, my goal was to investigate Callum's disappearance, and hopefully find him. What I would do today was an easy decision. In spite of Pete's instruction not to continue my investigation, particularly in the scrub area behind the hall, that is what I will do. My decision to ignore Pete's instruction won't go down well with him, but I needed to know more about what was going on in that clearing I found yesterday.

"It is an ideal place to hold a prisoner … or hide a body," I murmured aloud between sips of coffee. The possibility of finding Callum at the laydown area was a sobering thought, and one which reignited my concern for Emily. My call to her room went unanswered. Today was not off to a great start. Regardless, my first priority this morning is to check on her.

With the remnants of breakfast abandoned, I dressed and headed along the corridor to Emily's room. It was early and I didn't want to wake the other guests or draw attention to myself. I tapped gently on her door. No response. I knocked louder. A sound from inside the room told me someone was in there. As I was about to thump on the door again, a horrible thought occurred to me: how embarrassed would I be if, when she opened the door, I found she was not alone? I'll worry about it if it happens, I told myself – and raised my fist once more to pummel the door.

"Who is it?" Emily's voice called through the locked door.

"It's me, Sonny. I'm sorry if I woke you. I just wanted to make sure you were okay and to find out your plans for today before you disappeared."

I heard the chain on the door rattle, and a moment later Emily ushered me into her room. There is a god. She was alone and I didn't have to face the embarrassment of finding someone else there as well.

"When you didn't answer the phone, I became worried something might have happened to you."

"No, the only thing of note this morning is I overslept by a long way and must have been in the shower when you called. It was close to two o'clock when we arrived back here last night. The property we went to is further out of town than I thought, and time got away from us. Then we had the long drive back to Cranvale. The people we went to visit wanted us to stay, but Chris wanted to be back in Cranvale this morning. I imagine he already is busy helping organise the rally. It's now scheduled for some time around mid-morning. I didn't glean anything more about today's event."

"Don't worry about it. I'm sure we will know more in due course. What are your plans for today? Are you planning to observe the rally?"

"Yes, my friend, the local journo, heard the rally was rescheduled. He sent me a text last night suggesting I be in his office early today to avoid being out on the street when things start to liven up in town. I had better get a move on if I'm to be there as arranged."

"Take care. Keep safe. We'll compare notes later."

Back in my room, I toyed with the idea of ringing Pete to ask if I could look at his maps before I headed out. Then I remembered I wasn't supposed to go anywhere near the scrub today. Best not to alert him to my plans... As it was still quite early, a few minutes interrogating Google wouldn't go amiss. Reception was poor. Google took ages to load. Early morning probably was when most of the Cranvale area went online. Finding a map with details of the area I wanted took too long. I gave up and logged off.

After checking my backpack, I set out on foot again for the scrub. Today's route would take me directly to the hall. I wandered along part of the main street before cutting through to the service lane I used yesterday. Instead of entering the scrub from there, today I continued along it to the hall. Not wanting to be too obvious, I went a short distance past the hall as I tried to look like a tourist exploring the place while out on their morning constitutional. Then, I doubled back to the rear of the building.

From there, today followed much the same course as yesterday. I battled my way through the thick undergrowth while being attacked by all manner of biting insects. Vines clawed at my shirt. A couple of times branches snapped back to slap me in the face. At last, I could see the clearing up ahead. My trek through the scrub brought me out at almost the spot from where I observed the area yesterday. The place seemed unchanged ... and deserted.

After a few minutes straining my ears for anything to suggest someone was lurking in the laydown area, I decided it was safe to venture out into the open. Nevertheless, my pulse was rapid and my breathing shallow as I inched my way towards the demountable. Still no sign of anyone around. So, feeling bolder, I strode across in front of it. While the ground underfoot was hard, and looked deliberately compacted to create a suitable laydown site, patches of hard stubbly grass dotted the area. The nature of the ground allowed me to explore without leaving footprints.

While exercising extreme caution, I picked my way to the far end of the clearing before turning and working my way back to my starting point. On the return leg of my site inspection, I examined each of the shipping containers in turn. All had heavy locks to prevent unauthorised entry … all except one, that is. It also was the only one with a window. The window was useless as it was set too high in the side of the container for me to see into it. As this container wasn't locked, maybe a quick look inside might prove useful…

I hesitated. Would I be pushing my luck too far? Possibly … but this was the container that interested Black Leathers yesterday. Much taller than I am, he tried shining his torch in the window to see inside. When he couldn't see anything, he went to the demountable – presumably to fetch a key – before unlocking and opening the doors a fraction. I couldn't remember if he locked it again afterwards. Perhaps someone else since then left it unlocked.

Using a couple of tissues to prevent handprints, I heaved on the heavy doors. After a bit of huffing and puffing, the doors stood about forty centimetres apart. My small torch made little impression on the darkness, but it was good enough to reveal a bundle of something on the floor against the far end wall. A quick look over both shoulders to check I was still alone before I eased sideways through the narrow opening and rushed to the far end of the container. Being in and out of there as quickly as possible was critical. I did not want to be trapped in there if other people arrived.

It took no time for me to see enough. The bundle on the floor was a body. I felt my stomach tighten and my breathing approach hyperventilation as I crouched beside it. Had I found Callum? God forbid I should have to tell Emily the horrible truth. My heart skipped a beat as I rolled his head slightly towards me.

It wasn't Callum. Whoever it was had not been dead long. The body was still warm, but was a mess. He received a good going-over … possibly on a number of occasions … before he died.

If he had just died, someone was here within the last hour or so. Time I was out of this container – and off this site. By throwing my weight against them, the doors closed more easily than they opened. Then, wasting no time, I was on my way past the demountable to re-enter the scrub. As I passed it, I wondered if it might be worth a quick look inside that building as well. I hesitated. After scanning the area to confirm I was still alone, I started towards the door.

That's when I heard the sound of engines approaching. While they weren't close yet, it sounded like several of them coming my way.

"Forget the demountable," I muttered to myself. "Get back into the safety of the scrub."

Throwing caution to the wind, I raced across the several metres of open ground and crashed my way into the scrub to put a couple of metres of dense undergrowth between me and the clearing. I was still struggling to control my breathing when the first of the bikes made its appearance. Other bikes roared into the area behind it, and a large expensive-looking 4x4 followed them in.

Frantic activity broke out across the laydown area. Blokes rushed in and out of shipping containers, apparently oblivious of the noise they made. Despite the activity and noise, nothing told me why they were there. The throb of a powerful motorbike added to the noise as it joined the others already parked in the clearing. Above the sound of the motorbike came the sound of two more approaching vehicles.

With everyone engaged in whatever was happening, I took the opportunity to move further away from the site without drawing attention to myself. It took ages of watching where I placed my feet and easing my way through the undergrowth to move a safe distance away from the clearing. I stopped for a moment to listen for anyone following me. The wisest thing to do was for me to leave the scrub and return to the motel.

The other intelligent thing to do was not to emerge from the scrub too close to the hall. That required cutting across close to the edge of the scrub and to emerge on the service road behind those commercial buildings from where I entered the scrub yesterday morning.

Chapter 8

While out in the open and still vulnerable, I stood still for a few moments to regain my composure and to take stock of my surroundings. Everything was quiet. No one followed me or was waiting for me when I emerged from the scrub. Now I could wander nonchalantly back to the motel ... or so I thought.

By cutting through between two buildings, I found myself on the edge of the main street. It was a different street from yesterday. Today, quite a few people occupied it. Some milled about in groups of three or four, while others appeared intent on dealing with shopping or other business matters. A couple of dusty vehicles drove along the street. I hesitated, hanging back a metre or so between the buildings to watch proceedings until I judged the time was right to step on onto the street without being noticed.

The coffee shop was my destination. It was later than the lunch hour rush. I hoped there was something left for me to eat. A few people smiled or said hello as I strode along the pavement. To my relief, the coffee shop was deserted. I passed the last customer leaving the shop as I walked in.

"I know I'm late, but I'm hoping there is still something I might have for lunch."

"In case there was a latecomer or two, I've just made a couple of fresh sandwiches. Would you like one toasted?"

"Yes please, that sounds great. And, could I have another of your wonderful coffees to go with it?"

While Carol (I was polite enough to ask her name) fussed about attending to my lunch, I began a conversation to fill in time while I waited. "It's not the weekend already is it?" Carol gave me a confused look and shook her head. "Oh good; for a moment I thought I'd lost track of the days. Holidays can do that to you. Yesterday you told me the town only tends to come to life on weekends, and I noticed the street is a lot livelier today than it was yesterday."

"Oh yes. Today is the exception to the rule. I suppose you heard about the fuss around here over plans to extract coal seam gas by fracking."

"Yes, a couple of locals mentioned it. They were a bit hostile about the prospect of it."

"They would be. There aren't too many in the area support it. The reason there are more people in town today is there was supposed to be a protest rally this morning against fracking in this area."

"You said, *was supposed to be*. Does that mean it didn't happen?"

"Yep … and it's the second day it didn't happen. The rally was supposed to be yesterday, but something went wrong. The organisers received word of a problem early enough to call it off. No, that's not correct. They *postponed* it until today. Then some sort of problem occurred again today. Nobody found out in time to stop people coming into town. It must be frustrating for those involved, but it has been good for me. Today is the busiest I've been in ages."

A further setback, eh…? Pete Messell and his officers will not be impressed. For them, it meant another day of sitting around waiting for something to happen, when they could be back in Ralston getting on with normal duties. While I was dying to know more about today's setback, I didn't think Carol knew much more … and my lunch was ready.

Having decided to 'eat in' today, I sat at one of the small tables with my sandwich and coffee. You never know… Someone might come in and chat to Carol about what happened. I can't help overhearing conversations, can I? No one did come in. My plate and mug were empty, and I learnt nothing more. Time to retreat to the motel to try catching up with Pete Messell.

The walk back gave me time to review my morning. I needed to report the body in the shipping container, but to whom? I'm reluctant to deal with the local coppers again. From what I know of their attitude, I doubt they would take me seriously. On the other hand, from what I've seen of their approach to policing, I could find myself under suspicion and possibly occupying one of their cells. No, I don't think I'll be talking to the local coppers. That leaves Pete Messell…

In any other situation, my first thought would be to report my findings to him. Today, that will be a little awkward. Pete will not be in the best of humours after another day wasted in Cranvale. And, he would not take kindly to my having defied his instruction not to go investigating the scrub today. We are good mates, but he can be vicious when not best pleased with anyone. Nevertheless, Pete was my best – my only – option. I will just have to cop whatever he dishes out.

With some trepidation, I tried Pete's room. Trepidation turned to frustration when he didn't answer. "Why did I expect him to be sitting around in his room?" I muttered to myself. "He is on duty, not on holidays." Calling his mobile was not an option. Who knows what he might be in the middle of when I called? One thing was clear: I had to tell someone about the body in the shipping container. The danger was, if I didn't do so soon, the body might disappear before the police went to investigate.

When in doubt, call Ben Richards. It's my standard practice when I'm in a jam, so I might as well stick with past practice now. While Cranvale is not in Ben's Millhaven police district, Pete's receiving a call from Ben would meet with a better reception than one from me. I tried Ben's number. It went to voicemail. Bugger…! Now I am fresh out of ideas about what to do. For want of inspiration, and to help curb my rising frustration, I opted for a shower and clean clothes…

and a shower might relieve some of the itching from the insect bites I received this morning. I was picking through my limited wardrobe for something to wear afterwards when my phone rang.

"Now what disaster has befallen you?" Ben barked at me. "I thought Pete was in Cranvale now. Why aren't you talking to him? No … don't bother explaining. I'm sure it will be too complicated for a mere male like me to understand."

"Probably… but that's beside the point. I found a body this morning in a shipping container in an area I discussed with Pete last night. My problem is the local police will give me grief rather that show any interest in investigating … and I don't know where Pete is or what he is doing. If something doesn't happen soon, the body might disappear. I don't dare call Pete in case I interrupt something important."

"Oh, I see. But it is perfectly all right to interrupt anything I might be doing." I heard Ben heave a dramatic sigh. "Leave it with me. I'll see if he will accept my call."

"As if Pete wouldn't accept your call…" I snarled. But, there was no one listening except me. I had no doubt Ben would call Pete's number the moment he ended our call. So now I wait … but do I shower now, or find something else to do while I wait for Pete to contact me? A shower will have to wait. I have plenty of notes to write up, and I have no doubt I will need to refer to them when Pete begins interrogating me about my morning's activities.

It was about twenty minutes later when Pete called. "Are you at the motel? … Good; stay there. I'm about five minutes away. In the meantime, see if you can rustle up a decent pot of coffee."

With not enough time for a shower before Pete's arrival, I rushed to finish recording my notes from my last couple of days in the scrub. But first, a call to room service for coffee to be delivered as soon as possible. Their timing was perfect.

It arrived no more than a minute before Pete knocked on my door.

He didn't waste time on niceties. "What's all this about a body in a shipping container? Is it the missing Callum bloke?"

"Thanks for coming … and no, it's not Callum's body. We might need those maps of yours so we can pin down the location of the clearing I told you about."

After telling me to pour the coffee, he rushed to fetch his maps of the area. We spread the maps out on my bed – the only flat surface big enough except for the floor – and anchored them in place with any heavy objects nearby. Then, as we sipped coffee at my small table, Pete went through my notes which I was printing out when he arrived.

"What happened to not going anywhere near the scrub today?"

There it was: the question I had been waiting for since Pete's arrival. I tried to think of some smart response, but ended up settling for a shrug instead. It earned me an all too familiar Pete Messell disgusted look, but I was relieved it was the worst I would receive. Pete now was too focused on the body I found to be bothered about my defying his instructions. He bounded up from the table, almost sloshing my coffee everywhere.

"Show me on this map where you think the clearing is located. Were there any reference points – markers of any sort – to help identify its position?"

I shook my head as I ran a finger over the map in what I thought to be the direction I took from behind the hall. It was hopeless. Bashing through the scrub wasn't like taking a direct route. There were trees to dodge around, and detours to find less dense patches of undergrowth. "I can't be sure. Nothing on this map gives me a clue about the clearing's location. Wait a minute. There is something I haven't done." Without waiting, I brought my computer back to life and launched Google Maps.

Within a few heartbeats, it was asking me for a location. For want of any better idea, I keyed in 'Cranvale'. The good citizens of this area don't seem to bother the internet at this hour of the day. Speed was good, and an aerial map of the town soon filled the screen. By enlarging the image and then moving it about on the screen, I managed to identify the hall. The scrub stood out quite clearly against the built up town area.

"I don't know how long the clearing has been there and when it was turned into a laydown area," I murmured as I scanned the image.

"Is that important?"

"It depends on a combination of when it happened, and when this image was taken." I slid the image across and down a little more to search for the clearing. "Bingo! There it is. There's the clearing … and you can see the shipping containers and the demountable."

"Print it," Pete demanded as he scribbled in his notebook. "How do I get the GPS co-ordinates for the area?" It took only a few more seconds to print those out for him as well. "Enlarge this image a bit more if you can … Yeah, that's good … Now, in which container was the body you found?"

It was easy to point out the relevant container and the demountable building for him. The track into the clearing used by the various vehicles held my attention. They were not accessing the site from anywhere in town. As he started gathering up his maps and my printouts, I drew Pete's attention to the track.

"There is something else you might find interesting. See this track coming into the clearing…" I traced a finger over it.

"Yeah, what about it…?"

"A variety of vehicles use the track to access the clearing. The map shows it doesn't originate from anywhere in town. It looks as though access to the track is via an adjacent property. It might be worth knowing whose property it is."

Pete didn't reply. He was on his way out the door with his phone clamped to his ear. It's a safe bet he was marshalling his troops. I did hear him say with some emphasis 'no, leave the locals out of this'. If I didn't think it would be rejected out of hand, I would volunteer to guide them to the clearing. I knew that was never going to happen, so I contented myself with a shower and clean clothes.

While I was under the shower, it occurred to me I hadn't heard from Emily. With the scheduled rally a fizzer again today, I half expected her to be back in her room. Having agreed to compare notes on what we discovered today, I thought she would contact me by now. I suppose she could be spending the rest of the day with Chris, if he is still in town, or she might be with the local journo bloke.

As soon I was dressed, I tried calling her room. When there was no answer, I tried her mobile; no answer there either. My mind came up with any number of reasons why I couldn't contact her. Somehow, I wasn't buying any of them. My gut suggested something was wrong. While that might be the case, I have no idea where to begin looking for her. After a few moments, I realised that wasn't true. I could try her journalist friend. Even if she wasn't with him, he might know where she went.

Without a name, the telephone directory wasn't much use. The receptionist probably would know. I rang the bell on the reception desk and waited for someone to appear. The same bloke as delivered the coffee to my room earlier came to the desk. A few moments later I was on my way back to my room with the name of the journalist and his phone numbers.

Lance Prentice answered his land line on the second ring. The journalist was hard at work. He continued attacking his keyboard one-handed as he answered my call. If he was writing up copy for the next edition of the local newspaper, it was unlikely Emily was still with him. He confirmed my reasoning.

"No, I haven't seen Emily since soon after we learned the rally was cancelled. She went off to find Chris Tremaine in the hope he would tell her something about why it didn't happen. If she learned anything, she said she would come back to tell me. I haven't seen her since."

"Thanks, Lance. I'm sorry I interrupted your work. I only called you because Emily isn't answering her phone. I'm sure she will turn up eventually." If only I believed my last comment…!

Would I call Chris Tremaine if I had his number? Probably not, I decided. Thinking of Chris had me wondering if he was still booked in to the motel. Should I bother reception again? Of course I should. The same young man who helped me with Lance's phone numbers answered the phone at reception.

"I wanted to leave a message for Mr Chris Tremaine, but I can't remember his room number. It wasn't important, but we had talked about meeting in the restaurant for dinner tonight and I wanted to confirm the arrangement."

"I'm sorry Miss, but I can't help you with any of that. Mr Tremaine checked out late this morning. I'm not sure if he is still in town."

Okay, that information doesn't put my mind at ease in any way. Has Emily gone off somewhere with Chris? I checked my phone for messages; nothing from her. What do I do now? I don't want to involve Pete. Emily would be mortified if she was off somewhere having a lovely time with Chris only to have Pete Messell and his merry men come crashing in to rescue her. In the end, I tried her phone again, and left a message when she didn't answer.

There must be something productive I could do, but my mind was preoccupied with concern for Emily. After trying her number again and pacing around my room, I decided to sit outside for a while. I grabbed my computer and set up under the pergola by the pool. I wanted to know who owned the property from which vehicles accessed the laydown area … and, for that matter, whose laydown area it was.

Not much thought required to determine who owned the equipment in the clearing. It could only belong to the mining company causing all the fuss in the area at the moment. Identifying who owned the property providing them with access to the place proved another matter. It took a few minutes to work out how to go about it. At the end of those deliberations, all I was certain about was that it was hot and horrible outside today. As I retreated to my room, I decided my only course of action was to see what Google might do for me.

After bringing up the map I looked at earlier with Pete and locating the clearing marked on it, I moved my cursor to the property I was interested in and again expanded the view. The image was beginning to pixelate but it showed the location was occupied by various structures. While a few items were scattered around the place, a cluster of buildings in one corner suggested this was the homestead and its associated out-buildings. I was about to try interrogating the map further when my phone rang.

"Emily… where the hell are you? I've been worried sick something might have happened to you. When you weren't answering your phone, I thought you might have joined Callum in doing a disappearing act."

"What… No, I'm fine. I just read your message, and called you straight away. I'm back here in town and on my way to the motel. I'm just going to call in on Lance Prentice, my journo mate, for a few minutes on my way past."

Thankfully, as she ended the call, she didn't hear my huge sigh of relief. Sometime in the near future, I will make amends for being so terse with her. Still, the important thing was, she was safe and should soon be back here telling me where she had been for most of the day. My moment of relief was short lived. What about dinner tonight? I still haven't told her about Pete Messell and his officers being here, and I wasn't inclined to tell her just yet. It's a reasonable assumption Emily will expect the two of us to dine together tonight. It is what we would do under normal circumstances. But, tonight, I want to spend time alone with Pete catching up on all he learned from that clearing in the scrub.

Chapter 9

It was about forty-five minutes later before Emily returned to the motel. On coming to my room, her first move was to feel the coffee pot still on the table since Pete's visit earlier.

"Bugger … it's cold. I'm desperate for a coffee and I thought salvation was at hand."

Her message was a no-brainer. I called room service for another pot of coffee. With the important things in life taken care of for the moment, I felt it safe to ask her about today's abandoned rally. "Carol at the coffee shop said the protest rally didn't happen again today. I don't imagine Chris and the others who organise such events are too happy about the way things are going. Did you hear anything about it?"

"People weren't happy about the cancellation, especially those who travelled in from outlying properties. At first, I couldn't find Chris anywhere. It was about lunchtime when I caught up with him. If I'm generous, I'd have to say, the reception I received is best described as frosty. Part of it probably was due to his being cranky about the way things went today. But, there was something else behind it as well. All it did was make me more determined to find out what I wanted to know."

"He might have been disappointed, but it doesn't entitle him to take it out on you. I discovered he booked out of the motel this morning. So, I presume he will be heading back to his property, and won't hang around town any longer … unless they have another attempt at a protest rally tomorrow. Anyway, did you manage to prise anything about the cancellation out of him?"

"Only a bit… As far as I know, there won't be another attempt tomorrow. Yesterday's rally was cancelled – in plenty of time in advance – when they learned the key mining company people weren't going to be in town. Today, it was the mayor who wasn't in town. As a consequence, the mining company representatives didn't come to town again today. Today's big problem was, nobody knew about any of this until just before the rally was due to start. It left the organisers, including Chris, in a bad light and might make it difficult for them to raise much support for any future proposed rally. So, yes, I image Chris would be keen to leave town."

"It was convenient of the mayor to just happen to be out of town today. I wonder how he managed to arrange such a fortuitous time to be elsewhere. What caused his unscheduled absence? It seems to me, information from the protesters' side of proceedings is being leaked back to the mayor and his cronies, but a similar leak in the opposite direction isn't occurring."

"I did call in on Lance at the newspaper office on my way back to the motel. He didn't know much more than I did, but his information suggests the mayor left town in a hurry sometime late last night or early this morning. It tends to confirm your suggestion of a leak."

"Chris and the other protest organisers probably have come to the same conclusion by now."

"Yeah... I thought it worthwhile using Lance's information to try to extract further details from Chris. So, after leaving Lance's office, I scouted around town for Chris in the hope he hadn't left yet. ...And, I suppose I was a bit miffed to think he might leave without bothering to tell me."

"Oh dear, it suggests your friendship didn't mean much." The look on Emily's face told me his leaving without as much as a goodbye cut her deeper than she admitted. "I take it, you didn't find him?"

"Oh, I found him all right. He was at the big carpark area behind the supermarket. It's where the protesters left their vehicles, and where they were to congregate for the start of the rally. Chris was standing beside his vehicle … and was being *very* friendly with a gorgeous looking woman in skin-tight white jeans. I abandoned my quest and started back along the street towards here. Lance was coming out of his office as I was passing. He asked if I managed to find Chris. He probably hoped I had more from Chris to pass on. I explained the situation. His comments didn't help: *That would be Justine, his wife. She used to be a model, and I believe she appeared in a few TV sitcoms before they married. I think she still does a bit of work from time to time. Rumour has it she would be happier back down south working on her career.*

"It sounds like today wasn't a good day for either of us. Now, about tonight…"

"Ah yes; about tonight… I hope you don't mind, but I won't be dining here again. While I was chatting to Lance outside his office, his wife came along. She knew about me and about Callum's mysterious disappearance, and was interested. The three of us chatted for a while. They are having dinner in town tonight, and she invited me to join them. She seems really nice, so I accepted."

At least something has gone my way today. Now Pete and I will be able to eat alone. As I congratulated myself on my good luck, an odd thought drifted in from left field. I tried squashing it as soon as it arrived, but traces of it lingered to worry me: was Emily's friendship with Lance Prentice developing similar overtones to the friendship she recently enjoyed with Chris Tremaine? And, was Lance's wife sensing something similar happening – and hence the invitation to dinner. They still recommend keeping your enemies close as the best policy, don't they? Maybe Mrs Prentice viewed Emily as a potential enemy. I would need to keep a close eye on my friend lest she finds herself in all sorts of trouble.

Another idle thought to wander in related to Callum. Emily's mentioning his name in conversation a few moments ago is the first time I recall hearing it from her in a little while.

While a cooling of any potential relationship between them is welcome, I don't want her losing focus on why we are here. I need finding the missing Callum to remain the primary focus for her as well as for me if we are to have any degree of success … unless she decides to turn the whole matter over to the police and we can go home.

Emily stayed chatting with me until a little after five o'clock when she returned to her room to prepare for dinner with the journo and his wife. The whole time she was with me, I maintained the assertion my day had been a non-event. Somehow, I managed to avoid any mention of finding a body in a shipping container. A part of me felt mean about it, while the rest of me wasn't convinced she was sufficiently focused to deal with the information appropriately. In truth, her developing friendship with the local journalist had me a little wary about sharing too much with her.

Alone in my room, I decided to devote whatever time I had before Pete's return to analysing everything I knew – or thought I knew – in relation to Callum's disappearance. First, I made a note of a couple of vague questions drifting around in the back of my mind. They tried to develop after Emily told me of the mayor's sudden absence from town. The trouble is, those questions still aren't fully formed, and it has me unable to work out why they bother me.

Pete didn't return to the motel until around 7.30pm. It was fortunate he came to my room before heading to his own for a shower. It allowed me to order dinner for the pair of us from room service for before the kitchen went into its closing-down-for-the-night routine. A little later and we wouldn't have stood a chance of more than a toasted BLT sandwich. I ordered a bottle of a good red to go with our lamb shanks. Pete looked wrung out when he returned. A glass or two of a good cabernet might help restore his spirits.

Dinner was a fairly desultory affair. Little conversation interrupted our eating. The wine seemed to work wonders though and, by the time we placed our trays outside the door for collection, Pete was ready to work on into the night. My predictable first question for him: did they find the body?

"We followed your example and approached the area via the scrub. It was just as well the bloke was dead. A gang of flat-footed coppers crashing through the bush could never be described as exercising caution and stealth in the process. No one was around, so we went straight to the relevant shipping container and found the body still in situ. He had been dead for quite a while by the time we arrived."

"Your situation was a bit precarious. Some of the other mob might have arrived at any moment. I imagine their intention would be to dispose of the body in a more 'permanent' way as soon as possible."

"We had the place to ourselves when we arrived. The 'scene of crime' stuff took ages, as it usually does. Just as we were finishing up, company arrived. Two blokes in a van roared into the clearing and straight up to the shipping container. It was fortunate we heard them coming. We all dived out of the container and hid behind it until the two blokes opened the container's doors. That's when we scored ourselves a couple of prisoners. Their van came in handy for removing them and the body from the clearing."

"You followed the track out to that property?"

"Nah … when we arrived at the clearing, I sent one of my blokes to check out the track. Bit of the way along it, he found a little-used, roughly formed track leading off from the main one. The offshoot comes out in a deserted area on the outskirts of town. My blokes took the van and its cargo back to Langton, the neighbouring town, where they are billeted during our stay in the area. I called for a plane before we left the clearing. It was waiting at an airstrip when the van reached Langton. The van's cargo – two live and one dead – is now being processed back in Ralston."

"Okay, so you didn't have to go onto the property thanks to the offshoot track. I can't help wondering why the track exists when all their travel to and from the clearing is via the property and along the main track. Life might become interesting around here when they realise their two blokes haven't returned."

"Their thoughts on that one might be misdirected. The van the blokes were in is now ditched at the airstrip near Langton. Most people would be forgiven for coming to the conclusion the two blokes had abandoned the mob and absconded. What about you, did you manage to gain any further information on what happened with today's protest rally?"

"Very little; but it is interesting. And the information is probably about third-hand, so make what you will of it. Nevertheless, for me, it raises a whole truckload of questions."

The next few minutes were spent discussing Emily's information about the mayor's absence at a most convenient time, and the possibility of a leak from within the protesters' camp. Pete went quiet for a while. I knew he was mulling things over, so I remained silent until he spoke again.

"The mining company bigshots knew the mayor intended doing a flit last night. None of them turned up today for the big meeting postponed from yesterday. I think our friend the mayor could do with a bit of investigating. I'll have one of my staff dig up background information on the man – and whatever else they can find out about him."

"It might make for interesting reading. I admit my immediate interest is in ownership of the property from which the mob accesses the laydown area in the bush. Whoever owns it must be a staunch pro-fracking supporter."

"Ah well, we should know the answer to that by tomorrow. I asked my staff to check title records for the property. I hoped they would have something for me by tonight, but nothing has come through yet. If the gods are in our corner, we might even have an ID for the body in the shipping container by tomorrow as well."

With little else we could do, we called it a night and Pete left. It took a few moments to tidy the papers strewn about my room in the course of the evening, but I wasn't ready for bed yet. When a further interrogation of Google produced nothing useful to my investigation, I decided to sit quietly and review what I knew about Callum's disappearance, and everything of any consequence which happened since then.

After turning off the lights and opening the drapes, I pushed the lounge chair over to the window and sat down to think. While I kept telling myself I was at Cranvale to investigate Callum's disappearance, and what was happening with the mining company and fracking was none of my concern, I knew it wasn't true. My gut and the little voice in my head were telling me somehow the two matters were connected. If I could work out what the possible connection could be, I might gain some traction in this case. With every passing day – even passing hour – the risk to Callum's life might increase.

It was after midnight when I accepted my deliberations were going nowhere and sitting in the dark any longer was pointless.

*****

My first thoughts this morning were about Emily and her night out with Lance Prentice and his wife. I half expected her to knock on my door when she returned after dinner. She didn't, and now I found myself wondering about it … and imagining dark scenarios which might explain why it didn't happen. Best I touch base with her as soon as possible this morning for my own peace of mind – and to clear my head to be able to concentrate on other matters. What those 'other matters' might be I didn't have a clue about, and what else I might do today was just as big a mystery.

When Emily didn't respond to my knocking on her door, I went back to my room and tried calling her. She didn't answer her room phone, so I called her mobile. A thick, groggy voice answered. My stomach went into instant spasm. "Where are you?" My demand seemed to focus her attention.

"I'm in my room. Where did you think I'd be?"

Oh dear; her indignant tone told me she was not happy about my call. Best I try smoothing things over. "You didn't answer my knock on your door and, when you didn't answer your room phone, I became worried something had happened to you too. Are you all right … and may I come to your room talk to you?"

A dishevelled Emily opened her door to me. It was obvious she had climbed out of bed to let me in. "I'm sorry. I didn't realise you were still in bed. You normally are an early riser. Are you okay?"

"Yes, of course I'm okay … except I haven't had much sleep. It was after two o'clock when they dropped me back at the motel. I needed a shower before I went to bed. The restaurant at the pub was so hot and stuffy, I sweated all night. Still, it was a pleasant evening; lots of good conversation and laughs."

She ran through the menu choices on offer at the pub's restaurant and what each of them had chosen, and then recounted some of the highlights of the evening. Her final comment caught my attention: *I hope the Prentices woke earlier and in better condition than I did this morning.*

"Why is how and when the Prentices woke important?"

"They are flying to Brisbane today and the flight leaves early. Gail is going to spend a few days with her best friend who has been diagnosed with a terminal illness. Lance decided to fly with her, partly for support, but also to talk to a few of his journo colleagues. He is hoping to pick up some dirt on the mining company and their operations."

"So, Cranvale will be without its local newshound for a few days. Will they miss out on their weekly newspaper this week?"

"No. Lance is only away for the day. He will return either tonight or maybe tomorrow morning; whenever the next return flight from Brisbane is."

With Lance Prentice out of town and Chris Tremaine back on the property with his wife, I wondered what Emily's plans were for the day. She might well want to tag along with me. The only problem with that is, I don't know what I'm going to do. But, I am fairly sure I don't want her tagging along … at least not until I hear what information Pete's Ralston staff managed to dig up for him. When I asked the question, my expectations regarding her plans were wrong.

"I'm having coffee with a woman I met yesterday. And my friend, Claire, whom we stayed with at Winyard, is coming into town. If she is here early enough, she will join us for coffee. If not, I'll catch up with her later and we will spend the day together. She might stay in town overnight, but I won't know about that until later today. What are your plans?"

Now, there is a difficult question to answer. "I'm hoping to catch up with one or two people who might have useful information. Apart from that, I might spend more time exploring the scrub behind the hall again. I can't help feeling the area is significant to our investigation, but I have no idea why it would be."

It was only half a lie. I hoped to catch up with Pete. I'm hoping he has information about the body in the container, the mayor and/or the mining company. Anything on any or all of that would be most welcome at the moment. But, it is who owns the property providing the mob with covert access to the clearing in the scrub which tops my want-to-know list.

I dawdled over breakfast in my room in a bid to avoid making a start on anything. If I'm honest, I was stalling in the hope Pete might bring me information which would decide what to do today. At about 9.30, I gave into frustration. With still no sign of Pete, maybe another visit to the laydown area is my best option for at least some of the day.

After gathering up the few things I might need and stuffing them in my backpack, I was about to leave when Pete knocked on my door. He looked smug. He had information! I could have hugged him on sight … but didn't want to waste time. Besides, he probably would have a heart attack if I hugged him.

"Don't stand there looking smug. Come in and share what you know." I threw open my door and made an exaggerated welcoming gesture.

"Only if you order coffee. I haven't had breakfast yet."

I took the hint and ordered a full English breakfast and a large pot of coffee. The kitchen wasn't happy. They believed breakfast finished at nine o'clock. I set them straight on the matter and, about twenty minutes later, breakfast – and the coffee – arrived. His breakfast smelled so good, I wished I ordered two so we could breakfast together. My earlier cereal and juice just did not compare. There was no opportunity to learn anything from Pete while we waited for his breakfast. He took a lengthy phone call and followed it up with a couple of calls of his own. He had just settled at the table when his breakfast arrived … and my opportunity to ask questions was further delayed while he dispatched it.

At last, with mugs of coffee in hand, we faced each other across the table and I felt able to start delivery of the barrage of questions I had been holding back since his arrival. My first one was predictable. "Have you received any information yet from your Ralston staff?"

"Yeah, most of it came through last night. There was one bit I wanted confirmed, and that was the call I received just now. Where would you like to begin? I'm sure you're bursting to know it all, so you lead off with the questions and I'll answer the ones I can."

His last comment didn't fill me with confidence, but I launched into question time with gusto anyway.

"Do we have an identity for the body in the container?"

"Not one of ours… He is from interstate where he is known to police in at least two of the southern states. Appears he was something of a muscle-for-hire, and had run-ins with the law a few times through his membership of one of the motorcycle gangs. We don't know much else about him, but I think it's a fair bet he was one of the mining company's pack of bully-boys. What he did to cause his demise remains a mystery."

My first question about the body probably was the one I was least interested in. The mayor and ownership of the property providing access to the laydown area are of much greater interest. So, my second question related to ownership of that property. Pete chuckled and, after appearing to consider the question at some length, made a show of clearing his throat before answering.

"Ahem, well that is an interesting question and, if I'm not mistaken, your next one will relate to the good mayor of this town."

"I know you are enjoying this, so get on with it. Dealing with those two issues in any order will be okay."

"Good to know. You see, it is a bit hard to separate the one from t'other."

"The mayor owns that property…?"

"Now hold on. Who is telling this story? If you keep interrupting, I'll take umbrage and leave." I made a sweeping gesture to indicate he had the floor. "Right then, let's continue. Before we do, do you think your room's account could afford another pot of coffee?"

If only I could reach across and slug him one without ruining my chance of extracting any more information from him, I would. Instead, I smiled sweetly and ordered another pot of coffee from room service. I sent a mental note to my kidneys to assure them that, while they were already swimming in this morning's coffee and juice, they would survive.

Waiting for the coffee to arrive required about as much patience and restraint as I could muster, but Pete was enjoying himself and I was not about to let him get the better of me.

Chapter 10

With our mugs refilled, I gave Pete a hard look. He interpreted it correctly. After heaving a somewhat theatrical sigh, he launched into answering my questions about the mayor and the property.

"Okay, let's start with the property which interests us both. The Titles Office has it registered to and elderly couple, Thomas and Edna Newman ... which won't mean anymore to you than it did to me at first. Thomas Newman died a few years back, so Edna is now the sole owner. The couple were hard hit the last time this area suffered severe drought for a number of years in succession. After the drought, they struggled to rebuild their herd and re-establish the property. Already elderly, they found the struggle a bit much for them. They basically walked off the place and moved to live in Brisbane. They were well enough off to have a comfortable life for a while before moving into a retirement-type village. Enquiries suggest Edna is now quite frail and seriously ill."

"Unless she found herself in serious need of cash at this late stage of her life, I can't believe Edna supports fracking, or she is too happy about the property being used as it is by the mining company. I'm inclined to think she must be unaware of what is happening around here at the moment. In which case, how does the mining company come to be using the place ... or are they simply indulging in a form of squatting?"

"Well, there is more to the story and, as they say in all good yarns, the plot thickens. From what I understand, it seems Edna doesn't know much about anything these days. So, I agree it is unlikely she is aware of, or has authorised, the mining company's use of her land."

"What about her family? Might one of the kids have set it up? Like so many farming families, is it possible the kids didn't want anything to do with the property but now see the opportunity to make some cash from it?"

"It would be a possibility except the Newmans had no family. Therefore, there were no children to take it over and hence the reason the couple walked off it."

"I wonder what happens to the property when Edna is no longer around. Is she planning to leave it to someone, or is to be sold and the money to go to some charitable institution?"

"No, on Edna's death, the necessary documentation to transfer the property to a new owner is in place. As I said earlier, the Newmans had no children. But, they did foster a child for many years, and that child now features prominently in the future of the property."

While Pete seemed to be gathering his thoughts, I waited patiently for him to expand on the story of the foster child. I suffered more than a hint of frustration when he began speaking again. He left the matter of the foster child – and me – dangling as he turned his attention elsewhere.

"Now, to the matter of the local mayor... It seems our local mayor has done all right for himself over the years. His early childhood reads like so many other tragic stories these days: father disappeared from the scene before he was born, mother turned to whatever she could to support her and the baby, and died as a consequence of her lifestyle before the child started school. Young Roland Garnham, with no other known family to take care of him, was put into care, and it's where he remained until he was about six or seven years old. It was at about that time the Newmans considered fostering a child. They took cattle to show at the Brisbane exhibition, and decided to look into the matter of a foster child while in the city."

"Oh no, don't tell me Roland Garnham is the local mayor... Now that I think about it, I've never heard the mayor's name mentioned once during the whole time I've been in Cranvale. He is always simply referred to as *the mayor.*"

"Give the lady a prize! I'm afraid that's the truth of it. The young Roland Garnham was fostered by the Newmans while they were in Brisbane and returned with them to live here on the property. It seems it was a happy arrangement. Unlike a lot of other foster children who leave their foster parents as soon as they're old enough, Roland remained with the Newmans until well into his adult life. We failed to find any evidence of formal adoption, but the relationship between him and his foster parents appears to have been strong and enduring. The care facility where Edna is a patient reports frequent contact, including visits, by Roland. These continued until such time as Edna's dementia progressed to the point where she didn't recognise him."

"As you said, it's a sad story, but it sounds like Mayor Roley might do all right for himself in the end. I imagine there is more than a fair chance the property will go to him on Edna's death. It seems this also solves the mystery of how the mining company acquired permission to use the Newmans' property. I'm not sure Roley had authority to approve such an arrangement, unless he held power of attorney for Edna. Pete, what are your thoughts on the subject?"

"I share your thinking. A couple of other interesting snippets came to light in the course of my staff's investigation of the mayor's background. As you're probably aware, a number of the electoral boundaries in this state are being redrawn to even out the *per capita* balance between the various electoral divisions. This electorate is one of those affected. Next year's election will be an interesting one for Roland Garnham. Where he lives will be on the other side of the electoral boundary, meaning he can no longer stand for the position of mayor in this electorate. The Newman property will remain on this of the boundary."

"So, does that mean he'll have a foot in each camp, so to speak?"

"Unless he chooses to live on the Newman property, his only hope is to stand for mayor in the neighbouring electoral district. Rumour says it is what he intends to do. By doing so, he will distance himself from the furore he helped create in this division. The other suggestion is, no drilling will commence in this area until after the next election."

"If drilling is delayed until after the election, the mayor can't be seen to be openly supporting fracking. While, behind closed doors, it's exactly what he is doing, but it remains deniable by both him and the mining company. When drilling begins after the election, he could argue it only happened because he was no longer the mayor of this district and was not in a position to oppose it. I wonder what else it's costing the mining company for his support."

"While we have nothing to confirm it, it's likely a sizeable bucket of cash will go into Garnham's campaign fund for his election as mayor of the neighbouring district next year."

"Surely people will see through such a ruse… Nevertheless, the information your staff dug up gives us plenty to think about. I'm not sure how any of it assists in my search for the missing Callum Farquhar, but instinct tells me at least some of it is useful to my investigation. What are your next moves? Do you and your troops plan on sticking around for a bit longer?"

"I believe it imperative we do. After all, there is a missing person, and his disappearance may well be linked to everything else happening here. I'll review the situation again at the end of today. It might be that I'll only retain a couple of men here and send the rest back to Ralston. How do you intend to proceed with your investigation, and is Emily still around?"

"Argh, I wish I knew what to do next. My gut feeling is I will find some of the answers I need on that property we keep mentioning. I don't know how or why. All I know is it will be difficult for me to go poking around over there."

"What about Emily…? I haven't seen her or heard you mention her lately. Has she given up on finding Farquhar, or is she still assisting with your investigation?"

"In theory, and in a limited way, she remains involved. But, I have kept her sidelined a bit when it comes to sharing information. She gets on well with the local journo, and he is proving a good source of local information. But, he is a journo and I have no doubt he is chasing a story in return for information he provides. I am not keen for Emily to reciprocate … not that we have much to share so far. As a consequence, she is unaware I have returned to that scrub area a few times. She knows nothing about the clearing or what goes on there, and definitely knows nothing about a body being found there. Oh, in addition, she doesn't know you're in town and staying in this motel. I don't know how much longer I'll be able to maintain that situation."

"I'm surprised she isn't here this morning. What have you sent her off to do today?"

"Emily made her own arrangements for today, and it looks like she should be having a fairly social time of it – as opposed to worrying about finding Callum. I don't mean to sell her short, but her focus is all over the place rather than on the investigation."

Pete returned to his own room to make phone calls and plan the day's activities for him and his troops. Time alone in my room was welcome. It was fast approaching time for me to have a firm talk with Emily. If we are no closer to finding Callum within the next forty-eight hours, I believe it will be best to hand over the matter of his disappearance to the police, and for Emily and me to return to Millhaven to resume our normal lives. So far, I've been lucky there has been nothing urgent regarding possible new investigations, but I can't be away from my business for too much longer.

A decision about today seemed almost impossible. My mind wanted to focus solely on the property and how it might be involved in my investigation. While I knew I couldn't explore there, with it occupying my mind, it was difficult to think about any other possibilities. The only alternative I could think of was to go back to the clearing in the scrub and poke about a bit more. Maybe I shouldn't mention such thoughts to Pete.

In the end, what to do today proved not to be a problem. About twenty minutes after he left, Pete knocked on my door. I detected a degree of uncertainty in him when he explained the reason for his return.

"I'm not sure if you've decided what to do today, but I have a suggestion for you. Information just received suggests now might be a good time to pay a visit to the Newmans' property. On the proviso we agree a code of behaviour on your part, you are welcome to come with us. I have no idea how such a visit will go but, as soon as the warrant arrives in my inbox, I intend to find out. Are you interested?"

"What a silly question. I can't believe you asked it. Of course I'm coming with you. What do I need to know, and how long have I got to get ready?"

About an hour later, we were on our way to the Newmans' property. I travelled with Pete. His officers who drove over from Langton met us at the property's gate. On the way, Pete explained the last piece of intel he received suggested the place would be deserted for most of the day. The information suggested everyone would be attending some sort of mining company 'council of war' at a place about seventy kilometres away from Cranvale. I suspected Pete's terminology 'council of war' meant a strategic planning meeting but, in hindsight, his description probably was apt.

It was almost eleven o'clock when we gathered at the gateway to the property. While it was much later in the day than I like to start an operation, I wasn't about to comment on the fact. Before we drove onto the place, Pete devoted a few minutes to a briefing of his officers to ensure everyone knew where they were supposed to go and what they were supposed to do. I also received my specific instructions ... and I realised there was a fair chance noncompliance might soon occur. Still, there was no point in alerting Pete to it – not before it became a problem.

Entry onto the property was not restricted in any way. The once imposing gateway was now a neglected shadow of its former self. A high wrought iron sign arching across the driveway was a rusted mess and almost illegible against the sky. Two enormous wrought iron gates hung wide open at crazy angles, their hinges having rusted away some time in the ago. With Pete's vehicle in the lead, we rumbled across the cattle grid, under the property's sign and started along a rutted and dusty driveway.

After about a kilometre of bone jarring ride, a cluster of buildings appeared on the horizon. Nestled amongst big old trees, and dominating the group was a large central building which I assumed was the homestead. It was while studying the buildings up ahead, I noticed tyre tracks running adjacent to the right-hand side of the driveway. They created a well-defined and recently used track. I reached over and tapped Pete to draw his attention to the tracks. Our cavalcade halted.

While none of us exited the vehicles, both Pete and I craned our necks for a better look at the tyre marks. They snaked off into the distance … and towards a dense patch of scrubland. Across the dry brown paddock, now populated by tussocks of dead grass and weed regrowth, the scrub stood out in stark green contrast. But, our initial focus was to be the buildings up ahead. Pete veered off the original driveway to drive along over the more recent tyre tracks.

My eyes were glued to the driveway as we raced along beside it. After a short distance, I shared my observation with Pete. "There is no sign of traffic along the driveway in recent times. It suggests the mob uses a different access to the property, and not the main driveway. Could it be they use that offshoot track which you and your officers found yesterday when removing the body and the prisoners from the clearing?"

"It's a logical conclusion, but the offshoot doesn't show it's had much use, and nothing recently. We are going to have to explore further the mob's various tracks in and out of that patch of scrub. Before we do anything else, we need to investigate what has been happening here on the property and, hopefully, we are not going to encounter anyone eager to show us around."

I allowed my eyes to wander down to Pete's hip and the side arm holstered there. During the briefing session before we entered onto the place, I noticed that today all the coppers were armed. At the time, I felt a twinge of regret my weapon of choice was safely locked away in the safe at home. The fact they saw the need to come armed had me feeling a bit naked and vulnerable.

Nobody rushed out to meet us when we reached the tight cluster of buildings. After parking in the shade of the big trees, Pete's men broke into two pairs and went off in separate directions to explore the buildings. I followed closely behind Pete as he strode towards the homestead building. As he stomped up onto the veranda on his way to the front door, he gestured behind him for me to go off to one side. Compliance seemed a good idea. Neither of us needed worry; nobody was home.

Finding the front door unlocked, Pete retrieved the search warrant from his pocket. With it on prominent display in one hand, he used his other hand to deal with the door and swung it wide open one swift movement. While it was a neatly executed manoeuvre on his part, I couldn't help thinking he had left himself without a free hand to draw his weapon if we encountered an unwelcoming reception committee. Perhaps he knew more than I did. No one waited to greet us. Apart from the sound of the old house creaking under the heat of the midday sun, the place was silent.

From the moment we entered the place, it was obvious people were living here. Signs of occupancy were everywhere: a discarded magazine on the sofa, a shirt slung over a chair back, a filthy mug abandoned on the coffee table. The kitchen looked worse. Packets and boxes of food, some still open, cluttered bench tops. Piles of unwashed dishes adorned the sink and its draining board. Perhaps the dirty plates still on the table were left there due to a lack of space for anything more to be placed in or around the sink.

A big rambling house, the old homestead originally contained four bedrooms. At some point in time, a section of one side verandah was closed in to create an additional two rooms. They appeared to be an office and a storeroom. All of the bedrooms were in use. Some of the beds appeared to be some of the original furniture left in the house. Camp stretchers added in some of the rooms suggested a substantial recent occupancy.

What once must have been a well-appointed and comfortable home still reflected some of life here before it was abandoned. What it didn't have was any sign of Callum's ever having been there. With Pete engrossed on his copper's search of the house, I was free to wander through it alone. One of the officers calling Pete's name brought me rushing from a bedroom.

I arrived in the front room as what must have been a brief conversation between the two coppers ended. When Pete turned to face me, his face didn't reveal any secrets, so I felt compelled to ask.

"Any developments I might be interested in?"

"I don't know yet. They flew the drone over a fair area of the property. There is any number of small outbuildings dotted randomly about the place. In a flyover of one of the buildings, the drone seemed to pick up evidence of activity. It stood out because the other buildings appeared devoid of anything similar. He will fly the drone over it again at a lower altitude, but we will drive over recent tyre marks to be a little closer to the building before he launches the it. I assume you want to come along?"

Again, a silly question … but he already was striding across the front verandah towards his vehicle. I trotted to catch up with him. We followed the drone pilot in the other vehicle. While it was clear a vehicle made several trips this way in recent times, the ground was so dry and hard, its tracks were barely discernible. The lead police vehicle came to a sudden halt and Pete pulled up close behind it. He jumped out and joined the drone pilot beside his vehicle. After exchanging a few words, the drone was on the ground and being readied for flight.

Aware of my place in the order of things, I remained in the car until I saw both men move back a distance from the drone in readiness for its launch. They would examine the transmitted images from the drone on the computer the pilot had set up on the tailgate of his vehicle. I did not want to miss the show, so I scrambled out of the car and rushed over. The drone already was whirring its way across the landscape by the time I reached the two men. I imagined the pilot would stand out in the open for a clear view of the drone's flight. It seems I was wrong.

Instead of moving away to leave only Pete and I hunched over the computer screen, the pilot monitored its flight on the screen and managed its course from there. It seemed only a few moments had elapsed, before the pilot exclaimed, "There it is, Sir. That's the building. I'll fly around it. The signs of activity are clearer from this height than they were in the earlier images."

That was all I needed to hear. The little voice in my head was telling me this was important and I needed to see it. It was easier said than done. Two hulking blokes hunched over the computer left me little opportunity for even a brief glance at the screen. I elbowed a little gap between them just in time to see images of vehicle tracks leading to the hut's door and evidence of other activity around its entrance.

Parked up close to the hut, neither of the coppers made a move to get out of their vehicles. I took my cue from them and viewed it from the comfort of the car. After a few moments of sitting observing nothing happening anywhere around us, Pete slowly opened his door and prepared to slide out.

"Sonny, stay in the car until I tell you it is okay for you to come out. We need to give the place a quick once-over first."

While not too keen on the idea, I knew I had no other option than to do as I was told. Upsetting Pete was a sure way of being excluded from any future police investigation. I watched the two officers confer briefly while standing between the two parked vehicles. Then, Pete started towards the hut. His colleague followed close on his heels. Of all the inopportune moments…! Pete's phone rang. The procession of two came to a halt while he took the call. It was brief, but it initiated a flurry of activity.

"Back in the vehicle," I heard Pete shout at the drone pilot. "Get back to the homestead. Collect the others and be ready to move out."

As he raced back to where I sat bursting with curiosity, he made another call. I heard enough of it to cause my stomach to tighten: ...*Be ready to go as soon as the vehicle returns. Company is on its way. I want to be well gone before they arrive. I'll take the lead.*

He started the car and had made a wide turn by the time he ended his call. I hauled my seatbelt across and buckled it as Pete planted his foot. Then we were bouncing off potholes and porpoising over minor undulations along the track. The big boxy 4x4 was not designed for rally driving, but Pete wasn't about to let that be a problem as we flew across the landscape. Somewhere behind us, the other vehicle was shrouded in a thick cloud of dust.

I like to know what is coming at me. It is so much easier to deal with if you know what it is and can prepare for it. My preference counted for nothing today. Pete was driving hard and it was clear he was totally focused on returning to the homestead as quickly as possible – and with us both still intact. Asking questions about what was going on did not seem a good idea just then.

Our time at the main cluster of buildings was mere moments. Pete waited while the other officers scrambled into the second vehicle … and then we were off again, with Pete continuing in the lead.

Chapter 11

We raced along over the tyre tracks made by the mob's vehicles beside the main entrance road. I continued to sit in silence and kept a tight grip on my seatbelt to avoid being thrown about as we bounced across the rough ground. At the point where the tracks veered off across the paddock towards the scrub, Pete swung a sharp left, and we too were headed for the scrub. It wasn't until we neared the point where the track entered the scrub that Pete eased back on the accelerator and adopted a more comfortable speed. At last I felt it safe to ask questions.

"Might I ask what precipitated our sudden exodus from the property?"

"I received word the mining company's get-together had ended. Some of the participants already were on their way back to Cranvale. No one was sure when they left. It meant I had no idea how soon they might arrive back at the home-stead."

"Did it matter? You have a warrant to cover your being there. You weren't doing anything unlawful by having a look around."

"That's true, but I want to use this warrant in a different way. I want them there when I arrive brandishing my search warrant … and I want to tear the place apart in the course of our official search. It's all about catching people on the back foot, upsetting their confidence and, in general, it's about gaining the upper hand through catching them by surprise."

"You've lost me. If that's the case, what was today all about?"

"The best information we had indicated the occupants would be attending the company's get-together, but we couldn't be sure we wouldn't find someone at home when we arrived. Hence the need for the warrant – just in case. Today's exercise worked out perfectly. We now know the layout of the place and what appears to be happening there. Information we gained today will inform planning for our raid when it's time for us to make use of our search warrant … probably tomorrow."

"What about that hut? It was the only one of the outlying buildings showing any signs of activity around it. We should have looked in there."

"And we probably will look in there sometime soon."

"You have to admit it is suspicious. We should have had a quick look in there today."

"What makes you think it's suspicious? Odd … different … intriguing perhaps … Any of those things I'll agree, but why suspicious?"

"It's exactly the sort of place where you could hide something or someone. They could be holding Callum in there. He might be in a bad way, and we've wasted another day."

"You have nothing to suggest Callum is being held anywhere against his will, and nothing to suggest he has fallen afoul of the mining mob. In spite of what you might think, today was not a waste and, if it turns out Callum is being held on the property, we will find him when we execute our search warrant."

"Yes, but that may be too late for…"

"Aha, look at that. Now, isn't that interesting?"

Just as I was about to argue my case for Callum's being held somewhere on the property, Pete cut me off midsentence. I took a wild look around me to see what was so interesting – and saw nothing significant.

"What is so interesting? What am I supposed to see? We are driving along a track through the scrub and all I can see is more scrub."

"Oh yes, but there is an offshoot track heading off to the right from this main track."

"Yeah, I can see that. But you used the offshoot track when you brought the body and the prisoners out yesterday. What's so exciting about it today?"

"Ah well, no, we didn't. We didn't use this offshoot track. The one we used was further along, was over grown and hadn't been used in a long time. This offshoot is well-made and has seen plenty of traffic in recent times. I need to see where this one comes out."

He was right. As we travelled along it, I could see the scars on the trees where branches have been lopped off to provide unhindered passage and prevent damage to vehicles. While the track wasn't rough, it was a bush track and didn't provide the smoothest of rides.

"Aha, the end is near."

Pete's comment ended my sightseeing and brought my focus back to straight ahead where bright daylight suggested we would break out of the scrub and into open country. He slowed to a crawl. We eased out of the cool shade of the scrub and into bright sunlight and the heat.

"Oh yes, this is a much better option. I can see why this happened."

"What's so special? We are now behind some sort of big building at the local saleyards."

"The offshoot track we used yesterday exited the scrub on the outskirts of town, but in a very open area. Any traffic coming and going from there would catch attention. Where this one emerges is hidden by the saleyards. A lot of traffic uses the road just over there. It services the various properties out this way. Vehicles emerging from the scrub here simply enter onto that road and carry on to wherever they're going. The casual observer wouldn't waste a second glance on vehicles using the road. It's only if they knew where the vehicles came from, they might begin to wonder."

To demonstrate how vehicles from the property could merge into traffic into Cranvale, Pete drove a few metres along behind the saleyards before entering onto the road in question. Our two vehicles continued in convoy about 150 metres further along the road until we came to a large shed like building, the premises of the local stock and station agent. We drove in and parked in the area out front. Pete made a quick phone call to somebody in the other vehicle. The side of the conversation I overheard told me what I wanted to know: *From here we have a pretty good view of the road which snakes around behind the saleyards. Keep your eyes open for anything like a convoy coming this way and maybe heading for the track through the scrub ... I've no idea what the timing might be, but I don't think it will be long. Let's just sit tight for a while and see how it goes.*

Less than ten minutes later, three vehicles travelling together came along the road and disappeared from view behind the saleyards. Someone in the other car rang Pete to alert him. He confirmed having seen them.

"Yeah, I see them. It looks like each of the vehicles is filled to capacity. Gives us an idea of how many might be in residence on the property."

He instructed his officers to 'go home, have lunch and take the rest of the day off'. As he ended his conversation, I saw the other vehicle shudder into life. Moments later, it was on its way out of the carpark. Pete and I sat in silence until the other car disappeared from view. Then, he seemed to remember I was there.

"Back to the motel…? Do you think they'll muster up a late lunch for us?"

"Maybe a sandwich if you're lucky, but I doubt there'll be anything more."

"A sandwich…! I suppose it's better than starving."

I felt in need of a shower but, as Pete had planted himself in the lounge chair in my room, a shower was unlikely for a while. It was mid-afternoon and I didn't expect room service to be too happy with an order for lunch. With plenty of encouragement from Pete, I tried my luck. My earlier advice on the matter was correct. They would make us sandwiches.

"Ask for fries. Get a bowl of chips to go with it."

I thought fries might be a step too far for the kitchen but, with obvious reluctance, they agreed to the chips to accompany the sandwiches, large pot of coffee and carafe of orange juice I ordered. I gave them my room number, but was tempted to tell them to charge it to Pete's room until I thought better of it. I needed to stay in good with him for a bit longer yet.

All credit to the kitchen; the spread of sandwiches and chips they provided was excellent and huge – sufficiently huge to satisfy even Pete's hunger. Part way through lunch, he asked to go over my investigation into Callum's disappearance. To avoid the embarrassment of admitting to having made no progress, I tried dodging his questions. It didn't work, so I found myself forced to admit the truth.

"Much as I hate to admit it, this case has gone nowhere. After all this time, I still have no clues as to how, when or why Callum suddenly disappeared from the B&S ball. And, before you ask, no, I have no evidence to suggest anyone else was involved in his disappearance. All I know for sure is that he did not return to work as he was supposed to after their trip out here. I've come up with several scenarios to explain what happened, but none is based on even a shred of evidence. My thinking at the moment is to tell Emily to hand his disappearance over to the police, and then we both should return to our lives in Millhaven."

"How do you expect that to go down? Is she likely to concur with your thinking, or is it more likely she will argue to stay on and search for him?"

"I don't know. A couple of days ago, she would have refused point-blank to go along with the suggestion. Now, I don't know what her feelings are. I'm unsure how she might react. But, as we are doing nothing more than spinning our wheels with this investigation, I can't see any benefit in pursuing it any longer."

"I suggest sticking with it for another day. If we execute the search warrant tomorrow, the hut will be included. You will know whether Callum is there or, perhaps, if he ever was. See where things lead after that before you decide to hand the case over. Anyway, handing it over would be no big deal. Because you have told me about his disappearance, and we are keeping an eye out for him as we progress our own investigation. You must keep an open mind. Emily might return from her day of socialising with a load of new information to help further your investigation."

I didn't buy his positive outlook. I don't think he believed it either. Regardless of whether I shared his thinking or not, I did want to see what – or who – was in that hut. To do so, I needed to stay on the right side of Pete to ensure an invitation to join them again tomorrow. It was almost five o'clock when he went back to his own room.

For the next few minutes, I did nothing more than sit and reflect on both the outcome of today and my stalled case. My phone cut through the silence of my room and brought my reverie to an end. Emily was back from her day out. She suggested coming to my room after she showered.

"No. I need a change of scenery. Give me a call when you've freshened up and I'll come to your room. You can tell me all about your day out over a cold drink of some sort."

I wasn't desperate for a cold drink or to hear about her day out. What I didn't want was for Emily to come to my room just now. It was obvious two people had dined in here today, and I'm sure she would question me about the other person. For some reason, I remained reluctant to tell her Pete Messell and a group of his officers were here. While I felt a twinge of guilt about it, the little voice in my head kept telling me it was the right thing to do. So, my conversation with her this afternoon will focus on her socialising.

While I waited for Emily to call me back, I loaded all evidence of our late lunch onto the trays it arrived on, and parked the loaded trays out in the corridor … outside the unoccupied room two doors down from mine It might surprise the staff when they came to collect the trays but, hopefully, the move would prevent a whole lot of difficult questions from Emily. On the way to her room, I tried to work out what excuse I would use to avoid having dinner with her tonight. …Or, was this when I had to come clean about Pete's presence in town?

One of the staff carrying a bottle of white wine in an ice bucket and I arrived at Emily's door at the same time. I relieved him of his load and knocked on her door as the staff member beat a hasty retreat. Emily looked a bit nonplussed when she opened the door to find me holding the wine. "How did you...?" After my brief explanation, we got on with the serious business of dealing with the bottle.

With both of us comfortably settled with glass in hand, I led the conversation in the direction of her day out. "Tell me about your day of mingling with the locals. Who were they? How were they? Come on. Don't keep me in suspense. Share all the juicy gossip you picked up today."

"Well, I met Cynthia, the woman I told you I was having coffee with. She was already at the coffee shop when I arrived, so we started the day with an early coffee. Just as we were draining our mugs, my friend Claire arrived … so we had to have another cup of coffee. Carol, the woman who owns the shop, came and sat with us while the place was quiet. Later, we tried to discuss discreetly whether to stay there for a sandwich or to go to the pub for lunch. That's when Jenny arrived. She thought Cynthia might be in town and dropped into the coffee shop on the off chance. Jenny had a busy morning and was in desperate need of a coffee. We had another coffee!"

"You must've been bouncing off the walls after so much caffeine."

"Yeah, my kidneys were awash. Anyway, we had decided to go to the pub for lunch. Jenny had to drop off something at her accountant's, so we used that as an excuse to leave the coffee shop, and then dropped off Jenny's stuff on the way to the pub. I don't think the pub was too happy to see us turn up so late for lunch, but we were served okay. Cynthia and Jenny left at about three o'clock to drive back to their properties before dark. That gave Claire and me some time together."

"Wasn't Claire also concerned about going home before dark?"

"No, she is overnighting in town. A friend of hers has a cottage in the back street. Whenever Claire comes into town, she spends the night at the cottage with her friend. When the friend is away as she is now, Claire drops in to keep a bit of an eye on the place. …And that brings me to the next bit. Claire has invited me to have dinner with her at the cottage tonight. I'm taking my toothbrush. I've a feeling I'll be spending the night there. I'm sorry. I seem to be deserting you all the time. If you'd rather I stayed to dine with you, I'll cancel with Claire."

"Don't be silly. Of course you should have dinner with Claire ... And spend the night if that's how it works out. You know me. I quite like my own company. But you haven't told me what titbits you picked up during your socialising today. Did you learn anything interesting?"

"Sorry; I was just coming to that. Before Claire arrived this morning, Cynthia and I had an interesting chat. Before her marriage, she was studying to be a geologist. The company she worked for was putting her through university. She only had twelve months to go when her father became ill; cancer.

Cynthia abandoned her studies and came home to run the property. Soon after her father died, she met her husband-to-be at a cattle sale. He is off a property too but, as the second son, had no prospect of taking over the family's holding. He was working with the stock and station agent when they met and, after they married, he helped her run the place she inherited."

"Sounds like a nice romantic story, and I suppose it's heading for a happily-ever-after ending." I regretted the comment as soon as I'd made it. It was bitchy and uncalled for. I didn't want to know about Cynthia's private life. My interest was in anything she learnt that might be useful to our investigation.

"Bear with me. It might seem irrelevant information, but it is important background knowledge. Not surprisingly, Cynthia and I got around to discussing the furore over the planned fracking in the area. She doubts that's going to happen. Her knowledge of geology tells her extraction of coal seam gas in this area doesn't require fracking."

"Hard to believe the town would be in such an uproar about something that isn't going to happen because it isn't required. The rest of the town appears convinced the mining company plans to use fracking to extract the gas. If Cynthia is right, I'm wondering how the story ever got started. Did she have any thoughts on the matter?"

"She does have a theory and was happy to share it with me, in spite of the fact her husband told her not to discuss it with anyone. He's concerned the mining company might not be happy about it, and they seem to be a ruthless mob. Anyway, Cynthia's take on the situation is that it's political. While she is not sure how the story of the proposed fracking started, she suspects it was deliberate. Designed specifically to create the unrest it has done in this community. It will take time to explain her theory, and then for us to discuss it, but I am now running late for dinner with Claire. I'll do a bit of discreet digging tonight to see if Claire knows anything more. I'll tell you about it tomorrow."

There was no point in arguing, or making her any later for her dinner appointment. Besides, when we finally sat down to discuss Cynthia's theory, I wanted us to have plenty of time to explore it properly. In the meantime, Emily had given me something to think about, and something to run past Pete tonight if we have dinner together again.

The message light on the phone was blinking when I returned to my room. Pete's message suggested we dine in his room this evening. Sometimes things work out well. But before dinner, I want to spend time examining Cynthia's theory and the possibility she might be right. For the moment, I'm at a loss to understand how deceiving the community over the method of extraction could be about gaining political mileage.

I was no further enlightened by the time I left for Pete's room. All my deliberations had achieved was to give me a headache.

Chapter 12

I don't know what Pete did after dropping me at the motel. Whatever it was left him in a cranky mood. That, combined with my headache, didn't suggest a pleasant or productive night ahead. Conversation was stilted all through dinner, and only started flowing more freely during coffee afterwards. With all the dinner stuff back on the delivery cart and parked in the corridor outside Pete's room, it was time to test whether useful discussion was possible this evening.

"I caught up briefly with Emily after she returned. She's overnighting in town with her friend from university. I asked if she learned anything interesting or relevant to our case."

Food, wine and coffee had worked wonders on Pete's disposition. He was eager to hear the outcome of my meeting with her. I repeated her report of Cynthia's comments re fracking in this area. When I finished, he spent some time cross-examining me. Finally, in exasperation, I snarled, "Pete, that is all I know so far. Emily was running late. I received an executive summary of what she learnt to tide me over until we can discuss it."

He nodded and fell silent for a few moments. "Sorry about the questioning, but Emily's news is the first interesting information any of the locals has provided. It got me a bit excited. What do you make of it?"

"The short answer is 'nothing'. I'm inclined to believe Cynthia knows what she is talking about, and something tells me her comments are significant. My problem is, I don't know why they could be. Emily did suggest something political might be behind the fracking issue."

"Financial benefit I could accept. Political manoeuvring, I'm not so sure about. What might the mining company hope to gain politically? They already have politics heavily on their side. That's what allows them to come in, run rough-shod over property owners and take over large areas of agricultural land. I've no time for farmers taking the law into their own hands, but it's not difficult to understand what drives them to it."

"Please don't misunderstand what I'm about to say. While listening to you, a part of my mind went off-piste to do its own thing. The only political player it came up with was Roland Garnham, the local mayor. From the outset, my speculation was Garnham made a dodgy deal with the mining company that benefited only himself. Perhaps it might be along the lines of a significant donation to his campaign funds for next year's election. But, what if there were other significant back-handers involved?"

"Well, I think we determined some other deal is involved. I doubt the mining company would be utilising that property – property which Garnham virtually owns already – if some compensation wasn't flowing back to him. The way every-thing out there is so covert suggests whatever the deal is between the company and the mayor, it's probably dodgy."

"I'm trying to adopt a similar mindset to that of the majority of the locals at the moment. Losing the use of such an area of my land for crops or grazing would not sit well with me. If, as has been suggested, fracking will cause fur-ther complications, such as significant detrimental effect on underground water supplies, it would only exacerbate the hostility towards the mining company and its extraction methods. Such impact would mean any land still available for farming operations might be rendered useless. And anything that impacted on the property's water supply might result in the landowner and his family no longer being able to live on that property."

"Okay, it isn't too hard to understand how landowners quickly worked that out, and why they are compelled to fight against such mining activity in any way they can. In the end, it comes down to the government's wanting coal seam gas extracted and sold to both domestic and overseas buyers. The landowner doesn't own what's under his land. Therefore, any fight they might stage against such mining activity will be futile. I haven't followed too closely this business of extracting coal seam gas, but it seems the prospect of fracking in an area generates more antagonism than any other means of extracting the gas. I need someone to explain it to me."

"I suspect Emily could explain it quite well. While I don't pretend to understand it either, fracking does seem to have the potential for more significant and widespread impact on the land."

"Okay, but you might have to explain it a bit more fully if I'm to understand it."

"It would be better left to those in the know to explain it. Nevertheless, as I see it, where ever the gas is extracted on a landowner's property, an area surrounding the wellhead is fenced off. As extracting the gas from a lucrative seam might involve drilling hundreds of wells on a given parcel of land, the owner's livelihood will be impacted in much the same way as if fracking occurred. It's those other impacts associated with fracking which ultimately make that method of extraction the least acceptable process."

Rather than take us any further into the potential territory of misinformation, I suggested we park the subject until we could discuss it with someone who knew how it all worked. There wasn't much else to discuss after that. Pete confirmed he would return with search warrant in hand to the property again tomorrow. After assuring me I was welcome to join them, our evening came to an end.

Back in my room, I knew I was in for another late night. My mind was working overtime. So far, it hadn't produced any answers, but it was churning through my conversation with Pete, and would continue to do so after I went to bed. I remember seeing two o'clock slide by, but must have fallen asleep soon afterwards. The next thing I remember is being woken by my phone chirping loudly.

"If you're still planning on coming with us today, you had better get your backside into gear. I'm going to be leaving in about half an hour."

My breakfast tray waited patiently outside my door. The toast has turned to leather. I made coffee, woofed down the cereal and juice, dressed and was almost functioning normally by the time Pete knocked on my door.

"When I went for a run this morning, your tray was still outside your door. I reckoned it suggested you might need help to get moving today. I'm assuming you still want to come with us to see what we find out on that property."

"Of course I'm going with you. I especially want to look inside that hut, but anything else you find will be interesting too."

Conversation was almost non-existent on the way to the property, apart from one brief period when Pete laid down the ground rules regarding my behaviour. His rules had a heavy focus on what I shouldn't say or do. I knew I would struggle to comply, but I would try hard. I did not want to end up alienating myself from him. This morning, he seemed tense and withdrawn. I doubted it has anything to do with searching the property. Over the course of his career, he must've been involved in hundreds of similar situations. It occurred to me something else might be causing his present mood.

Peter dragged a group of his officers from the Ralston precinct all the way out to this far-flung area of his region. After so many days here, he had little – only one body so far – to show for it. In the absence of any further evidence, he was unlikely to spend more than another day or so here before packing it in and returning to Ralston. That scenario caused me some concern. Without Pete's involvement, I had little hope of finding Callum. And, I did not intend ruining my chances of his help by alienating myself from his investigation by doing the wrong thing.

The silence wasn't wasted. I found the lack of conversation presented an opportunity for my mind to roam free. It promptly returned to last night's mental gymnastics. I again examined Cynthia's comments about fracking. Somehow, I was convinced it was an important factor. Establishing how it was relevant was another matter. In spite of the time involved in the long drive to the property's homestead, I progressed no further with unravelling the implications of her comments.

As we passed through the gateway, I felt my excitement start to build. Won't be long now, I told myself; just the rough driveway to the homestead before the search can begin. About halfway along the track, another less exciting thought occurred to me. In executing the warrant, the police would make the acquaintance of those in residence at the homestead. It's logical their search would begin there before moving to the surrounding outbuildings. The more distant huts dotted around the property would be the last searched. That put my hut – the hut I desperately wanted to inspect – way down towards the bottom of the list.

Curbing my impatience until it was my hut's turn to be searched was going to be a challenge. With more officers, they might have broken into teams to complete the searches sooner. But, with only Pete and his four officers, they barely made one decent search team. It would be late in the day before they got around to my hut. How far away from the homestead was it? The little voice in my head suggested I keep an eye out for an opportunity to escape unnoticed to mount my own search. I might keep its suggestion in mind.

Our arrival at the homestead didn't receive red carpet treatment from the residents. I expected people to rush out onto the verandah as soon as we drove up, but nobody came out to meet us. Pete ordered me to stay in the vehicle until they gained entry to the building. It seemed sound advice.

Evidence to date suggested this mob wasn't too familiar with the concept of the sanctity of life. So, apart from unclipping my seatbelt, I remained in my seat … with one hand on the door handle for an immediate exit the moment it was safe to join the others.

Pete thumped heavily on the front door. For about a minute, nothing happened to suggest anyone was at home. Just as Pete prepared to bang on the door again, it opened a crack. That was all the coppers needed. The next few seconds were a scene straight from a cops-and-robbers movie. Two constables threw themselves against the huge wooden door. The inhabitants offered some resistance. The door swung open about a quarter of the way before coming to an abrupt stop. Pete and one other constable then added their weight to the argument. It was all that was needed. The door crashed wide open. A few moments of chaos followed.

From my safe vantage point, it was impossible to tell what was happening, but it involved quite a lot of noise. I interpreted it as those in the house being none too pleased about visitors at this hour of the morning. The confrontation was soon over. With the rough stuff appearing to be done with, I deemed it safe to assess the situation from closer quarters. Out of the vehicle and onto the verandah, I tiptoed to the front door now standing wide open.

Pete had control of the situation. In a strident voice, he ensured the residents knew what was happening and why. I risked a quick look inside. A number of the residents were perched on the sofa and other lounge chairs in front of Pete, who was in full flow of delivering his message. The constables had spread out and now engaged in the actual search. Did I want to venture inside to join them?

It seemed a strange time to be asking myself that question. What was a point of coming if I didn't want to be a part of the action? Deep down, I knew why I hesitated. I was torn between two thoughts. I wanted to be in there to see what was found and what people did, and to hear anything that was said. On the other hand, for me, all of that was secondary to examining that hut in the back paddock.

If I didn't go inside to see and hear everything first hand, I could find out about it later from Pete. The alternative was to slip away now and make my way to the hut on foot. The latter option held most appeal. With everyone so busy with proceedings, no one would notice I wasn't there. Then rational thought kicked in. Pete would not be happy if I sneaked off to the hut alone – and possibly contaminated a crime scene. Getting Pete offside was likely to result in his refusal to share with me any information about the outcome of their search. I quietly slid into the room and stood against the wall adjacent to the door. Nobody acknowledged my presence.

A few minutes later, one of the constables strode past me on his way out the door. He carried a number of evidence bags in his hand. I assumed he went to one of the vehicles and, when he returned a few moments later, he carried a fresh supply of bags. On his way past, he whispered a few words in Pete's ear. Whatever he said was important. After barking a warning to the residents not to move from where they were sitting, Pete followed the constable into the next room.

Apart from wanting to see what was so important in the next room, I didn't feel too comfortable being the only member of the troop left alone with the mob. Without taking my eyes off those still seated in the lounge room, I followed the others into the next room. I need not have worried. As I was about to slide into that room, I heard Pete order one of his constables 'to go out there and keep an eye on them'. One of the constables strode past me as I hovered near the doorway.

When I finally entered the next room, I found Pete and a constable huddled over a chest of drawers in the far corner. I cleared my throat to alert them to my presence, and hopefully avoid sustaining physical injury after taking them by surprise.

"Good to see you decided to join us." My mind generated a whole flock of smart comebacks in response to Pete's comment but, before I was foolish enough to issue any of them, Pete continued. "Come and have a look at this little lot. I had no idea they were such a tidy mob; not much evidence of it anywhere else in the place."

They had the top drawer open. It held a small armoury. What looked like an old quilt lined the bottom of the drawer. Nestled among its folds were a rifle, sawn-off shotgun, two hand guns, and a new looking shotgun, as well as boxes of ammunition to suit the various weapons. After photographing the drawer's contents and instructing the officer to bag the lot when they finished investigating the rest of the drawers, Pete closed the top drawer and opened the next one down.

This one contained obvious drug paraphernalia: two small electronic scales, bags of pills and some containing white powder, a box of syringes, and a half-empty box of small plastic bags. There were also another handgun and a couple of lethal-looking knives. Again, everything was photographed and earmarked for bagging. As I watched, an officer clicked off a myriad of photos. I couldn't help wondering what else of interest to the police the chest of drawers might contain.

It didn't take me long to find out. The third drawer appeared reluctant to open. After jiggling it a bit and then giving it an almighty heave, the drawer shuddered partially open. A brick of banknotes came out through the gap. In part, it was responsible for jamming the drawer. More jiggling and tugging finally had the drawer open. I'm sure my mouth fell open at the sight that greeted us.

One end of the drawer was occupied by a couple of expensive-looking tote bags, now crumpled and showing signs of having seen much use. While they looked a bit forlorn now, in new condition, I would have died to own either one of them. A small backpack, a 'bum-bag' and a messenger type bag also were crammed into that end of the drawer. But, the contents of the remainder of the drawer were the focus of everyone's attention.

Some stacked neatly and others just jammed into large plastic bags were more wads of banknotes than I had ever seen. Pete let out a low whistle as he fanned the end of one of the bricks. It was a stack of one hundred dollar bills held together with a rubber band. Most of the money was one hundred dollar notes, but there was also a good representation of fifty dollar notes as well. A lot of the money in the plastic bags was in neat rubber-banded rolls.

"How much do you think there is?" It was an inane question to ask, but I couldn't help myself. In my stunned state, it just slipped out.

"I couldn't even hazard a guess, but somebody will be kept busy for a while counting it." Pete slapped a wad of notes on the palm of his hand as he spoke. "By the look of all this, business has been doing well. Quite a few people might be upset when they discover their source of supply cut off … hopefully!"

More photos were taken before the officers began clearing out the drawers, starting with the stash of cash in the bottom drawer. Pete left them and went back to the lounge room to talk to the residents.

I heard him say, "Good work, Constable," as the sounds of a scuffle drifted my way. The Pete bellowed, "You were told to stay where you were. Now, get back and sit down. Don't any of you move. We have a few things to talk about, and my officer here will make sure you stay put to participate."

For me, it was decision time again. While two of the officers recorded and bagged everything in the drawers, one moved off to continue searching the premises, and the fourth one remained with Pete in the lounge room. Should I tag along with the one continuing the search to see what else was found, or should I join those in the lounge room? Proceedings in there could be interesting, but once again I was aware later

Pete probably would share with me anything he learnt. On the other hand, helping the constable with his search could be exciting.

In the end, a decision wasn't necessary. Pete recalled the constable from search duties to record details and finger-prints of the mob still occupying seats in the lounge room. I couldn't work out what he intended doing with them. There were too many of them to take them to the local lock-up in the two vehicles we came in. All became clear when I overheard a phone call he made from out on the front verandah. A light plane with extra officers on board would put down on the property's airstrip in about an hour's time.

A vision of the airstrip from our visit to the property yesterday flashed through my mind. "That's interesting…," I murmured aloud.

"Did you want something?" Pete asked as he brushed past me on his way back into the lounge room.

In response, I gave him a shake of my head as I went past him in the opposite direction. An old squatters chair further along the verandah looked like a good place to sit and think, so I made myself comfortable and got on with my thinking.

Only a few moments later, Pete stuck his head out to see where I was. "Are you okay? I noticed you weren't anywhere inside."

"I'm fine. With so much happening in there, I wanted to keep out of everyone's way. This chair was too inviting to ignore. I'm happy to sit out here while you lot do whatever you have to do. You might have to wake me when you are ready to leave here though. This chair is very comfortable."

Pete's look suggested he doubted the veracity of my reply but, after a moment, he nodded, turned on his heel and disappeared inside again. I'm not surprised he held some doubts. I wasn't sure how much truth was in my explanation. Nevertheless, first, I wanted to take a minute or two to sort out a couple of things in my mind. There was something bothering me about the prospect of the police's small plane landing on the airstrip here. Something in the distant reaches of my mind begged me to drag it to the fore. In the peaceful solitude of the verandah, with only the flies annoying me, I let my mind run free.

That vision of the landing strip from yesterday bounced back squarely to front and centre. I knew what was bothering me about it. *Neglected i*s the best description of the property – or, perhaps *abandoned* might be more accurate. The only evidence anyone had been here in years were the tracks made by the mob's various vehicles. All previous driveways and tracks on the property were now either overgrown, or so rutted and potholed as to be unusable … but not so the airstrip!

Its present condition suggested it saw quite a bit of work in recent time. Putting a plane down on it now would present no problems at all. I think it reasonable to assume the mining company had need of an airstrip out here. Why else would they invest so much work in revitalising an airstrip in such a neglected environment? Still, I imagine any light planes flying in and out of a supposedly deserted property might raise the odd eyebrow around Cranvale. That had me wondering whether the strip had been used, or whether it was prepared on the off chance it might be required at some time.

I debated whether I should go back inside to see what had developed during my absence, or stay out here and think of something else to. The latter option won out after no more than a moment's consideration. While the coppers were so occupied inside, it presented the opportunity I required to slip away unnoticed. On my way past Pete's vehicle, I helped myself to a bottle of water from the cooler compartment in the centre console, and grabbed my hat and sunglasses off the back seat. Then I was jogging across a parched and uneven paddock in an attempt to put as much distance between me and the homestead as quickly as possible.

The day was far too hot for jogging. I dropped my pace to a brisk walk. How far away was that hut? It hadn't seemed so far when I thought about it earlier this morning. Now, I wondered if my attempt to reach it on foot might be foolhardy. I felt the sweat trickle down my spine. Moments later, my shirt was plastered to my back. A couple of strands escaped from my poor attempt at a ponytail and glued themselves to my face. I had no doubts my face already glowed red, and there was still a long way to go.

Chapter 13

With my eyes glued to the outline of the hut in the distance, I tried ignoring the heat and my aching legs to concentrate on maintaining as much speed as possible. Bowled along by the only breath of breeze I felt since leaving the homestead, a piece of prickly tumbleweed flew directly at me. It broke the rhythm of my hard slog by necessitating a few fancy steps to avoid contact with it. Then, I was off again and striving to regain my rhythm from before the unexpected visitor. The hut now appeared no more than about two hundred metres away. Its proximity provided the encouragement needed to pick up my pace again.

Approach with caution a little voice on a continuous loop chanted in my ear as I slowed to a walk for the last hundred metres. An approach from the rear of the hut seemed the safest bet. Even so, I felt my stomach tightening as I closed in on my destination. About five metres away from the rear of the hut, I stopped to survey the area. Nothing but a vista of relatively flat parched earth broken only by the presence of an occasional stunted and gnarled tree surrounded me.

No movement intruded anywhere in my field of vision. Good; either they haven't missed me yet, or they are too preoccupied with other things to come looking for me. I knew Pete would know exactly where I had gone. I told myself, standing there behind the hut was achieving nothing. True, I didn't know what might await me on the other side, but standing around wondering what to do next only added to the growing lead ball in the pit of my stomach. "For God's sake, get on with it," I chided myself aloud. "Move your feet!"

My feet crunched quietly on the dry ground as I picked my way along the side of the hut and around to the front.

A quick scan of the area out front told me little, but the tyre tracks held my attention. Yesterday, the jumble of tyre tracks and footprints created a suspicious montage over an area in front of the door. Today, while it was difficult to be sure, I was almost certain more marks were added since our visit yesterday. The uncertainty held me glued to the spot for the few heartbeats it took for my potential vulnerability to occur to me.

If something unpleasant awaited me in the hut, standing out front in the open as I was probably presented an invitation for whatever was inside to come out to meet me. I unglued my feet and tiptoed to the front wall of the hut. With my back planted hard up against the wall adjacent to the door, I took a couple of deep breaths while I tried to work out what to do next. Should I reach for the handle, fling open the door and barge in, or should I knock and wait to see what happens?

For some reason, the latter option appealed. I knocked. Nothing happened. I knocked again, more vigorously this time. Still nothing happened. Okay, I tried the polite approach with no result. My preferred option had failed. Time to try something more robust. After one more deep breath to steady my nerves – and allow for any tardy response to my knocking – I reached for the door handle.

The next few seconds were a blur: grab the handle, fling open the door, rush in. …And nothing happened, except I then was standing in the middle of the hut … alone. "Bugger! This is not what I expected to find," I told the empty hut before even having time to investigate the place.

Standing in the middle of the hut with my hands on my hips and swivelling from the waist, I scanned the interior of the building. It was a basic unlined timber shack with what had once been a hearth at one end. A two-burner camp cooker now occupied the small alcove. The opening through which smoke from a fire in the hearth once travelled through to an outside brick chimney structure remained evident. In more recent times, with an open fire in the hearth a thing of the past, a sheet of ply had been nailed over the flue opening.

Devoid of a bathroom, a kitchen sink, or any other of usual facilities, the hut had become intended for no longer than overnight stays. It had no electricity. The stubs of several candles and the wax trails left by others, adorned the many 'shelves' provided by the exposed wall girts. Furniture was in short supply. An unpainted and scarred wooden table about the size of a card table stood against the wall further along from the fireplace. Two straight-backed wooden chairs accompanied it. Even sadder-looking than the table, the chairs' many breaks were plated over with ply offcuts.

The only other furniture was an old iron-framed single bed against the wall opposite the fireplace. I started towards the bed. The sound of a plane circling overhead made me stop and listen. Then it was coming into land. Time for the homestead residents to depart the property. It gave me the confidence to carry on exploring the hut without worrying about being discovered or interrupted. I knew where the coppers were. They would be at the airstrip overseeing the evacuation of the mining mob members from the homestead. A little more relaxed by that knowledge, I continued across the hut to examine the bed.

Up close, a thin mattress did nothing to make the bed look more enticing than it did at first glance. Its filthy striped ticking featured many rips which allowed the mattress' coir stuffing to escape in various uncomfortable looking places. I couldn't help thinking that, while the hut now had not been in use for many years, it probably was just as forlorn and uninviting in its heyday.

As I stood beside the bed, something caught my eye. A pile of dirty rag appeared to have been kicked in under it. I used the heel of my boot to drag it out a little way. Reluctant to touch the rag with my bare hands, I applied my boot to open it out for a better look. It wasn't just a pile of rag, but was once a fine cotton bedsheet. Why was it under the bed, and why was it here in this godforsaken hut in the first place?

Using the toe of my boot, I stretched out an area of the sheet to examine some of its stains. I caught my breath. The stains were recent. Somebody was here and had used this sheet. Somebody had slept on this bed. My stomach tightened. I felt my breathing become shallow. Is it possible the 'someone' was Callum? Surely not… Why would he hide out here in this horrible place? … Ooh, perhaps he had no choice. Perhaps he was held here.

Okay, that's possible … But why…? Why would anyone – presumably the mining mob – hold him captive? What had he done, seen, said or heard to make him a potential risk if left at large? There was a more disturbing question begging for attention: if Callum was kept captive here, where was he now? Possible answers to that question flooding through my mind made me weak at the knees. I needed to sit down … but not on that bed. I was halfway across the hut on my way to sit on one of the chairs when I heard it.

A vehicle roared up at pace. There was barely time to dash across and stand against the wall beside the door before I heard a car door open and then slam closed. With nowhere else in the hut to hide, my only hope was I would be hidden by the door when it opened. Nevertheless, my chances of being able to slip out from behind the door unseen and make a dash to safety were negligible. And, my chances of staying alive seemed equally non-existent.

Footsteps crunched up to the door – and stopped. Then, after about a second's delay, a tentative tap on the door followed. I bit my lip and held my breath. Perhaps they will go away. It's what happens in all the best movies … But not in the real world … Not in my real world of the here and now. The door handle rattled before the door slid slowly open about thirty centimetres.

In spite of the impossibility of it, I tried oozing myself

into the very fabric of the wall. It only required whoever was out there to stick their head around the door for me to be discovered. I prayed: please don't let them come in; please don't let them see me. Apparently the communication channels were closed. No one heard my prayers. The door was pushed wide open. A large shadow fell across the floor. My visitor was almost certainly male. From behind the door, I heard him take a couple of steps into the hut. In an instant, a hand grabbed the edge of the door and swung it almost closed, fully exposing me in the process. My strangled shriek sounded loud in the empty hut.

"What the hell do you think you're playing at? What are you doing here, and why didn't you tell anyone you were leaving the homestead? Well, don't just stand there. I want answers."

I had never seen Pete quite so angry. If I'm honest, I deserved it, and I shouldn't have expected anything else. The overwhelming feelings of both relief and fear rendered me speechless … and further antagonised Pete. He was about to release another tirade when I finally found my voice.

"I'm sorry. Yes, I should have told someone I was going, but everyone was so busy back at the homestead. I didn't want to get in the way or interrupt anything. So, when I found myself just hanging about on the verandah, it occurred to me that I could do something worthwhile, and maybe save everyone having to traipse out to this hut after finishing-up at the homestead." My ever-so-humble-and-apologetic demeanour wasn't sufficient to earn me a favourable response.

Pete continued to berate me about my lack of a number of personal attributes – common sense, respect, appropriate behaviour – for a little longer before his demeanour underwent a sudden change.

"Well now, having thoroughly contaminated my possible crime scene, what have you found?"

"For your information, I haven't contaminated the scene. I haven't touched anything except the outside door handle. As for finding anything, I think I found something just as you arrived." I gestured with my chin towards the sheet on the floor. "I haven't touched it, but I feel someone who was here recently might have used that sheet. Maybe forensics will tell us more."

Following my example, Pete used his boot to spread the sheet further. "You might be right. The stains on this sheet don't appear to be old. This place is not exactly the Ritz. I hope whoever spent time here recently didn't pay too high a price for his accommodation."

The thought behind Pete's comment wasn't lost on me. Of course I thought this might be where they held Callum. If that were the case, where was Callum now? Without having asked Pete about it, it's a fair assumption their search of the property didn't find him. That realisation had my stomach doing flip-flops. How high a price did the recent resident of this hut pay? …And, in whatever condition he might be, where was he now?

While I pondered such dark thoughts, Pete went to speak with his officers. A few moments later, every surface of the hut was being dusted for fingerprints. Pete left me alone while he examined every square inch of the place. I leant up against the wall near the bed, and let my eyes roam over the interior of the building. It hit me like a sledgehammer. How could anyone stay here for any length of time? There were no facilities. No bathroom, no toilet, no electricity (maybe not so important), and no water.

How could anyone stay in this hut without water? I knew every square inch of the interior of the hut, and there were no taps, no sink or wash-basin, or anything else that might hold water. More importantly, I wasn't aware of a readily available source of water outside the building. I hadn't seen the complete exterior of the place. Maybe there is a tank or a pump of some sort outside somewhere. That thought was enough to have me mobile again.

I pushed myself off the wall and, in a slow aimless way, meandered towards the door. No one noticed. No one even glanced in my direction. I continued out the door and around to the side of the hut I hadn't seen before. There was nothing there; no outhouse, no tank, no pump, no sign of anything to suggest a water supply. The only thing of note I found were the foundations of a brick chimney once attached to the wall to service the fireplace inside.

As I was already outside, I continued with a circuit of the building, ending up back at the door. I barrelled headlong into Pete as I strode into the hut.

"Where the hell have you been this time? Go and sit in the vehicle and don't move from there. I can't take my eyes off you for more than five seconds without you disappearing. Stay in the vehicle until we finish in here and come out to join you."

My whinge about it being too hot to sit outside in the vehicle didn't win me any favours. In truth, it was only a half-hearted complaint. There was nothing more for me to see or do inside the hut. Sitting alone in the vehicle with the air-conditioner running provided an opportunity to review in comfort what I now knew – or thought I knew – about this hut and its possible connection to Callum's disappearance.

When the coppers emerged from the building, there was urgency about their demeanour. They all piled into the vehicles. Pete hit the ignition and had the motor purring almost before planting his backside properly on his seat. With no longer any need to cover our tracks, the two vehicles drove around the hut and headed back towards the homestead. The silence between Pete and I lasted the few minutes before I could restrain myself no longer.

"Pete, is it likely Callum spent time since his disappearance in that hut? I know you didn't find anything definite to support the idea, but what are your thoughts on the subject?"

"Argh, if I have to give you an opinion, I suppose it might be possible … And if I don't give you an opinion, you will probably nag me all the way back to the homestead. So, perhaps it would be more productive if I asked you for your thoughts on the matter."

"As I said, I found nothing to suggest Callum had been there, but I feel certain someone spent time there recently. I can't think of a reason why anyone would stay there by choice. It is such an inhospitable place to spend even a night. If it were Callum who was there, the question is, was he there of his own free will? I believe he was not. If I'm right, it would suggest he was being held there in some way; somewhere he wouldn't be found easily."

"I agree all of that is possible. The only problem I see with it is that we didn't find any sign of Callum anywhere else on the property. …And, before you ask, yes, we did keep an eye out for any trace of him while we carried out our search for material related to our own case. So, do you have any ideas – no matter how fanciful – on where he might be, or how you might progress your investigation?"

"Leave that question with me for a while. The hint of an idea is trying to develop. I need to think on it a bit longer before I'll know if it makes any sense."

Something was not right. Pete's mind seemed to be elsewhere when he spoke to me. It made me nervous. Was I unaware of something that was happening? Did their search of the property produce something that now had Pete on edge? My queries about what was on his mind brought assurances he wasn't concerned about anything. Accepting there was no point in pushing him further, I let silence descended between us.

It allowed me to concentrate on Callum, his disappearance, and what might have happened to him since the B&S ball. I was convinced Callum had been in that hut. I felt it in every fibre of my being. Proving it was another matter. I tried to step away from all thoughts about the hut, focusing my thinking instead on where Callum might be now. It seems I must accept he is nowhere on the property. So, where else is there? Where might they hide him? A perplexing thought rushed in. What if this was all down to Callum, and the mining mob had nothing to do with it? What if Callum orchestrated his own disappearance and everything which has happened since then?

Why would he do that? Such thoughts made no sense. While I might accept he found someone more exciting to be with than Emily – his reputation didn't preclude such a possibility –I doubted he would be so cruel about it. No, I don't believe his absence is of his own making. But, that doesn't answer the question: where is he now? Through all the murkiness filling my mind, an image slowly emerged.

"The laydown area…!"

"What? Sonny, what about the laydown area…? I assume you mean that clearing in the scrub where we found the body in one of the shipping containers."

"Yes, the clearing in the scrub… What if they moved Callum into one of those containers? Perhaps someone was around yesterday when we visited the hut. Who knows what we might have found if we had gone inside then instead of waiting until today?"

"Are you criticising the way I do my job … trying to tell me how to do it?"

"No, of course not. A couple of thoughts bother me at the moment. One of them is that no one other than Callum is responsible for his disappearance." Pete turned and gave me a confused look. His eyebrows slid almost together. I ignored him and continued. "If he were in the hut when we drove up yesterday, he might have made a move overnight to somewhere he considered a more secure hideout."

"And, if that isn't what happened, what other scenario have you come up with to explain what you seem quite convinced is evidence of Callum's presence in the hut?"

I chose to ignore the sarcasm in his voice, but remained silent for a few moments. I wasn't sulking. It was a case of taking time to clarify the half-formed alternate scenario lurking at the back of my mind. I still wasn't sure I had sorted it out when I responded.

"I think there might be two *what-ifs* involved in my potential second scenario. The first is, what if someone was in the hut with Callum when we were there yesterday and they organised to move him elsewhere? My other possibility almost reverts to my first scenario. What if Callum was alone at the time but, later yesterday, he told one of the mining mob about his close encounter with unknown visitors, and that person relocated him to somewhere safer?"

"Okay, so how do you think it happened? I mean, where do you think they might take him?"

"As I said, maybe they considered one of the containers in the laydown area in the scrub a safer and more secure place."

"I'm not sure I agree. They must know we found the body and have taken a couple of their members into custody. Why would they still think of the laydown area as somewhere safe?"

I caught my breath. "What if…?" I croaked, and then paused for a moment to regain control of my vocal chords. "What if it doesn't matter if we find Callum at the laydown area? What if he can't tell us anything, but they hoped moving him would shift the focus away from their hideout on the property?"

"Are you suggesting that, if we find anything at the laydown area, it will be a body and not someone alive and well enough to tell us what's been going on around here?"

"Argh, yes … but I wish you hadn't said that. It sounded so much worse when you said it aloud than when I thought it. All I know is my gut is telling me the laydown area is the place to look for Callum."

Pete shot me another one of his looks, but a couple of heartbeats later he reached for his phone. I heard him give a short, sharp command to an officer in the following vehicle.

Chapter 14

While the track to the property's gate was rough and required many sudden sharp manoeuvres to avoid the worst of the washouts and potholes, bouncing across the long neglected paddock was worse. For the second time in as many days, I found my tightly fastened seatbelt couldn't keep my backside firmly on the seat.

After his ten-second phone call to the other vehicle, Pete reefed the steering wheel over hard. We were off the track and heading for the scrub. I knew, that from a distance, what looked like a flat paddock was something else. Covered in lumps and hollows, tussocks of dead spiky grass, and almost hidden logs, it made for a bone-jarring ride which didn't allow traversing the paddock in a straight line. We were constantly thrown about – up and down and from side to side – as Pete maintained high speed in spite of frequently swerving to avoid the worst of the obstacles.

The tortuous trek felt like it lasted forever. In reality, within a few minutes, we picked up the mob's tracks from their many trips to the clearing in the scrub. Thanks to the frequent use, their tracks made the rest of our journey almost comfortable. I felt myself relax, and tried releasing my death grip on the shoulder strap to reach for the clip to undo my seat belt. Nothing happened. After having clung white-knuckled to the strap during the paddock crossing, it required a few moments of exercising my fingers to restore their circulation before they felt inclined to comply.

Once we reached the trees, Pete eased off the accelerator a little to enter the scrub at a sedate pace compared to our earlier death-defying mad dash.

"Keep your eyes peeled. We don't need any surprises jumping out of the trees in front of us. I doubt we'll find anyone waiting for us at the site, but I would prefer a stealthy approach."

He had to be joking. How could two big, gutsy four-wheel drive vehicles crashing their way along a rough track through the scrub make a stealthy approach? "Accept it, Pete. That ain't going to happen. Might be better to just go for it, but be prepared for whatever reception awaits us at the clearing." My comment brought a throaty chuckle from the driver, but no noticeable change in speed.

Then, the light ahead suggested we were about to break out of the bush and into the laydown area. Our speed dropped to a crawl. Pete was on his phone to the other vehicle for another brief call as we entered the clearing. No vehicles about. No one came out to meet us. When we were a few metres into the area, Pete pulled off to one side to allow room for the second vehicle to enter and park beside us.

"Stay in the car … and this time I mean it, Sonny. Don't even think about getting out until I tell you it's safe to do so."

There was that tone of voice again. And this is another one of those times when I wouldn't dream of arguing with or defying Pete. This doesn't mean I was happy to remain in the car. It simply meant I had learned to read my long-time friend well over the years, and know when to do as I'm told. I undid my seatbelt and slid down in my seat as I watched the coppers go about their business.

While there was no obvious sign of life at the site, they employed extreme caution as they moved towards their main target: the demountable building. One tried the door. From what I could see, it appeared to be locked. The men briefly regrouped out front of the building before fanning out and to begin a search of the site. Pete stayed close to the demountable, only allowing himself to venture as far as the nearest shipping container. After picking his way carefully around it, he tried opening its huge double doors. They too were locked.

An eerie silence hung over the clearing. The coppers made no sound as they searched the whole area. No one called out. No one laughed, or coughed, or sneezed. It was as though I watched a movie with the sound muted. After a few minutes, they emerged into the open at the far end of the area and began making their way back towards Pete. From some distance away, they gave him an all-clear signal.

He turned to face the vehicle and beckoned to me to join him. No second invitation required. I looped my bag over my shoulder, slid out of the car and eased the door closed with a soft click. After taking a moment to scan the area and listen for any stray sounds, I dashed across the open space to stand beside Pete.

"It seems we are alone," he murmured as he continued scanning the laydown area. That was all he said, and I had no opportunity to comment before he was gone.

Pete moved a few paces away from me to meet his officers as they returned from their search. I heard the murmur of voices but, they spoke so softly, I couldn't hear what was said. They had to be reporting the outcome of their search. I was desperate to know what they said … and what they found. But, this was police business. There was nothing I could do for the moment, except remain where I was and hope Pete would return to share their information with me.

At last the police huddle broke up and the officers again began making their way around the many shipping containers on their way towards the far end of the site. Pete strolled back to me. The stony look on his face told me they found nothing. I felt my heart sink as I tried to prepare myself for the bad news.

"As quiet as a morgue… Oops, sorry, perhaps not the best choice of phrase. My blokes found no one and no sign of anything to arouse their suspicions. Looks like our cross-country drive was for nothing. Feel free to wander around if you like. You won't find anything, but I need time alone to think about what out next move might be."

"He has to be here. I was sure he would be here. I felt it in my very core. Where else would they take Callum? Unless they have some other hidey-hole we don't know about yet, this is the only other place we know to be associated with that mob. I don't doubt how well your officers carried out their search, but I will have a nose about on my own anyway … while I leave you alone to do your thinking."

Such a determined plan is all well and good, but where do I start? I've no doubt the coppers found every shipping container locked. The keys to every one of them probably are in the demountable, which also is locked. If only I could get into the demountable … and, if Pete weren't around, I would. The tools I needed were in my bag, but Pete was unlikely to stand around watching as I picked the lock. At that point, Fate decided to intervene.

Out of the corner of my eye, I saw Pete start to move away. I stood watching him for a few moments. There wasn't any particular direction to his wandering. He just wandered past the first container and continued until he disappeared amongst the many others along one side of the clearing. This was my chance … risky, but my only chance.

With one last look to be certain Pete wasn't around, I raced to the demountable building and tiptoed to the door. My gentle tap on the door wouldn't have caught the attention of anyone with even the slightest defective hearing. No time to waste. I didn't know how long Pete's perambulations might last. One quick scrabble around in my bag and, a moment later, I had tools in hand. A deep breath to steady myself, and I went to work. The lock was not complicated. A split second later, I eased the door open wide enough to slip inside.

No one accosted me. Pete wasn't yelling at me. So far so good…! But I needed to take stock of where I was. The building was small; probably only intended as a site foreman's office. A small open area immediately inside the door was set up as an office. I suspected a bathroom area lay behind the door separating it from the main area. No need to confirm the facilities, my interest is in what I might find in the office.

It comprised a desk, chair, metal filing cabinet, and a small wooden cupboard, all well-used and bearing the scars of a hard life. The makeshift key rack mounted on the back wall behind the desk held my attention. A metre-long length of 100mm x 15mm timber sporting a row of hooks was screwed to the wall. Most of the hooks held keys. Two keyrings were on the desk, but I counted six empty hooks on the keyboard. That called for a spot of mental gymnastics.

Before becoming too alarmed about the empty hooks, I needed to explore my memory banks. How many shipping containers were there? It didn't matter how hard I thought about it, I couldn't be sure. …And, I didn't have the luxury of wasting time while I thought about it. No matter what I try to tell myself, one thing remained possible: if Callum was in one of the containers, whoever stashed him there might have kept the container key. Some sort of register or map identifying what each key belonged to would be useful. There had to be something correlating the numbered tag on each keyring with its respective lock's location.

Time to achieve anything was slipping away, I reminded myself before turning my attention to the desk and the two keyrings on it. Again, their tags were of no use without some form of reference. One of them caught my attention. Its keys were different from all the others. They were not for a padlock. I glanced over at the door. Aha…! This key opened the door of this building. The lock was one of those, where to lock the door when leaving the building, you push in the button and pull the door closed behind you. No key is required to lock it from outside… but a key is required to enter again. Someone out there must hold a key to this building.

With nothing more to be learned from the first keyring, I turned my attention to the other one on the desk. This one was for a padlock. Which padlock, is the question. Its tag said '7'. It might mean the seventh shipping container, but there was nothing to suggest – apart from my breed of logic – that the containers were numbered in order of their position on the lot. Apart from frustration, I was starting to feel desperate. Pete could return at any moment and find me in the building. That would not go well for me.

Forget the keys, I told myself. Look for a register. The three drawers down one side of the desk held little, and nothing of interest. Half expecting the filing cabinet to be locked, I left it until last and turned my attention to the wooden cupboard. This had one drawer at the top, with cupboard space underneath. The cupboard held nothing but dust and a couple of torn scraps of paper. The drawer, binding on its runners, required an almost herculean effort to wrench it open. At first glance, my heart sank. It too held little. The only thing of possible item of interest was a small notebook.

Thanks to having found nothing thus far, my last hope was the filing cabinet. My fervent prayer was for it to contain as little as all the other furniture. If it held any quantity of material, it would take far too long to sort through it in the hope of finding a key register. And it might be locked, thereby delaying things even further. Why rush in when you can procrastinate? A quick flick through that little notebook won't take long, and who knows what it might reveal.

"Thank you, God!" Someone had drawn a mud map on the inside cover of the notebook. It showed the layout of the entire laydown area. The demountable and all the shipping containers were identified. Various areas along the opposite side of the clearing were labelled 'Pipes', 'Valves', 'Fittings' and 'Bolts & Joiners'. I paid particular attention to the numbering of the containers. They hadn't been numbered in a continuous sequence, but probably were allocated a number when they arrived on site. The early arrivals were spaced wide apart. Later arrivals were slotted into spaces in between… or so it appeared.

Key number 7 was on the desk. To me, this suggested it was the most recent one used. Maybe they were in a hurry and threw it on the desk rather than waste time putting it back on its hook. Maybe they intended returning quite soon later to use the key again. Maybe … Maybe … It was all so much speculation. Maybe the issue was whether container 7 was likely to help locate Callum. Of course I will check it out.

Halfway to the door with key 7 in my hand I stopped. Should I take a selection of other keys with me as well? Rational thought stepped in. I hadn't worked out how I could check inside container 7 without attracting attention and incurring the wrath of Pete. It was pointless expecting to open random containers without being noticed. Decision made, I continued to the door with only one keyring in my hand. While standing with my hand poised to open the door and exit the demountable, a new difficulty occurred to me.

Would Pete be waiting close by outside, possibly a bit frantic by now if he realised I was missing? A window or two would be handy to see what was happening outside. In the absence of windows, there was nothing for it but to trust my luck. I opened the door a crack. No one waited out front, but my view was restricted to a narrow strip. With the door about a quarter of the way open, I risked sticking my head out for a quick look around. No one in sight; no one yelled at me.

With my heart in my mouth and my breathing almost non-existent, I dived out through the partial opening, pulling the door closed behind me without locking it. After racing down the steps, I made straight for the nearest shipping container. I took a moment to settle my breathing a little before taking a quick look around both corners of the container. That caused me pause for thought. Still nobody in sight … but there should be five coppers roaming about. Why aren't any of them visible? I would expect at least one of them to be out in the open.

How much time did I spend in the demountable? I had no way of knowing. Part of me wanted to think it was a quick visit, while the rest of me believed I took a while. The cops completed their initial search of the area before I broke into the demountable. If they were ready to leave, but couldn't find me, would they drive off without me? Possibly; Pete knew I had walked through the scrub to this clearing a couple of times on my own. Maybe they thought, in my disappointment, I abandoned the search and returned to the motel on foot. Perhaps they left to check the motel.

No, I don't buy that, I told myself. I didn't hear a vehicle while I was inside. They must still be here somewhere. My stomach went into spasms. If they were still here, but not visible, had something happened? Might *they* now be occupying one of the containers? Was someone other than us here all along? That thought chilled me to the bone. My stomach was now a squirming mass.

"Standing here wondering about it will not do anyone any good," I murmured. That's when clear thinking – or good old common sense – kicked in. Were the vehicles still parked at the entrance to the clearing? I couldn't remember seeing them as I dashed out of the demountable and raced over to the container. From where I stood between two containers, I couldn't see the area where they parked the vehicles. I slid along the far side of the first container and peered around the front of it. The vehicles were still there. Okay, they haven't abandoned me. But, where the hell are they? Pressed hard up against the side of the container closest to the scrub, I took a couple of moments to consider the situation … and work out what to do next. The answer was simple; the task maybe not so much.

"I need to look in container 7, and I need to find out where everyone is." That decision brought a new concern: what had happened to everyone? Along with my resolve to get on with my mission, and a large dose of apprehension, I began sliding along the container towards its far end.

Tentative, my progress was slow. When I reached the far end, and with still nothing untoward encountered, I stepped up my pace. After moving past three more containers, I stopped to listen. Still no sound from, or sight of the five coppers who arrived here with me. In front of me, the next container had a small 7 spray-painted on the back of its lock. The little voice in my head was giving me a hard time: *Go for it. Look in the container and then worry about the others.* I couldn't dispute the logic of its message.

Placing one foot in front of the other in a careful and deliberate way, I positioned myself for action. It was the moment of truth. I inserted the key into the padlock of container 7. It clicked open smoothly and without effort. A quick glance over my shoulders, and I was dragging open the huge doors.

Disappointment hit me like a hammer blow. The container was empty … or so it appeared at first. Reluctant to enter, I stood in the doorway using my tiny pocket torch to scan the interior. While it was not being used to store anything, something on the floor in the far corner suggested it had been used. I ached to investigate what was on the floor. But, the thought of someone slamming the doors shut once I was inside prevented me from stepping in there. Where are the coppers? It's true, there's never one around when you need them.

I pushed the doors closed without a sound and slid the padlock into place without locking it. Not only did I need someone around while I investigated the interior of the container, but my concern for my companions was escalating. First things first, I decided. Find the coppers. I began picking my way along the rest of the containers until I reached the far end of the clearing. Stunned and perplexed, I stood at the rear of the last container and looked around me.

Nothing…! Not a murmur; no sound of boots on compacted ground … nothing except the sounds of the bush greeted me. The birdsong continued undisturbed, and the breeze, which had freshened a little since we arrived, played its own tune as it blew through the trees. Apart from that, the only other sound was the pounding of my heart as my panic level headed for record heights.

Another quick peek around the corner of the container showed the rest of the clearing remained devoid of people. I stepped out into the silent open area and stood there scanning for any sign of movement. Nothing and no one…!

"How could I lose five burly big blokes?" I asked the universe. "How could five police officers just disappear without a trace and without making a sound?"

Stupefied, I don't know how long I stood there. Another thought to fuel my concern developed in the dark depths of my mind. What if – somehow – they were overcome and locked in one of the containers?

"That's silly," I chided myself. "It would take half a platoon to overcome those blokes … and they would not go quietly." But, the debate between me and the universe continued. "What if there was a fuss and they hadn't gone quietly? Would I hear it from inside the demountable?"

Common sense insisted the idea was rubbish, but I couldn't let go of it. Yes, I had walked past every shipping container in the clearing, but I hadn't checked whether they were locked. The only one I checked was 7 and, as expected, it was locked. It was fair to assume any of the containers now storing equipment also would be locked. Perhaps they kept them all that way to prevent curious intruders. If the five missing blokes had been bundled into one of the containers, I'm sure their assailants would lock it. So, without opening every one of them to check, how would I know if they were being held in one of them?

"Standing here debating with myself achieves nothing. Move yourself. At least go and inspect the containers more closely."

My feet responded, and I marched around to the doors of the last container. It was locked. I pounded on the door in the futile hope anyone inside they might respond. They didn't. A mixture of disappointment and relief flooded over me. Okay, keep going, I told myself. Check all of them. I had taken a couple of steps when the sound of something crashing through the bush made me freeze.

Sandwiched between two containers as I was, it was difficult to determine exactly from which direction the sound came. Of more concern was that, in my present position, I was fully exposed to anyone moving through the clearing. There was nowhere to hide … except in the scrub. I moved around to the far side of the container and eyed off the distance between it and the first of the trees. It wouldn't be any more than three metres, but I would be fully exposed crossing it. When there was no other option, it was worth a try.

Once I moved out from between the containers, it was easier to pinpoint the direction of the sounds. It took a couple of heartbeats for me to decide. If I go now, I would be in the scrub before whatever was approaching reached the clearing. Without wasting time or energy on breathing, I took to the toe and hared across the open space to crash into the undergrowth. Not one of my most elegant moves, the resultant scratches would require attention later.

Ignoring my wounds, I moved to position myself for a clear view of anything entering the clearing from the far end. Within moments, I heard voices; unhappy voices. Then, as their owners broke out of the scrub and entered the clearing, an all too familiar voice cut across the bitching.

"Jesus, you sound like a mob of old women. So we didn't find anything. Point noted. I get it. Just stop whinging for a few minutes please, while I think about it." Pete's level of frustration was clear. If his blokes knew anything of Pete, they would know to comply.

Unsure whether to laugh or cry, I bounded out of the scrub to confront the group. "Where the hell have you been? I was half out of my mind with worry when I couldn't find you."

"Good to know we were missed," Pete snarled.

"Missed…? No, not you; only the car keys. I was contemplating walking back to the motel through the scrub if you didn't show up again before dark."

Chapter 15

"Since we are discussing people having gone missing, where were you earlier on? I looked for you to tell you what we were doing, but you were nowhere to be found."

Judging by Pete's attitude when they emerged from the scrub, something had not gone according to plan. My comments were not helping matters. I would do myself a favour if I backed off a bit.

"Sorry; it was just that I was worried about what might have happened to you all. Did you find something to cause you to go off into the scrub?"

"Yeah, you might say that. The boys found some vague tracks leading off from the far corner of the clearing. They looked recent and worth investigating. Turned out to be nothing. They didn't go anywhere and disappeared after a while; a wild goose chase. All we have to show for it are a lot of mosquito bites. Anyway, this whole area hasn't produced anything of use. We are no further advanced now than we were when we left the property. Unless you have something more useful to contribute, we should cut our losses and head back to town."

"Uhmm … I'm not sure, but I might have found something. Perhaps it's worth a quick look before we leave."

"If you insist. What is it?"

While Pete followed me around to container 7, his officers made themselves comfortable on various bits of equipment close by. I knew I was in for a rugged time when we reached the container, as I was sure they had checked and found all of them locked. Pete would definitely want to know how number 7 now came to be unlocked. To answer to that question, I would need to tell him about the demountable as well.

Our arrival at the doors of container 7 went much as I anticipated. Pete must be tired, or frustrated. His response to my explanation was nowhere near as fierce as I expected. In fact, he accepted my explanation without even raising his voice, but he was not happy. I knew I would be hearing more about it in the future. Once we managed to move on from that part of the exercise, Pete helped me swing the doors open.

I shone my torch down into the far corner. Its small beam barely managed to illuminate the object on the floor there. "I don't know what that is. It could be nothing – at least, nothing to do with why we are here. Nevertheless, I thought it worth a look. I didn't want to go in there without having someone out here to cover my back."

Pete called one of his officers over to join us. "Lewis, stay out here and keep watch. Make sure no one closes these doors while we are inside. Right, Sonny, let's investigate that mysterious object of yours."

'Mysterious object' was a misnomer. There is nothing mysterious about a filthy torn piece of rag ... not at first glance anyway. Pete used the toe of his boot to spread the grubby heap out on the floor. "Not the most exciting thing I've ever found... If there is nothing else you want to show me, perhaps we should be on our way."

He was right. At first, the rag didn't impress me either. I went down on my haunches to examine it on the off chance it should prove to be significant. As I played my torch over it, something about it grabbed my attention. It didn't matter that I told myself it was just a filthy piece of rag. My gut wouldn't agree with me. I don't know how long I inspected the cloth, but it was longer than Pete thought necessary.

"Do you think we might be on our way now? It hasn't moved. I'm pretty sure it's dead and there's nothing we can do for it. I doubt the worker who dropped it here is shedding any tears over its loss. If you're so attached to it, take it with you and give it a decent burial later."

"There's no need for sarcasm. A-n-d, I think it might be misplaced anyway. We saw a cloth like this earlier today, back at the hut on the property. What we found there looked like part of a bedsheet. This piece looks like it might belong to the same bedsheet."

"Eh…? You can't be serious. How did you come up with that idea?"

"Come down here and have a look at it. I'm willing to bet this piece is torn from the same item as the material we found in the hut. The grubby marks on it are the same. Another thing tying it to the other piece is this mark here. It looks like blood to me – fresh blood."

No further persuasion required. Pete removed a plastic bag from his pocket, carefully folded the rag and shoved it in the bag. "Right, now what else have you got to show me?"

As we closed the container and locked it again, I decided to chance my luck. "I don't have anything else, but I wonder if we shouldn't check the other containers before we leave. It would be better to know there is nothing else here, rather than wasting time wondering about it in the future."

"…And I suppose the keys to those also will miraculously appear."

"No miracle involved. We will go and collect them from the demountable."

"Of course we will. Lewis, get the rest of the blokes up off their backsides and follow us to the demountable."

After placing the key to container 7 on the desk, I looked for something in which to carry the rest of the keys. A lid from a box of paper was under the desk. I laid the keys out in the lid according to their position as shown in the little notebook. Then, the slow march along the line of containers began. The process of unlocking and checking the interior of each one seemed to take much longer than I expected, but at last it was done.

With Pete's approval, I returned the keys to the keyboard, and threw the key to the demountable onto the desk beside the key to container 7 so they were where when I found them. Pete reached over and snatched up the demountable's key. "Might come in handy. You never know when we might want to come in here again."

Pete rounded up his men for a quick conference prior to our departure from the place. It only lasted a couple of minutes, and we were on our way to the vehicles when Pete received a phone call. His officers, striding out ahead of us, continued to their vehicle and climbed aboard. I was standing next to him when he answered the call.

"Sam, to what do I owe the pleasure of this call? If it's bad news I don't want to know. … Oh, in that case, yes, I do want to know. What can you tell me?"

The look I received from Pete suggested I should move out of earshot. I headed towards the car, but didn't get in, choosing to lean up against the front mudguard instead. I had no doubt the call he received was from Sam Keller, his lead detective at the Ralston precinct, and who was the officer holding the fort in his absence. While I didn't know where they took the mob they rounded up on the property this morning, I assumed they were flown straight to Ralston. In which case, Sam oversaw their arrival and incarceration.

Too far away to hear what was being said, I had to rely on Pete's body language and facial expressions to gauge whether the call delivered good news or otherwise. Sam's call lasted several minutes. I didn't detect anything in Pete's behaviour to suggest bad news. When the call ended, he remained standing where he was and stared off into the distance. After a while, he slipped the phone into his pocket and started towards the car.

Only a few feet away from me, his phone rang again, Pete checked the caller ID before answering.

"Ah, I wondered if I might hear from you today. So tell me, what have you to report? Anything interesting happening at your end?"

With nothing to tell me who the caller was, and bursting with curiosity as I was, I feigned great interest in the surrounding bush – but kept my ears pricked – as I continued to lean against the car. I'm not sure listening to the one-sided conversation did me any good at all. If anything, it was frustrating and only served to heighten my curiosity. The caller appeared to have a lengthy report to deliver. That call lasted longer than the one from Sam.

Pete looked pleased with himself, and even was smiling, as he strode to the car. "Come on, climb aboard. There is nothing more for us to do here. I don't know about you, but I think we blokes could do with something to eat."

Moments later, our cavalcade of two vehicles was on its way out of the clearing and bouncing along the track through the scrub. Pete was humming a tune I couldn't identify as he drove. A good sign I suppose, but infuriating. What had he learned from his phone calls to so lift his spirits? It got the better of me. I couldn't restrain myself.

"Those phone calls obviously were good news. You're a different bloke from the one who emerged from the scrub not so long ago. Does it have anything to do with our case … finding Callum, I mean … or was it just about your case?"

"Hmm … I don't really know about Callum, but I suppose I've come to accept somehow your investigation is linked to mine. If I'm correct, over the next day or so, both of us might learn something to our advantage. Interrogation of the mob we rounded up this morning has begun in Ralston. What we might learn from them, and how long it might take to prise anything out of them remain a mystery. But, with Sam on the job, I feel confident we will learn something."

"Your last call seemed to please you no end. I assume it delivered good news."

"I'm not sure I'd call it good news, but it suggested a breakthrough in my case soon might be possible. I'll drop you at the motel, and then follow the others to the neighbouring town where they're staying. I'll be back in time for dinner, so order dinner in your room for about half seven. Might be best if we eat alone, if you can manage that without upsetting Emily too much."

While putting off Emily yet again tonight was easier said than done, I agreed to the arrangement. I didn't want to upset Emily, but I did want the opportunity to find out more about those phone calls Pete received. Trying to think up some way to avoid having dinner with her would keep my mind occupied all the way to the motel.

About the time I started worrying about Emily and dinner, we were at the point where, about thirty metres ahead, a track branched off to the left. Pete slowed a little before reefing the wheel to take us onto the side track. As we bumped along with branches swiping at us from every angle, I continued trying to extract more information from him about his phone calls … and he continued being evasive and smug. I suppose we were about halfway along the side track when Pete's phone again chirped into life. This time, with the call played through the car's audio system, I heard both sides of the conversation. I recognised Taylor's voice.

"Hey Boss, are we on the right track?"

"Yeah, we are going into Cranvale. While you carry on out of town, I'll drop Sonny off at her motel and then follow you."

"O-k-ay … but why didn't we take the other track that comes out behind the saleyards?"

"Eh…? What are you on about?"

"You went past the turn-off to the track to the saleyards. This one emerges way out on the outskirts of town."

"Argh, it doesn't matter. Don't worry about it. This one still takes us to where we want to go. Think of it as the scenic route. It doesn't change anything; stick to the plan."

Pete's scowl as he ended the call was priceless. At about halfway through the call, I realised what had happened. I dissolved into a fit of the giggles. I tried restraining myself during the call, but the look on his face now destroyed my self-control. Pete and I had been too engrossed in our game: my trying to winkle information out of him and his trying not to give anything away. It resulted in our driving straight past the first turn-off which would have brought us out of the scrub behind the saleyards.

The rest of the journey into Cranvale and on to the motel was notable for the heavy silence filling the vehicle. A couple of times along the way, more giggles escaped me. Pete remained unamused and shot me a dark look each time it happened. He let me out on the street in front of the motel. His only comment as I scrambled out dragging my bag after me: "Just see you order something decent for dinner … and a damned good wine to wash it down."

Even as I let myself into my room, inspiration continued to elude me. Maybe I should just be honest – within reason. I could say I had caught up with an old friend and we arranged to have dinner together. It was the truth. I can't help it if Emily interprets it as my having unexpectedly bumped into an old friend. In the event, an excuse of any sort wasn't required. As I dumped my bag on the bed, I noticed the blinking message light on my phone. A feeling of sheer relief surged through me when I learned it was from Emily. She was having dinner again with the local newspaper editor and his wife. Some-times the gods smile on you!

Part of me felt obliged to call Emily to thank her for her message and enquire after her day. A larger part of me was overcome with cowardice and guilt. I resolved to take a long shower before giving her a call. Having spent so little time together over the last few days, we were in danger of becoming strangers. I continued to be surprised by how quickly Emily's interest in, and concern for Callum had mellowed. Maybe I was selling her short but, now she seemed more interested in participating in Cranvale's social life.

With the shower turned full on, I stood for a long time enjoying its needle-like blast on my skin. It wasn't idle time. While I stood motionless under the shower, my mind worked overtime. First, it reviewed everything that happened today, before moving on to analyse why our search for Callum came up empty. My gut kept insisting we were in the right place, but hadn't looked well enough; had overlooked something or somewhere.

I brought my hand up to wipe my face. The fingertips were white and as wrinkled as prunes. A hasty change of plan had me reach for the tap instead. Then I luxuriated in drying myself with today's fresh, fluffy white towel. With my wet hair wrapped turban-style in the towel, and still with no idea what I was going to say, I headed for the phone to call Emily. The message light blinking again spared me the trouble. It was Emily again.

Hi Sonny, me again. I tried calling your room but you weren't there. I just wanted to apologise and explain why I was abandoning you again tonight. I am hoping Lance might have something useful to share. Anyway, it would have been rude to turn down their invitation to dinner. I imagine it will go late, so I'll try to catch up with you tomorrow, or at least let you know what I'm doing. Hope you had a good day. Bye…

At last things are going my way today. If I can manage to order something nice for dinner – and maybe an expensive wine to go with it – I might make Pete more amenable to sharing some of whatever he learnt today. Apart from those phone calls at the clearing, which almost killed me with curiosity, I suspect whatever he was up to after he dropped me off might be of interest as well.

It was 7.30pm exactly when Pete knocked on my door. His timing was great. He came straight to my room on returning to the motel, and our dinner, which should have arrived at the same time, was running late. It gave us time to sit and relax with long glasses of cold mineral water. Our meals arrived about ten minutes later.

Dinner's arrival precipitated the usual faffing about with setting everything up, pouring wine and passing condiments back and forth. We ate in relative silence, due in part to the fact we both were starving after our day of little food – or anything else. The roast beef was cooked to perfection and delicious. The wine was excellent and a perfect accompaniment. I gave dessert a miss, but ordered Pete's favourite for him. After he finished it, conversation resumed between us ... I made sure it did by leading it off.

"You must be exhausted tonight. It has been a long day for you, and you've done a lot of driving over rough country. You're probably looking forward to a long hot shower tonight."

"It wasn't too bad, and dinner helped revive me somewhat."

"Was the day worthwhile at all for you. I know we didn't find Callum, but did you manage to progress your investigation? Late in the day, it looked as though you received at least some good news."

"So far, none of the mob rounded up this morning is saying anything, but Sam thinks a couple are starting to weaken. They will continue to work on them tonight, so we might hear something from Ralston in the morning. I have another bloke in Langton keeping an eye on the mining company's headquarters there. I suspect they are aware everyone on the property was rounded up and it – or something else I don't know about – seems to have caused a flurry of activities. The headquarters had an interesting visitor today. A visitor trying not to be seen or identified, and who slipped in through the back door. A visitor who should not be anywhere near that place today.

There might be some interesting follow-up to all that in the next day or so … depending on how other issues pan out."

He ended with an infuriating tap on the side of his nose. It was obvious he would not elaborate any further this evening, so I changed the subject by asking what he had planned for tomorrow.

"I'll let you know in the morning if we are doing anything of interest to you. Whatever we end up doing, it won't be an early start. I need to hear from a couple of people before any decisions are made. They are unlikely to call until after nine o'clock. Are you likely to be around if we decide to do something of interest to your investigation?"

I made it clear I was interested in tagging along with them regardless of whatever they decided to do. Our conversation after that was light and of no consequence to either of our investigations. It was still early when Pete announced he was desperate for a shower and bed. After putting our dinner trays out in the hallway to be collected, I surfed TV for something to help me switch off before going to bed.

A few minutes into that exercise, I realised I hadn't lodged my breakfast menu for tomorrow. While it was later than the cut-off time for handing it in, as I already had filled it out, I decided to take it to reception anyway. That nice young man was on duty. I donned my very best smile and, waving my breakfast menu at him, marched up to the reception desk.

"Oh, that looks like a beauty. Is it yours?" An expensive looking drone was sitting on the lower level of the desk in front of the lad.

He looked about ready to burst with pride as he ran a hand over it. "Yes. It's probably the best one in this area at the moment."

"I've fancied buying a drone for some time, but I've held off as I'm not confident I could learn to fly it. I'm sure you're an expert. Did it take you long to learn?"

"I wouldn't say I was an expert, but I'm pretty good. There's a big competition in Ralston next weekend. I've arranged to have the weekend off so I can compete."

"Good for you … Do you have to practise for such competitions, or do you just turn up on the day and have a bit of fun?"

"No, this is a serious competition. I practise flying it whenever I'm not at work. All this week and right up until I leave for Ralston, I'll fly it every morning."

"Could I come to watch you?"

"Yeah, of course. I'll be at the open area next to the hall at seven o'clock tomorrow if you want to come along. If you're game, I might even give you your first flying lesson."

How could I refuse such an offer…? Of course I'll be there in the morning – and I'll continue working on him to ensure I do engineer a chance to fly his drone. "Maybe I should have my breakfast delivered a little earlier. Would you mind changing my slip to the earlier time?"

Chapter 16

So far, so good this morning; breakfast arrived early, and I was now on my way on foot to be at the other end of town by seven o'clock. I don't know why I decided to walk instead of driving, but something made me think it was the right thing to do. As I approached the hall, I saw the car of my friend from reception was already at the launch site. His drone flew overhead as I joined him in the clearing.

He didn't lack skill. I stood in silence as the drone demonstrated its capabilities, including weaving in and out and through an obstacle course he prepared for it. Then he landed it a couple of metres in front of where we stood.

"Is that a camera strapped on underneath?"

"Yeah. It takes amazing photos from up there. Everything looks so different from when you see it from here on the ground."

"How does it work? Do you start the camera before you launch it, and then sort out later what images you want to keep?" He found my question hilarious, and fetched the drone to show me the camera.

"I suppose you could have the camera running from the moment it was in the air, but you would be restricted to short flights. It would require too much storage to be filming for the whole time it was in the air. So much of what was captured would be rubbish anyway. The pilot needs to control what happens up there."

"Okay, so you need to tell the camera when to take shots. How do you know what images it might capture? You might find it missed all the targets you wanted to shoot." More raucous laughter from the pilot.

"This screen on the control panel lets me see what the camera sees as it flies over the area. If something worth shooting catches my attention, I send the drone back over that location and tell the camera to capture the image. Anyway, do you want to have a go? I've done enough for today. You won't be interrupting my practice session."

Now the difficult part begins. I need to deliver an almost Oscar-winning rendition of a woman who knows nought about drones and has never touched one before. True, I don't own one, but my mate, Ben Richards, owns a big expensive model, and I have flown it several times.

"Okay, I'm up for it … and I promise I'll replace it if I crash and destroy it. But, you will have to be patient if I'm slow at learning how to do it."

The young bloke had more patience than I expected, and was an excellent instructor. After not too long, I launched my first flight. There were no fancy manoeuvres, and the flight wasn't long. I pretended to be a bundle of nerves as I brought it in to land. He was polite enough to claim to be amazed at how quickly I mastered it. It seemed like the right time to ask him to explain the camera operation to me. Several minutes later, I captured a couple of images of the two of us standing in the clearing below.

While everything had gone well so far, I hadn't achieved the real reason I was messing about with the drone this morning. I was struggling to work out how to progress things in the direction I wanted. Then, his phone yodelled loudly from where he had left it in his car. As he turned to rush back to his car, I asked, "Would you mind if I took the drone for another short flight?"

"Help yourself. It might be a long phone call. It's probably my girlfriend."

Wonderful timing! Now let's get this bird in the air. As it rose off the ground, I risked a quick glance at the lad. He was leaning against the car with his back to me. Perfect… Let's see what I might find while he isn't watching. I sent it off high above the scrub towards the laydown area clearing. A quick scan of that l area showed no changes since yesterday. Reluctant to be caught flying his drone over the scrub, I started it on its return flight.

I caught my breath. What was that? I'm sure there was a glimpse of something. A quick flick of the controls and the drone went back to hover over the clearing. Then, I started it back towards me again, this time slower and higher. "There it is! I did see something." I checked over my shoulder. It didn't look like the lad heard me. While it was tempting to photograph what the drone hovered over, it wasn't my camera. Not wise to alert someone else to what caught my interest. Time to bring the drone home, before my friend's phone call ended.

No sooner had the drone landed than I heard a car door slam. His phone call over, my new friend strode back to me. His face told me the call had not gone well. "I didn't bend it, so that's good news, but it looks like your call didn't go so well. Your face is as long as a football field."

A wry smile tugged one corner of his mouth. "No. It was my girlfriend. She's not happy about spending the weekend alone while I'm in Ralston."

"Take her with you."

"I told her she could come too, but I wouldn't be able to spend much time with her. The weekend is about competing with my drone and talking to other owners to pick up tips and ideas. What should I do?"

"I'd be the last person you should ask about relationship matters. This drone flying lark is quite addictive, but I know someone who would not be impressed if I took it up." I was thinking of Ben Richards, and I wasn't going to mention my interest would be in using a drone to aid in my investigations. I'm sure Ben would manage to find something illegal about it.

"Yeah, it's my problem. The whole relationship thing is a problem. Maybe this weekend will sort it out once and for all." As he spoke, he walked over and picked up his drone. "I'm sorry, but I have to go to get ready for work. I can drop you at the motel on my way if you like."

"No thanks. Staying in a motel involves a lot of food and drink. I need all the exercise I can get if my clothes are still to fit me when we leave. Besides, this is the nicest time of the day for a walk."

A minute or two later, he was on his way and I was standing alone in the cleared area beside the hall. The dilemma I struggled with as I began my stroll back to the motel was when to ring Pete. My initial thought was to call him as soon as I returned to my room, but there were a couple of problems with that plan. Pete might have left the motel by the time I arrived. He might come to tell me his plans for the day but, when he found I wasn't there, he would head out without me. By the time I'd hoofed it a couple of hundred metres along the road, a simple solution occurred to me.

Peter answered his mobile on the second ring, not giving me much time to compose what to say. "Good morning, Sir. Are you still at the motel or out and about?"

"Still in my room waiting for phone calls… Why do you ask?"

"I've been out for a walk and thought I might have missed you before you set off for the day. I need to talk to you as soon as I return to the motel. I should be there in about another ten minutes at the latest."

"Okay. I'll be here in my room. Come and talk to me."

My pace quickened, and it didn't take me anything like ten minutes to reach the motel. I marched in through the backdoor and straight along the hallway to Pete's room.

"Did you run all the way? I'm sure it wasn't ten minutes ago you called me. Could I interest you in a cup of coffee? I've had a fresh pot delivered." I helped myself to coffee while my mind tried to work out how to tell Pete what I think I discovered. "Okay, now we are all set with coffees, what was this urgent matter you wished to discuss with me."

"At the risk of being hopelessly wrong, first, I'll tell you what happened this morning."

I gave Pete an abbreviated version of meeting the lad from reception and flying his drone a couple of times. Then I paused. I still didn't know how to explain what I saw. Pete wasn't helping. He gave an impatient nod when I ended the story about flying the drone, but now he was giving me a 'give me more' gesture. Nothing for it, but to charge in and hope it all goes well.

"While the lad was on the phone, I flew the drone as far as the clearing in the scrub to check it out. There was no one around and no sign of activity since we were there yesterday. As the drone made its way back to me, I thought I glimpsed something in the scrub. I retraced its flight, and had it hover over the site where I saw this thing. It was part way along the first offshoot track from the clearing, the track that emerges behind the saleyard. That's the turnoff we missed on our way out of the clearing yesterday."

"Okay, so you saw something along that track … for Christ's sake Sonny, get to the punchline. What …did… you… see?"

"Keep your shirt on. I'm trying to give you all the details of what happened; a full report. Not too far along the track was a dark coloured SUV. It wasn't going anywhere, so it should still be there when we go to investigate."

"What makes you so sure?"

"The vehicle was being quite friendly with a large tree. I didn't see anyone around it."

"Well don't just stand there. Come on, grab your gear, and let's take a drive through the scrub. My officers are on their way into town. I'll let them know to meet us on the track."

Pete was already speaking on the phone as I left to collect my bag. With scant regard for the speed limits around town, Pete headed for the saleyards, and we were soon bouncing along the track to the clearing.

"How long before your officers are likely to be at the scene?"

"They are probably there ahead of us. They were close to the saleyards when I called them, so they would have turned straight onto the track."

He was right. Their vehicle blocked the track. We parked behind it and made our way on foot towards the crash site. His officers stood at the ready but hadn't inspected the vehicle yet. When we were beside the officers' car, Pete strode ahead while yelling back at me, "Stay there, Sonny. Do not come any closer."

For a few minutes, all five men seemed to congregate around the car and peer in its windows. No doors were opened; no one touched the vehicle. After wandering around the car as much as possible with the big tree occupying so much of the front of it, Pete stood beside the driver's door.

I wanted to shout, is it Callum? The grim faces around the car made me bite my tongue. I'm not sure how long I was subjected to the agony of not knowing before Pete called me.

"Perhaps you should take a look at this. It's not pleasant though, I warn you now."

A wave of trepidation flooded over me and made me hesitant. As I approached the rear of the vehicle, I slowed my pace and glanced in through the rear windows as I passed. A woman's body was sprawled in the cargo area. The little voice in my head was screaming *this is not going to be good news*. I tried to ignore it as I took a few baby steps to stand beside Pete.

The driver had fallen sideways and was sprawled across the centre console, with his left arm spread across onto the passenger seat. He was face down, but I could tell it was

Callum. A nasty gash near the wrist looked recent. Perhaps that's where the blood on that piece of rag came from. His right arm remained tangled in the steering wheel. No gashes were visible on that arm, but chafing and scarring were.

"Are they both dead?"

It was a stupid question, and I knew that the moment I asked it. The car had not been opened. Nobody had checked either of the people in it, so how would they know? I looked back at the woman in the rear of the vehicle. From where I was standing, I couldn't see all of her, but I could see a lot of dried blood in her matted hair. Pete broke the silence that hung over the scene.

"Is he the Callum you've been looking for?"

Too choked up to be able to speak, I just nodded. All of a sudden, I had visions of breaking the news to Emily. While I wasn't sure how she would react now her interest in Callum seem to have cooled, it would still come as a shock for her.

"Right men, get your gloves on and let's find out what happened here. Stand back, Sonny, I'm going to open this door. It doesn't look like he will tumble out on top of us, but you never know."

Callum didn't tumble out. In fact, Callum didn't move at all. He was so still, I wasn't sure he was even breathing. From the moment I saw him, I suspected he wasn't … and wouldn't be breathing ever again. Pete reached in and tried for a brachial pulse at Callum's right wrist. It was obvious he didn't find one when he immediately reached over further and tried for a carotid pulse.

"Not in good shape, but still alive … for the moment anyway. Medical evacuation from here in the scrub will not be easy. Let's see how the woman is before I make a call, so I can tell them how many require evacuation."

With that, he stepped around me and went to the rear of the vehicle where the rear hatch stood wide open. Again, there was no sign of life from the woman sprawled in there.

This time, Pete went straight for a carotid pulse. I saw the grim look on his face lighten. I hoped it meant the woman was alive too.

Waving his mobile phone about above him in search of enough reception to make his call, Pete walked back towards our vehicle. I watched him climb into the car and start the engine. Then, while I couldn't hear him, I could see him speaking. I guessed the car's antenna found him just enough reception for the call. After his short call, he was back with us beside the crashed vehicle.

"The news is not good, boys. It seems we are out of luck with receiving any assistance to evacuate these two. Do you think we might be able to take them out in our vehicles?"

After a bit of shuffling of four pairs of feet, Taylor replied. "I think we can manage it. There are two points of concern: will we worsen their condition by moving them, and how do we get out of here? We now seem to be wedged in. I doubt either of us is keen to reverse all the way back along the track."

"Both good points… In response to the first one, we don't have any option but to remove them from the scene ourselves. Neither of the victims is in good condition. Leaving them here any longer will only result in one outcome. It will require some delicate handling to avoid worsening their situation. As for how we get out of here, I'm thinking we might just about be able to sneak through the narrow gap between the scrub at the edge of the track and the rear corner of the damaged vehicle. We'll worry about it when we get the patients loaded. In the meantime, and as quick as you can, we need to collect basic evidence such as fingerprints and whatever else might be lying around."

Two officers were delegated to dust the crashed car for fingerprints, while the other two were to help Pete transfer the patients to our two vehicles. Devising a plan of action took a few minutes. In the end, it was decided to remove the rear bench seat from the crashed vehicle and use it as a makeshift stretcher to carry the injured woman to the nearest car. Some debate followed on whether to transport her still lying on the seat, or risk further injuring her by removing her from it and placing her flat on the floor of the cargo area. As they would need the seat cushion again to transfer Callum to Pete's vehicle, the latter option was adopted.

Extracting Callum from the vehicle was more complicated than extracting his female companion. It wasn't a matter of simply lifting him across from where he was on to the long bench seat. He would need lifting completely out of the car before being placed on the seat placed on the ground beside the car. Another complication was the distance involved in carrying Callum to Pete's car. After some discussion, it was agreed the officers should try sneaking their vehicle past the crash scene in order to clear the way for Pete's vehicle to move closer.

In spite of a few anxious moments, the manoeuvre was successful, but it did result in the officers' vehicle received a few solid wallops from young saplings growing over the edge of the track. With the first vehicle out of the way, the delicate operation of transferring Callum to Pete's car began.

Once Callum was out of his vehicle and arranged on the makeshift stretcher, Pete called a halt to operations while he folded down his car's rear seats. With the seats flat, they could slide their 'stretcher', complete with Callum on board, straight in through the cargo area hatch without needing to rearrange the patient. He would be transported out of the scrub still lying on the seat from the crashed vehicle. With that vehicle locked up and the keys removed, our two-vehicle convoy was on its way.

Callum's transport arrangement made for a slow and careful trip. Both Pete and I were aware any swerving or sharp turns could roll Callum off his soft bed onto the hard floor of the cargo area. In spite of our slow speed and the careful driving, the journey out of the scrub seemed twice as rough and nerve wracking than before. With the crashed car still occupying the saleyards track, we were obliged to use the other less travelled one and exited the scrub on the outskirts of town.

We drove in silence for most of the way. It wasn't until I could see daylight up ahead that I felt it safe to ask the two questions which had travelled with me from the crash site.

"What are your plans for getting the two patients to a medical facility? The medical centre in Cranvale doesn't appear adequate to cope with what these two might require."

"I agree. I doubt it would be up to the job, but we won't be finding out. Apart from being anxious for the patients to receive urgent medical attention, I'm also keen for them not to hang around in this area for any length of time. The way things are, I can't guarantee their safety if they remain in Cranvale or even in Langton. That's why I arranged for them to be flown out. My first approach was to the Flying Doctor Service, but they have one plane out of action and the other on a long haul flight with a patient. The air-sea rescue helicopter from Ralston is flying out to collect them for us. I'll feel a lot happier when I know they're back in Ralston."

"Amen to that. What about retrieving the vehicle? I'm assuming you will want it taken somewhere for forensic investigation, so how will it happen?"

"There might be a bit of extra activity in Cranvale by tomorrow. You'll see a few more people and several bits of heavy equipment in the area. Included in that will be a large bulldozer to widen some of the tracks through the scrub, and a car trailer to transport the crashed vehicle to Ralston."

"Does it mean you will be heading back to Ralston in the next couple of days as well?"

"Not that I'm aware of… Why would you think that?"

"I thought, with your investigation completed, you and your mob would be heading home."

"No, it's your investigation that might be over. You are here to look into Callum's disappearance, and now he's been found. Unless your brief extends beyond that, I imagine you might be leaving town quite soon. My investigation, and the reason for me and my men to be out here, is a long way from being wrapped up."

"Oooh, I see."

It was the only response I could come up with because it was at that point I realised I still didn't know what Pete was investigating. I'd worked out earlier, they hadn't come out to help me look for Callum, but I hadn't asked about why they arrived so soon after Pete found out about his disappearance. The only other thing of interest to the police happening out here would be something to do with the unrest fracking is causing in the community. While I'm inclined to sympathise with the locals, I doubt it's anything illegal.

"So, you have an interesting task to complete tonight." I shot Pete a surprised look. I had to wait for him to stop chuckling before he explained. "You have to tell Emily about the condition of her boyfriend … And his female companion. That should make for an interesting few minutes."

Oh God, I hadn't thought about that. Still, it might not be as bad as he thinks. How bad, or otherwise, will depend on how well I've read Emily's behaviour over the last few days. I hope I'm right in thinking the passion has dissipated.

In what seemed like only a matter of minutes, the chopper set down in the open area on the outskirts of town where we waited. The patients were loaded on board, and were whisked off to hospital in Ralston.

Pete dropped me at the motel before following his officers out of town. I had the luxury of a laid-back afternoon catching up on emails and calls, and writing up my case notes.

Chapter 17

This evening saw a return to normal – whatever that might be. Pete called to say he would not be available for dinner tonight. I wondered if I might have the luxury of eating alone for once. Then, a bit after five o'clock, Emily called. She would be back at the motel soon and hoped we might have dinner together. I don't know whether the news I had for her would come as a relief, or if it would bring a sombre atmosphere to our table.

I have to admit to looking forward to returning home to Millhaven now Callum has been found and the case closed. While I'm not sure how Emily will react to the news, with nothing to keep her here now, I imagined she would head back to Millhaven. My resolve was strong as I strode to the dining room. I intended telling Emily about Callum as soon as we were seated at our table.

She looked tired and admitted the social whirl she experienced over the previous few days was catching up with her. We were barely seated when she announced she was thinking of going home – maybe tomorrow or the day after. It was the opening I needed to give her the news about Callum.

"We will both be able to go home. Callum has been found. So, there is nothing more for us to do here."

Her reaction to the news was not as I expected. In fact, I thought it hadn't registered with her. She didn't react at all, just sat silently straightening her cutlery for a few moments. I became concerned.

"Emily, did you hear what I said? Callum has been found."

"Yes. Yes, I heard you. I'm sorry, I … I don't know what I feel. I think it's relief. Yeah, it is relief. Relief he has been found, and he didn't just run off and abandon me out here.

As you say, we both can go home now, and with a clear conscience."

"A clear conscience…? Why wouldn't we have a clear conscience?"

"Well, if he were still missing when we went home, we would feel guilty. We would feel we had let him down; hadn't done enough to find him or to find out what had happened to him. At least, that's how I'd feel anyway."

"Okay, I think I see your point. Emily, I think your level of interest in Callum, and all that happened to him since the B&S ball, has diminished somewhat. I'm not prying into your private life, but you still haven't asked me how he is or what happened to him. It's okay. If you don't want to know, I won't burden you with it, and I'm sorry if you think I'm intruding. Given your relationship with him and your obvious concern after his disappearance, I feel obliged to give you as much information as I have about what happened."

"Sonny, I do want to know, but I'm also frightened to find out. You are right. These last few days gave me time to reassess my relationship with him. I think my feelings for him were a lot stronger than his ever were for me. More importantly, I think it gave me time to come to terms with something I always knew but didn't want to accept. I believe I was nothing more than a number to Callum – a conquest maybe; just one in his string of interests. Hindsight is a wonderful invention. It allowed me a clear view of events leading up to our decision to come out here for the ball."

"That's an interesting comment. What did your review of events highlight for you?"

"Well, I think coming out here for the ball facilitated some other plan or intention of his. While I was keen to see Claire again, Callum was quite eager and pushed for us to come for the weekend. I'm not saying his disappearance was part of some grand plan, or something orchestrated in advance, but I don't think his motivation for the trip had anything to do with the ball."

"Only you can assess that, but I would be interested in why you think so. Is it something you've seen, or has happened, since his disappearance? Is there something to suggest an ulterior motive for the weekend?"

"No-o-o, not that I can put my finger on; it's more like a feeling I have. If I'm honest, I think I've suspected something since before we left Millhaven. To put it succinctly, I think I am now officially over Callum. I feel guilty about dragging you into all of this and having you spend so many days out here when you could have been home running your business. And you are right. I haven't asked after him. How is he and what's his story?"

What better place to start my report than with his current condition? It ensured I had Emily's full attention before I moved on to how he came to be rescued. Details of finding and rescuing him took me into difficult territory again. Should I mention the female who was in the car with him, or not? I suspect she was not a romantic interest, but played a more sinister role in his disappearance… But, I had nothing to prove it one way or the other.

Emily and I have always been open and honest with one another, never shying away from the truth regardless of what the consequences might be. There was no reason to do otherwise now. My mention of the woman was brief. After all, what could I tell her about the female in the car? The best I could do was stress the fact we still didn't know who she was, why she was there, or what part she played in Callum's disappearance.

"It wouldn't surprise me if it did start out as some sort of romantic liaison. Now my 'rose-tinted glasses' are off, I can see I probably was keener on establishing a meaningful relationship than he ever was. Still, everything you've told me, Sonny, is upsetting. While I still don't know how I feel about it all, right now I do feel concern for him. If you don't mind, unless you've something else to tell me, I'd prefer not to discuss it further. As it is, I suspect thinking through the whole thing will keep me awake for some time tonight."

Conversation was sparse during our meal. For once, Emily passed on dessert, and we left the table for our rooms much earlier than we normally would. We walked to her door. I was prepared to stay with her for a while, but she insisted she wanted to be alone. It wasn't hard to understand, so I said good night and continued to my room.

Over a couple of fingers of single malt Scotch, I reviewed everything from during our dinner together. Instinct told me there was more to Emily's response to my news of Callum than she admitted. Whatever else there might be that she hadn't told me about continued to elude me, and I knew it wasn't going to be conducive to sleep. Rather than taking myself off to bed for an early night to toss and turn for hours, I decided to sit up and record my thoughts about tonight before calling it a day.

As I rinsed my glass, there was a knock on the door. There goes any hope of an early night anyway, I told myself as I hurried to open it. I expected it would be Emily waiting outside, having decided she wanted to talk after all. It wasn't Emily. It was Pete.

"Have you eaten? It's a bit late. I'm not sure they do room service at this hour."

"Room service is fine. I called ahead to order something. It should be delivered in about fifteen minutes. I'll give them a call shortly to ask them to deliver it here instead of my room. In the meantime, do you have coffee, or preferably, something stronger?"

"I don't have coffee, but I do have a single malt."

"Perfect… It will fill in time until my meal arrives. If I'm going to call room service, is there anything you would like me to order?"

"If you want wine with your dinner, you will need to order it, and perhaps a pot of coffee would go down well."

Once Pete sorted out everything with room service, we relaxed with our drinks. I could see he was strung out, and not knowing what caused it made it difficult to work out what to say or do. I wanted to ask him what happened after he left me earlier this afternoon, but instinct told me to allow him a while to relax before firing questions. Shortly before his dinner arrived, he seemed to come to life again. Conversation time had arrived. He initiated it.

"So, what happened here this afternoon? Did I miss anything exciting?"

"Nothing I'm aware of; I spent the afternoon here in my room writing up my case notes, and then went to dinner with Emily."? How did that go?"

"If I'm honest, I don't know. Her reaction to the news and subsequent comments weren't as expected. I questioned her about it, but her explanation doesn't sit well somehow. When you knocked, I thought, having changed her mind about wanting to talk, Emily had come to pour her heart out to me. After we had eaten, we went to our rooms. I haven't heard from her since. I'll try a little gentle prodding in the morning to see if I can get to the bottom of whatever is going on. So much for my afternoon, what about yours?"

"Not much to tell; it was a bit like yours. I followed my blokes back to their accommodation. We reviewed the morning's activities over lunch together. Then, they had tasks to undertake, and I had to meet up with a couple of people. My meetings went much like yours with Emily: not as expected and left me wondering."

My attempts at empathy didn't loosen any further details about his meetings. The intrigue he hinted at increased my level of frustration. I made a mental note to return to the matter of his meetings later, perhaps over coffee. Then room service arrived causing the usual lull in proceedings.

They had included two bread rolls with his meal. I decided he didn't need two, and helped myself to one of them. I'm not sure he noticed. If he did, he didn't comment ... and that was unlike Pete.

Later, as we sat sipping coffee, he opened the door for me again to pursue the matter of his meetings. I knew he wouldn't share all the details, but even some clues as to who he met with would be handy. But, before then, I had to answer the difficult question he asked.

"Now your search for Callum is over, I assume you will be heading home tomorrow. Have many cases built up in your absence?"

"There are three or four potential cases; none of them serious. I do need to get back to my office though. Nevertheless, I doubt I'll be leaving tomorrow. I think it's likely it will be the day after. What about your investigation, will it keep you here much longer?"

He shrugged and then shook his head. I think he was about to say something but changed his mind. I waited a few moments to see if he might reconsider. When he didn't, I gave voice to the latest thoughts running through my head.

"It just occurred to me, the thing that brought you and your officers out here was a call from Ben Richards after I reported Callum's disappearance to him. While Callum now has been found, the circumstances surrounding his disappearance remain a mystery. I assume what you're investigating will include exploring those circumstances as well. Whatever the scope of your investigation, I suspect you're going to be out here for some time yet."

"You're right up to a point. It was Callum's disappearance brought us out here but, once we were here, a number of incidents in the area added to the work we needed to do. I don't mean we've got more than one case on the go at the moment. It's just one big case. But, Callum is connected with everything else. I just need one small piece of information to untangle the whole mess. I had hoped to receive it this afternoon. Our stay out here might extend for a while yet if we don't dig up something useful in the next day or so."

"I am a bit concerned about Emily, so I intend staying in Cranvale until I know what her plans are. In any case, I will be here tomorrow at least, and maybe the day after. If I can help in any way with your investigation, I am available."

"Let's see what tomorrow morning brings. You might find your time taken up with Emily. I have paperwork requiring attention, and I'm still hoping phone calls might deliver some good news, so I doubt I'll be leaving the motel before mid-morning at the earliest. Give me a call when you know what you're doing for the day."

There wasn't much else to say or do. Pete looked as if it was way past his bedtime. It was now too late for the early night I had planned, but I wouldn't be out of bed long once Pete left. We must've been of one mind. He announced he was in need of a shower and sleep. We loaded the tray with everything from room service and Pete placed it outside my door on his way out.

*****

Unsure what this morning might bring, I hung around in my room for a while instead of going to breakfast. When I hadn't heard from Emily after waiting a reasonable amount of time, I went to the dining room alone. I was halfway down the hallway when my phone chirped. Emily. I braced myself for what might follow.

"Are you all right? I've been waiting for you to come for breakfast and became worried when you was so late."

Relieved when she sounded so normal, I rushed the last few metres to the doorway and waved across the room to her. "I had some stuff to do in my room, so I decided to get it out of the way first thing. Thanks for waiting for me. Both of us probably are starving by now, so let's get some food into us before we do anything else."

Once we were settled with our breakfasts, I jumped in with the first question. "What are you doing today? Do you have anything planned?"

"I don't have anything scheduled for today in Cranvale, but I'd be cancelling it if I did. I'm going to check out of the motel straight after breakfast. I'm packed and ready to go."

"Okay, so you're heading home today. I haven't yet decided whether to check out later or leave it until tomorrow."

"No, I'm not heading to Millhaven. I'm going to Ralston to see what's happening with Callum. From what you said last night, his condition was serious. It's possible I won't be allowed to see him unless his situation has improved, but I feel I need to be there when he regains consciousness … or, perhaps that should be, *IF* he regains consciousness. What can you tell me about the woman in the vehicle with him?"

"I don't know anything about her other than she didn't appear to be 'with him' in the strictest sense of the phrase. Emily, I don't know how she fits into the picture. All I know is Callum was in the driver's seat. She was in the cargo area, not the passenger's seat. To me, it suggests there was no close relationship between them. In fact, I'm inclined to think whatever association existed was hostile, and possibly a danger to Callum. I haven't answered your questions, but it is all I know."

She bit her lip and fiddled with the salt and pepper shakers on the table. I remained silent as she struggled with her own thoughts. Then she looked up at me. The pleading in her eyes almost broke by heart.

"I don't know any more than I told you, Emily. I'm not holding anything back. There is a long and involved story associated with his rescue. It doesn't answer any questions, perhaps poses a whole lot more. The only thing I haven't told you is that the Ralston police played a big part in rescuing him. You remember Pete Messell, the top cop in Ralston…?" She nodded. "After the first day or so, when we had no evidence of what happened to Callum, I called Ben Richards. He, in turn, called Pete. Pete and four of his officers from Ralston precinct drove out here the same day. I have been working with Pete and his blokes since then."

"Did Sam Keller come with them? If she did, I'd like to say hello before I leave."

"No, Sam is holding the fort at Ralston in Pete's absence. He has only four uniformed officers with him. The important thing for you to know is, the Ralston police are up to speed with everything. When you arrive at the hospital, you probably will find police guarding both Callum and the girl. I'll ask Pete to let them know you're coming."

She shrugged to indicate her indifference. Her despondency concerned me. "Emily, you don't have to go to Ralston. If you don't want to be there – for whatever reason – don't go. Go home. Go back to work as you as are supposed to on Monday. Call the hospital occasionally to check on Callum's progress, and maybe talk to him when he is well enough to take calls."

"It's not so much that I don't want to go to Ralston, it's about my feelings for him. Last night, I wasn't sure how I felt, but I did some thinking overnight – honest thinking and assessment."

"Sounds serious – and doesn't appear to have done you much good. Dare I ask what conclusions you came to?"

"Nothing good; apart from anything else, I'm disgusted with myself. My objective assessment of Callum makes me wonder why I ever got involved with him; what I ever saw in him. He is slick, but not honest. It's all about show, and working situations to suit his own ends. In fact, he is mostly what I don't like in people. Apart from all that, I doubt I was anything more than a convenience to him. No, I don't know what I mean by that, other than I don't think I *meant* anything to him. All I provided was a means to achieving something he wanted. In the beginning, I think I was just another conquest, but then I became an opportunity to come out to this area. While I talked about how nice it would be to see Claire again and it would be good to be out here on the weekend when something special was happening, it was him who kept on about coming out for the ball. I'm not stupid. I should have seen what was going on; seen through his subterfuge."

"You can go on beating yourself up for as long as you like, but it won't change anything. Perhaps you should see it as a hard lesson learned, and move on. For what it's worth, I think your assessment of Callum is reasonably accurate. And, I don't think he is a one woman kind of bloke. All that aside, I am curious about why he was so keen to come here."

"You mentioned something about his writing articles for a publication of some sort. Do you think he might've been looking for material for an article?"

"It's possible, but I don't know what would interest him out here. As a geologist, the only thing of interest might be something to do with the mining company's proposed fracking in the area. Something tells me it's too early to write about it yet. A more 'meaty' story might be possible closer to when the company begins operations, or shortly after they commence extraction. Did he mention wanting to see or talk to anyone in particular while out here?"

"No. He spent all his time trying to convince me what a great time we would have over the weekend, and how he was just coming along to enjoy it with me. How naïve could I be?"

When she checked the time, Emily's beating-her-self-up-session came to an abrupt end. "Look at the time. I had better check out and hit the road if I want to be in Ralston at a reasonable hour. Yes, I am going to Ralston. For the sake of my conscience, I will check on Callum's condition in spite of the fact he probably won't know I'm there and can't speak to me anyway. I won't hang around in Ralston; probably overnight there and then head back to Millhaven tomorrow. I'll call you this evening with whatever I learn."

There was a definite resolve in her demeanour as she strode out of the dining room.

Chapter 18

A quick wave to Emily as she drove off, and I was on my way back to my room. On the way past, I stopped at Pete's door. I couldn't hear any sounds from inside. Had he left already? I knocked lightly.

"Good morning. I thought I would let you know I won't be leaving Cranvale today, but Emily just left for Ralston. She will go to the hospital to check on Callum's condition."

"I'll let my blokes know she is coming. I spoke to the hospital earlier. They say, while his condition improved overnight, he still has a long way to go. Unless there is something of a miraculous improvement by the time she arrives, it is unlikely Emily will be allowed to see him. What are her plans? Will she hang around in Ralston for a while?"

"Dunno … I don't think she knows either. She says not. My gut feeling is she won't stay long; maybe no more than a day or two. I know she is due to return to work on Monday, and I believe she intends to."

"Who knows, by tomorrow, she might be able to see him, and he might be able to talk to her. I can't see much point in her hanging around in Ralston unless she is hopelessly infatuated with the lad."

"It seems she isn't. On a different note, if you need some help – or just company – I am available. While technically my investigation achieved its objective – Callum has been found – I doubt I'll consider the case closed until I know the circumstances surrounding his disappearance. I suspect he was held captive on that property. I want to know why, and what precipitated the course of events which led to that."

"Well then, it's likely we share some aspects of a common goal. My suspicion is Callum's disappearance is somehow associated with my investigation. His disappearing act might have brought us here, but our investigation changed tack after we arrived. I'm not saying we weren't interested in locating Callum. It's more like, once we were out here, we found there were other – bigger – 'fish to fry' as they say. I expect another phone call in a couple of minutes. After that, I'll have a better idea of what we might be doing today. Then, I'll come to your room for a chat."

"Would be nice to know what we might do today," I grumbled aloud as I checked the contents of my bag. "At least then I would know if I'll need any of this gear." After adding a fresh bottle of water and a new pocket-pack of tissues, and checking the batteries in my camera, my gear sack was ready to go. I spent the next twenty minutes sitting around waiting for Pete.

"Are you right to go?" he asked as soon as I opened my door to him.

"Yes; but where to, and to do what?"

"I'll tell you about it on the way. Come on. Hurry up. We've wasted enough time this morning."

We roared out of town as if a posse was close on our heels. Pete's set jaw suggested silence was best. So much for telling me what we were doing once we were on our way! My mounting curiosity had me in danger of bursting. All I knew was we were heading out of town – towards the neighbouring town of Langton Crossing I presumed. This was where Pete's officers were based since their arrival. It also was where Pete indicated he had stationed a man to report on goings-on in the town. Langton Crossing also was where the mining company's local headquarters were located.

After about ten minutes of deafening silence, I could bite my tongue no longer. "Is our destination a secret ... and likewise, what we are to do when we get there?"

"Eh...? I thought I told you. We are going to Langton Crossing."

"I don't know this part of the country well, but even I managed to work out where we were going. What I want to know is why."

"I think I mentioned a bloke I had keeping an eye on goings-on in Langton. He is an ex-copper who was injured in the line of duty. His recovery took months and left him permanently disabled and in a wheelchair. He came back to work for a while, but found it difficult being desk-bound while watching his colleagues doing all the things he used to do. After a while, he gave up, took a package and retired. I've used him a few times since then, usually on stakeouts. It just so happens, he is a talented artist and photographer … just what I needed for this assignment."

"I assume he still lives in Ralston…"

"Yeah, we flew him out here and installed him in a cottage off the main street. You wait until you see the park they created in the centre of Langton. It's always full of birdlife. There's a pond in the centre of it, and a number of bird feeding stations and birdbaths dotted throughout the park. Hugh is in his element there. It's the sort of place he loves – and it's a perfect fit with his watching brief. The mining company's headquarters are across the street from the park."

"While hanging about in the park is a perfect cover for an artist and a photographer, for what exactly is he watching? All right, even I can work out he is watching all things happening at the mining company's headquarters. What I don't understand is how, from over in the park, he is going to know what is happening inside the building. How can he help with your investigation?"

"It only took a couple of days for him to become part of the landscape. People walking their dogs chat to him on their way past, and the birds gather around him for the seed he throws them. But, nobody takes any notice of his continued presence or questions why he is there. It's excellent from the point of view of my investigation. He might not know what goes on in the building, but he sees everyone who comes and goes over there … and, when possible, records them on his camera. Some interesting people visit that building."

"So, we are to have a chat with your man, Hugh. Is there something particular we will chat about, or is it purely a social visit? It would be helpful if I knew before we talk to him what was going on. …Or, am I supposed to standby looking interested but saying nothing?"

"What…? No, it's not like that. Argh, I'm sorry. I've been distracted; trying to sort through a couple of things in my mind. Let's start again, shall we? Sam called this morning with an update. Callum is improving but is still under heavy sedation. It is unlikely Emily will be able to see him. Sam's other news was they are having some success with their interrogation of one or two members of the mob we rounded up from Cranvale. Details remain sketchy, but suggestion is someone from Cranvale is keeping the mining company informed of everything happening in and around the town."

"We know … I mean, we suspect the local mayor, Roland Garnham, is in contact with them other than as the mayor. That's not news."

"I thought so too, and shared those thoughts with Sam. From my earlier discussions with her, she arrived at the same conclusion and pressed the detainees to confirm her suspicions. The response she received left little doubt: *of course he is; everyone knows that.* After a bit of trial and error, the only others Sam could think of who might be in the know were the coppers. Now, it just so happened, Hugh noted Sergeant McClelland sneak into the mining company's headquarters building via the rear door. There was sufficient about his behaviour to start Hugh's alarm bells ringing. It's nagged me ever since Hugh told me about it. I'll revisit that conversation with him again this morning. Beyond that, we will have to see what else he has to share with us before we know what else we'll be discussing."

While still unsure why we were going to Langton this morning, I now knew why. Pete has me wondering whether, from the outset, his investigation was about possible corruption, and Callum's disappearance was a secondary issue to investigate.

There was no time left to plan how our conversation with Hugh might proceed. We were driving past the welcome sign and making our way along the main street. As we drove past, I had a brief glimpse of the park Pete mentioned. At this time, when all the surrounding area was dry and dusty, the well-maintained park stood out like a green oasis in the centre of town. I expected Pete to find a parking space somewhere close to the park. He didn't look for one, but continued along the street almost to its end before easing into a space in front of what appeared to be a coffee shop. I shot him a curious look.

"We can't just march into the park, bowl up to Hugh and start a conversation. He is undercover, and it is up to us to make sure he remains so. It's almost lunchtime. We'll pick up some food and drink from here before going to the park for a relaxing lunch. When we are part way through our lunch, if we should happen to notice Hugh going about his business, we tourists might feel compelled to talk to him about what he's doing."

"I see. I assume Hugh knows we are coming and what our plan will be so he might happen to position himself at the right place at the right time?"

"That's about how it goes. We go talk to him about his art stuff, and then invite him to join us for lunch and to talk about the park … and other matters which shall remain unmentioned for now."

The range of food on offer at the café was quite good, but not so extensive as to make choosing lunch difficult. In the end, we both over ordered, and ended up with almost enough for four people. Carrying our lunchtime feast, we walked along to the park and settled ourselves at a covered picnic table. Then came all the usual faffing about setting out our lunch, unwrapping our sandwiches, and getting down to the serious business of eating. I was about halfway through my first sandwich when Pete spoke – and loud enough for anyone within five metres to hear.

"That bloke over there in the wheelchair looks busy. Seems like he might be an artist of some sort. Might be worth a look while we're here."

"I'll mind our lunch while you take a look at what he's doing. If it's interesting, then you can look after everything while I have a look."

Without hesitation, Pete took a leisurely stroll across to where Hugh was sketching a collection of ducks on the pond. Their animated conversation lasted a few minutes before I interpreted proceedings as Pete inviting Hugh to join us for lunch. Hugh produced a box from his bag and waved it at Pete; probably indicating he brought lunch with him. Persuaded to join us at our picnic table, Hugh's electric wheelchair kept pace with Pete as they came towards me. Arranging ourselves around the table to accommodate Hugh and his chair and with Pete sitting close to him took a couple of minutes. Then we moved on to our two main objectives: eating lunch and receiving Hugh's latest intelligence report.

Anyone out of earshot watching us would be forgiven for thinking our time with Hugh was to learn about the park's wildlife. While delivering his report, Hugh only glanced at Pete occasionally. Most of the time as he spoke, he was pointing to various clumps of trees, or the pond, or other landmark features within the park. Whenever it was his turn to speak, Pete, for his part of the charade, pointed at images on Hugh's camera and appeared to ask questions about them.

My role in the performance wasn't a speaking part. All I did was to look at whatever Hugh pointed to, or lean over to look at his camera when Pete pointed to an image on it. While it might sound like a recipe for boredom, it was never boring. As Pete had met with Hugh only the previous day, I didn't expect Hugh would have much – if anything – new to report. I was wrong. Not only did he have a wealth of new information, but he was riveting to listen to.

As Pete worked his way through Hugh's photos with him, there was a sudden and dramatic shift in my role in the exercise. One of the images caught Pete's attention. It also made me lean in closer for a better look. Tricked up like an escapee from a cheap western movie, the figure in the image looked familiar. At first glance, it was difficult to tell why that was the case. The man in the photograph wore an oversized straw 'cowboy' hat with an elegant turned-up brim on both sides. Jeans, a pair of showy colourful boots, and a belt with a large fancy metallic buckle completed his costume.

It appeared the image was taken in a small carpark at the rear of the mining company's building. It was shot as the man paused by the side of his car after alighting from it. Out of the corner of my eye, I saw Pete moving his head around in the hope of gaining a better view of the man.

"Do you know who this is, Hugh? Do you recognise the car at all?" Pete asked.

"Nah, I can't say I'm familiar with the car. It might have been here before, but I can't say I noticed it. It's a common make and colour; not what you would expect our Wild West hero to be driving. I reckon I'd remember someone in that get-up if he'd been there before."

"There is something familiar about the bloke. I don't know whether it's his build or the way he's standing, but there is something about him."

I too tried looking at the image from different angles without success. Then I tried almost closing my eyes and squinting at it. "Got ya…!" Through my laughter, I managed to say, "Of course he is familiar. It's our very own Sergeant McClelland. Maybe he should have chosen a different disguise if he wanted to blend in with the surroundings."

"Jesus, you're right. It is Ted McClelland … and he seems keen no one should know it's him. Now why would he be paying a visit to mining company executives … and in fancy dress no less?"

"McClelland, eh…? Well now, that's a familiar face. He's been here a few times, mostly in civvies, but once in uniform; drove a different vehicle on those occasions though." Hugh flicked through his photos, stopping at a number of shots of McClelland along the way.

Both Pete and I sat back for a few moments before Pete returned his attention to Hugh and asked if there were any other images of interest.

"Yeah, there are a few other interesting ones. Some of them won't arouse your interest too much, but the last couple might set your pulse racing." As he spoke, Hugh waved his arm in sweeping gestures towards a distant clump of trees. He was convincing. An onlooker would perceive Hugh explaining where the bird or animal in his photograph usually hung out.

"Okay you two, have a look at this image. Tell me what you see."

Hugh's sinister grin told me there was more to the image than was obvious at first sight. I took my time examining the photo, glancing at Pete a couple of times while I did so. Pete leaned in closer for a better look at the image. I followed his example, but still nothing of note jumped out at me.

All I saw was a hire car arrive at the mining company's headquarters and drive around to the staff carpark at the rear of the building. His choice of parking spots allowed Hugh a clear view to take his shots. They showed a bloke in a snappy jacket, pork-pie hat at a jaunty angle, and sunglasses. Alighting from the vehicle and obviously cautious, he stood beside the open car door and scanned his surrounding for a few moments before slamming the door and rushing into the building. Pete's assessment of the shots matched mine.

"Hugh, this is fun, but all I can see is a spiv who arrived at the mining headquarters in a hire car. What am I supposed to see?"

"Is there nothing familiar looking about him?"

"No. All I see is a dandy sporting a lot of bling on his left hand. …And he needs a haircut."

I focused my attention and looked hard at the image. "That's it!" I squeaked.

"That's what…?" Pete snarled.

It was obvious Hugh's guessing game was wearing thin with Pete. I rushed in to try to rescue the situation.

"The man has his left arm stretched out to push the car door closed. On his wrist is a huge watch, and he has an ugly big ring on his ring finger. I've seen those bits of adornment before. To me, they tell me the man is Cranvale's mayor, Roland Garnham."

"Garnham…?" Pete barked a little too loudly, and then looked around to see if anyone might be listening. "What's the date stamp on this image?"

Hugh indicated the date and time in red across the bottom of the photo. Pete leaned in for a closer look and shook his head in mock bewilderment. "Now that is interesting. When this photo was taken, Garnham was supposed to be meeting with mining company representatives in Cranvale. The meeting was cancelled because, sometime during the night before, Garnham disappeared. Word was he left town in response to some personal emergency. Yet, here he is in Langton meeting with – presumably – those same mining company executives."

Hugh's giggling made him struggle to speak. "Well spotted, Sonny. I said you might find the photo interesting."

"Judging by his fancy get up, and the hire car, he didn't want anyone recognising him," Pete murmured more to himself than to us.

"Why was he driving a hire car? I know he has a Council vehicle as well as his private vehicle. If my memory serves me correctly, I think I saw him driving a cute little sedan on one occasion. Carol from the coffee shop said it was his wife's. So, why does he now need a hire car as well?" As I finished speaking, I looked up to find my two companions grinning at me.

Pete gave me a resigned sigh. "Think about it, Sonny. He went to great lengths to hide his identity. To then turn up in one of the cars you mentioned would undo all the good work he had done on his disguise."

Hugh added to my embarrassment at my lack of thought before speaking.

"Yeah, it's all about disguise … even to the extent of donning a wig. Here's a shot I took of him a few days ago. His hair was a slightly different colour and wasn't so long then." Hugh flicked back through a number of shots of the mayor. "Even if you didn't already know he was up to no good, you would have to consider his behaviour suspicious."

While perusing Hugh's gallery of shots of the mayor's visits to the mining company's headquarters, we discussed Garnham's possible involvement with the mining company outside of his mayoral responsibilities. He wasn't a regular visitor, but he was there often … too often for it to be on official business.

Finally, the official part of the exercise was over. Hugh had delivered his report and Pete had asked his questions. We returned our attention to our neglected lunches. I was thankful for the bottles of juice and water we brought with us. By the time we got around to eating them, the sandwiches had dried out and curled at the edges, and the lettuce was limp and tired-looking. It would require quite a bit of liquid to wash them down.

Over the next half hour while we ate, light conversation of no consequence to Pete's case included such topics as the weather, the drought, and the foresight of the local council in developing the park. With nothing more to do in terms of our meeting, and to maintain the subterfuge, Hugh announced loudly, "Well, all good things must end I suppose. I should be getting back to work. Thanks for your company. Maybe next time you're over this way we'll catch up again."

As we made our way back to the car, I deposited our lunchtime rubbish in one of the many decorative bins dotted throughout the park. The silence between us continued for quite a while beyond Langton's town boundary.

My mind had shifted to hyperdrive the moment Hugh left our picnic table. While the information he passed-on related to Pete's case, I began seeing possible connections with my case; with Callum's disappearance. A 'what-if' game was in full swing in my head.

Chapter 19

What if Callum's interest in coming out here was to investigate the fracking issue for an article he might write? What if, as a geologist, he might want to investigate the practicability of employing fracking out here? What if his intention was to spend time exploring the impact fracking would have in this area? What if he asked too many questions of the wrong people – or, perhaps, the right people – and they took offence? One last major 'what if' slammed in from left field. I let out an involuntary yelp, almost startling the life out of Pete who was lost in his own thoughts.

"What if …!

"What…? What if what? What are you on about?"

"I just had a horrible thought. What if Callum's 'disappearance' was of his own engineering? What if he chose to throw in his lot with the mining mob and somewhere along the line, for whatever reason, the situation turned sour?"

"Why would he throw in his lot with the mining company? What was his motive? What did he hope to gain?"

"If I knew, I wouldn't be struggling with all these 'what if' scenarios. I can think of a few reasons, but none of them makes any sense."

"Well, spit them out. Maybe they'll make more sense if we talk them through. You never know, we both might gain some inspiration from the exercise. I certainly could use some at the moment."

"Why are you searching for inspiration? I thought you said what Hugh gave you was valuable. Are you now saying it wasn't useful?"

"No, that's not the problem. It was useful. Now I have to work out how to act on it to achieve the best outcome. Leave it to one side while we deal with your problem. Let's go back to Callum's possible motivation for getting involved with the mining mob."

"If I knew Callum better, I might have a clearer understanding of how he thinks. So, anything I say at this time is based on little knowledge of the man or his likely motivation. Regardless, the first two possible reasons I thought of have monetary gain as their basis."

"Money is often what underlies decisions people make. Why would it be more significant in Callum's situation?"

"He is a geologist. Maybe he sees 'greener pastures' in working for a mining company into coal seam gas extraction than in coal mining. Perhaps he sees it as the way of the future. With the strengthening anti-coal mining sentiment about the country now, he might see CSG mining companies as an alternative that offers future career stability. I don't know how their pay rates compare to other mining companies', but Callum might see a better opportunity with this mob."

"Okay, I see where you're going with this one, but you said there were two possible reasons. What's the other reason?"

"Callum moonlights as a writer. Over the last few years, his work has appeared in various journals and magazines. I don't know what sort of money such work brings in, but I imagine it is a useful addition to his salary. Perhaps his visit to the fracking hotspot at Cranvale was to gather material for another article; an expose perhaps."

"If he managed to corner the right people, and they were drunk enough to say more than they should, he could end up with material for such an article. As it turns out, he was barely in Cranvale long enough to talk to anyone of any consequence before he disappeared. It would be worthwhile asking Emily who he associated with in the short time before his disappearance."

"Until they went to the ball, their time in the area was spent at Winyard. I don't think he picked up anything useful out there. His only opportunity to buttonhole likely targets was at the ball … And we don't know how long he was there before he disappeared. Again, I think he had little opportunity to gather information."

"Another possibility is for Callum to be pro-fracking, or at least pro-CSG extraction. Maybe he saw opportunity to join that side of the argument."

"Are you suggesting Callum's involvement with the mining company is for philosophical rather than monetary reasons…?"

"I'm just suggesting it's a possibility. Has he ever expressed an opinion on fracking? It's worth finding out."

"I'm not aware of it. If he supported the practice, I doubt he mentioned it to Emily. Still, she might have picked up on something. I will ask her about it."

Conversation came to a halt at that point. There was so much to think about, almost too much to get my head around. Talking it through with Pete hadn't solved any problems. It created additional questions to occupy my mind. Pete also remained silent, and appeared deep in thought. Perhaps our conversation gave him food for thought as well.

The heavy blanket of silence over us persisted for quite a few kilometres before I shattered it by asking a question. "What are your plans for what's left of today?"

"I need to check in with Ralston, and touch base with my blokes out here. And, I need to record notes from today and spent some time thinking about Callum's situation. The latter issue might trigger a couple of phone calls for information. What about you, what are your plans?"

"My first priority is to contact Emily. She's probably visited the hospital by now and might have updates on Callum's condition. As a result of our conversation, I now have questions for her. I doubt I'll gain anything of consequence from it, but it's worth a try."

"It seems we both have things to do back at the motel. Let's work to our own agendas until we meet up again for dinner at, say, seven o'clock in the dining room?"

"Sounds good; now Emily is no longer here, it will be nice to eat dinner in the restaurant again."

At the motel, my first priorities were a shower and coffee in that order. Once I was seated comfortably with coffee at my elbow and phone in hand, my thoughts turned to Emily. I had no idea where she was at this time of day. What she discovered at the hospital in Ralston would determine whether she overnighted in the city, or headed home to Millhaven. It didn't matter to me where she was, as long as she was able to take my call. I wanted to be able to report some progress to Pete at dinner tonight.

As I was about to call Emily, an alternative occurred to me. I flicked through my contacts for Sam Keller and called her instead. Sam and I worked a case together in Ralston back in the early days of her career as a detective and, later, both Emily and I spent considerable time with her during her stint at the Millhaven precinct. She even stayed with me for a while after her posting to Millhaven while she organised her accommodation. Now back in Ralston, she was Pete's second-in-command. I was about to end the call when she answered.

"Hi Sam, this is Sonny. Are you free to talk for a couple of minutes?"

"I've been expecting you to call. Yes, now is a good time to talk."

I explained my involvement with the situation at Cranvale before moving onto the reason for my call. "I thought it worthwhile to talk to you before I called Emily, so I'd be prepared if she had bad news to share. Have you spoken to her, and how is Callum?"

"No, I've been too busy to catch up with Emily, but I've left a message about maybe having dinner together this evening.

I didn't have a chance before she arrived at the hospital to talk to the police guards on duty there, so I think she might had a bit of a rough time at first. I called them in the middle of it all and squared it with them. Then I called the hospital and approved for them to share information on Callum's condition with her … as far as professional practice allows, I mean. So, she should be a bit happier now."

"Okay, so how is Callum, and was it possible for Emily to see him today?"

"No-o-o, I doubt she could see him. They keep him heavily sedated, so he is bombed-out the whole time. It's to help him amend physically as well as psychologically. Physically, the damage is not too bad, but the degree of psychological trauma he suffered is unknown. My understanding is it will be a few days before he regains consciousness."

"What about the woman who was with him in the vehicle, what is her situation, and do you know anything about her?"

"We managed to identify her and ran her ID. What an interesting bundle of tricks she is. I won't go into details now. Suffice to say, she didn't spend her life before Cranvale in a convent. When Callum regains consciousness, he might have an interesting tale to tell. In the meantime, the woman is being kept in an induced coma. Her head injuries were severe enough to necessitate surgery. They are unsure about her prognosis. It might be a few days before they know how things will go and, if she progresses well, it will probably be sometime after that before they try to bring her out of the coma. The doctors have indicated there may be some – even considerable – permanent damage."

Emily answered almost on the first ring. She sounded out of breath and I was a bit concerned.

"Oh no, I'm fine. I checked into a motel and then decided to go for a walk along the Esplanade. I ventured further than I anticipated and I was just coming along the hall to my room when I heard my phone ringing. I forgot to take it with me when I went out."

She confirmed she would stay in Ralston overnight, but wasn't sure about extending her stay beyond tomorrow. After our call, she would confirm Sam's dinner invitation. Emily echoed Sam's comments about having a rough time on arrival at the hospital. While things improved after Sam's intervention, she wasn't able to see Callum. They did update her on his condition and likely progress over the next few days. It appeared nobody mentioned the woman who they brought in with him, and it seems Emily didn't enquire about her. While I found that strange, I didn't query it.

Then, I moved our conversation on to those questions about Callum arising from my 'what if' interlude with Pete during the trip back from Langton.

"Thinking about events at Cranvale gave rise to a couple of questions. I'm not sure you can answer them, or shed any light on them at all, but they might be relevant to what happened to him." She agreed to tell me whatever she knew, but doubted there was anything more to tell. I pushed on anyway. "When you arrived at Cranvale, you went straight out to Winyard. Amongst the people you met and talked to while out on the property, was there anyone there associated with the mining company, or who seemed less troubled by the prospect of fracking than the rest of the community appears to be?"

"No. There was only a handful of people involved: Claire's family and Terry from the neighbouring property … Oh, and Terry's mate, Chris Tremaine. Every one of them is involved with a property in the area. The last thing they want happening is fracking."

"Did Callum ever express opinions about coal seam gas extraction, or about fracking in particular? I mean, did he make comment at any time, not just while you were at Cranvale."

"He never really commented but, no, there wasn't anything to suggest he supported the practice. If anything, he seemed intrigued they were planning to use the fracking method out there. He never said why he thought it strange, but his comments suggested that was his view."

"What about when you went to the ball, did Callum spend any time during the evening with anyone who might have been involved with the mining company, or who supported its initiatives?"

"Not while he was with me. When we first arrived at the hall, there was the usual flurry of introductions to people whose names I would never remember afterwards, and then we were swept inside with the rest of the crowd. Once inside, conversation wasn't possible. The music was so loud, those who wanted to talk had to yell. When we weren't dancing, Callum and I spent our time huddled in the quietest spot we could find. That's why we were leaving early. The sound was deafening and we had reached our tolerance level. We were on our way out when I was asked for a dance. Callum indicated he would wait outside for me and left. That was the last I saw of him. Everything else happened after the ball. At least, as far as I know, after he left the ball."

"Okay, so he didn't spend time with anyone of interest up until then. Of course, he might have struck up a conversation with someone outside the hall while he waited for you."

"I suppose it's possible. The problem is, we don't know what happened after he walked out of the hall. It was a while before I could escape to join him outside but, in hindsight, it doesn't seem it was long enough for him to create a situation that would result in his disappearance."

"How long do you think you will stay in Ralston?"

"It will be days before anyone is able to talk to him. There is no point in my hanging around here. I'll return to Millhaven tomorrow, and will check his progress with the hospital probably on a daily basis after that. The doctor looking after Callum said he would let me know if there was any change in his condition. I'll play it by ear; maybe return to Ralston when he is able to receive visitors."

There wasn't much else to discuss and Emily sounded exhausted. It had been a hard day for her. I ended the call and thought about the unhelpful report I would give Pete over dinner. The call produced nothing more than I already knew. More importantly, it confirmed whatever happened to Callum occurred during the short time while Emily had that last dance before going outside to find him. It was all after he left the ball."

My call to Emily continued churning through my mind as I made my way to the restaurant to join Pete for dinner. I had hoped for something – anything – to give him which might be a clue about what happened to Callum. Pete was perched at the bar when I arrived. We had one drink before moving to a table. There were few diners tonight, so our table in the back corner had us some distance from the others. I opened the conversation once we were seated.

"I was hoping to have something positive to pass on after calling Emily this afternoon. It seems it was wishful thinking. She contributed nothing more than I already knew – and that's not much. How about you, did you gain anything positive from today?"

"Quite a bit of interesting stuff was gained. I'll admit most of it was during our time with Hugh. A call to Sam Keller later this afternoon also produced a glimmer of hope. It seems one of the mining mob we rounded up doesn't like being locked up. He decided being cooperative might go some way to earning him his freedom. So far, nothing much has been forthcoming, but he did confirm the identity of the woman who was in the vehicle with Callum."

"Did he say what the connection was?"

"Not yet; it seems he needed to have another think about whether he should talk to us and how much he should tell us. He did indicate he thought a romantic encounter brought them together."

"A romantic encounter…? He was supposed to be spending the weekend with Emily. Argh, what am I talking about? That's about what we should expect from him. His reputation indicates he's incapable of focusing on only one woman at a time. Still, this must be something of a record, even for Callum. When I first tried establishing what happened, Emily estimated they were separated at the ball for no more than twenty to thirty minutes."

"I see what you mean about his being a slick operator. It was such a short timeframe. Did the woman target him? Did they know each other previously?"

"I suppose it's possible they knew each other before the ball, unbeknown to Emily. He would not tell a conquest – Emily, I mean – about his others women whether current or past. My gut tells me it was a chance encounter with a stranger. What my gut doesn't tell me is what happened after they met. I'm happy to listen to your thoughts on the subject."

"Nah, I'm fresh out of ideas. Nevertheless, I am inclined to agree with your suggestion of a chance meeting. I don't think Callum and the woman knew each other before the night of the ball. So, we have two possibilities: either he is a very smooth worker as you suggested, or one of them did or said something to trigger a chain of events culminating in both of them being in hospital."

"What are your plans for progressing the investigation? Now one of the mob looks inclined to be persuaded to talk, will you be returning to Ralston?"

"No, not for a while yet; there is still quite a bit of work to do out here. I don't know when we'll return. What about your plans? Are you still thinking of returning to Millhaven tomorrow?"

"I had hoped our discussions tonight might clarify my thinking. My initial thought was to leave Cranvale tomorrow but, while it remains a strong possibility, I feel there still might be more to discover out here. I'm not quite sure what my brief was for this case. If it only was to find Callum after his disappearance, then the case is closed. If finding him also involves finding out what happened and why, then my investigation still has some way to go. I know some of the answers might be available once he regains consciousness, but I'd like to be more informed before I talk to him."

"What about your cases back in Millhaven, are there any screaming for attention?"

"No, there is nothing current or urgent requiring attention. There are a couple of minor cases I will need to start work on by the end of next week at the latest. Apart from those, there are a couple of potential cases which might become realities sometime soon, but there is no guarantee they will."

"It sounds like you just about talked yourself into staying in Cranvale a bit longer."

"Yeah, I think it might be worth another day or two. What happens with your investigation might have some bearing on how long I stay."

While Pete tucked into his dessert, the prevailing silence gave me valuable thinking time. I had answered my questions. There was no reason for me to rush back to Millhaven. The administrative side of my business I had attended to while I was here, and there was no reason why that couldn't continue. By the time dinner was over and we were heading back to our rooms, my mind was made up. As we walked along the corridor, Pete chuckled.

"So, what's the final decision? Will you still be here tomorrow, or are you planning to leave?"

"No, I'll still be here tomorrow, but I'm not sure how long afterwards, or exactly why I'm staying."

Pete's earlier chuckle developed into a belly laugh. "Five minutes after we sat down to dinner, I could have told you that's what you would do. As you are planning to stay a bit longer, I suppose I should plan on having you tagging along for at least some of the time you're here."

Smug sod, I thought as I let myself into my room, but it seems he accepts I will want to be in on whatever his investigation involves. That should eliminate some of the arguments which usually arise.

Chapter 20

The extension to my stay at Cranvale did not start the way I planned. It began with the rare phenomenon of my sleeping in way past my normal wake-up time. Running late, I rushed through all the morning rituals, including breakfast, in order to be ready when Pete wanted to leave for whatever we were doing today.

As I put my empty breakfast tray outside my room, I decided to check what time Pete wanted to leave. Out in the hallway, the young lad from reception called me. He was loading empty breakfast trays from outside rooms onto a trolley.

"Good morning, Miss Whittington. I don't know if you're interested, but I intend to have some last minute practice with my drone this morning. You're welcome to join me. I finish work in about half an hour, and will go straight to the usual area. That's where I'll be if you would like to fly my drone again."

"Thanks. I'm not sure what I'm doing today but, if nothing urgent is on the agenda, I might take you up on that."

I was about to knock on Pete store when the lad called out to me again. "He's not there. He went out … uhmm, it was a while ago now. It was early, and I haven't seen him come back."

After thanking him for giving me a heads up, I tried Pete's door anyway – and received no response. Unsure what to do next, I opted to wander out to the motel's car park to see if his car was still there. It wasn't. I silently swore about having slept in. Perhaps he intended I shouldn't go with him today. If he'd knocked on my door or called my room, I would have woken and gone with him. So much for what I thought we achieved last night.

Well, if Pete went off to do his own thing without me, it was up to me to work out what I was going to do to fill in my day, and hopefully progress my case. More out of habit than anything else, on returning to my room I checked the gear in my backpack to make sure it was ready to go. …But, to go where? "I might as well go to have a play with the young bloke's drone. Maybe inspiration will dawn on me while I'm about it and I will be able to turn today into something useful," I told my empty room.

The morning was already hot. The sun had a fierce bite to it. I decided to drive to the clearing beside the hall rather than walk. If I'm honest, I drove in the hope some possible lead to investigate might occur to me. If my car was there, I would be able to follow it up without first having to return to the motel to collect the vehicle. It was a nice idea, but the gods didn't oblige me.

As I watched the lad putting the drone through its various manoeuvres, I again was impressed by his skilled handling of the controls. He seemed to have refined his light touch since the previous time we were there. He would acquit himself well in the competition on the weekend. I made a mental note not to enquire whether he had sorted things out with his girlfriend. He seemed pleased with himself as he brought the drone in to land at his feet.

"Come on, Miss Whittington, it's your turn now. Show me what you can do with it. I didn't watch you fly it the other day; too busy with that phone call."

He ignored my protest about my lack of ability, and insisted he wanted to watch me 'take the bird for a flight'. "I don't suppose there is any chance of another phone call to save me from having to demonstrate my lack of ability?"

"Not that I'm aware of, but if there is, it won't be from the same caller. Now, get that thing in the air so I can see what you can do."

Any procrastination to delay the matter seemed worthwhile. "So, does it mean you sorted out your girlfriend's issues about the weekend?"

"Yeah, I sorted them out. I like her company, but she was trying to own me; to control me. It was sort of like being married. I'm not ready for that yet. I'll be on my own for the weekend, and I'm happy about it."

I made what I hope was sympathetic noises about his romantic situation before rushing to launch the drone. Anything was better than running the risk of hearing details of the breakup of his love life. …Besides, another flight over the clearing in the scrub might be a good thing. I didn't expect to see any change, or any activity there, but I told myself it was worth a look.

As the drone took to the air, I began a chatty conversation in the hope of distracting him from paying too much attention to my skills or lack thereof. "You must be starting to feel a bit of tension about the weekend competition. I imagine there will be an impressive line-up of competitors. Hey… what's the range of this thing, and are there rules about where you can fly them?" While I chatted, I kept the drone flying an elliptical course that took it closer to the scrub area with every circuit.

He appeared to enjoy airing his knowledge. Over the next few minutes, he increased my knowledge of drones and the rules and regulations about flying them. In the midst of it, the drone flew a loop over the laydown area in the scrub. Having achieved my objective, I recalled the drone and landed it cleanly. I paid particular attention to the screen when it flew over the clearing. No sign of movement there today.

If all else fails, I could hike to the clearing for a better look around but, as the flyover proved, I don't have reason to do so. I suppose I live in hope Pete will involve me in whatever he is doing. While I dealt with my own thoughts, I stood off to one side watching the lad pack up his drone. Practice was over for the day. A few minutes later, I watched him drive off before starting towards my own vehicle. I didn't hurry. After all, I had nothing else to do; nowhere else to go. I climbed in and sat with my hands clasped over the steering wheel and my forehead resting on my hands.

Maybe extending my stay in Cranvale was a mistake. For want of something better to do, I'll go back to the motel and ponder that decision over a coffee. The sound of a car's horn interrupted my quiet moment alone. Then a vehicle roared in and parked beside me. I looked up half expecting to see the drone pilot returned for some reason. It wasn't.

Pete leapt out of the vehicle, stormed over and wrenched open my passenger side door. "Don't you have anything better to do than sit here slacking off while the rest of us are hard at work?"

"Of course I have things to do. So many things, I was taking a moment to work out what to do first." My tone was a bit shorter than I intended, but Pete was not one of my favourite people this morning.

"I could help you decide. I have some action about to go down. I thought you might be interested in being a spectator."

Without allowing him time to explain, I told him to follow me back to the motel so I could dump my car before we moved on to whatever he had planned. After that, we didn't go far; just as far as the Cranvale police station. With our destination only about three blocks from the motel, when we arrived, I remained no wiser about why we was there.

As soon as we stopped, Pete jumped out of the car and rushed up the police station's steps. He shouted over his shoulder, "Come on, I haven't got all day."

No further encouragement required. I followed his example and scampered up the steps behind him. Apart from Pete and me, the station was deserted. I expected the two local coppers would be there. The empty station brought me to a sudden halt. "Why are we here, and where is everyone?"

"All will be revealed soon. Either one or both of the local coppers will be joining us. Feel free to take notes as our meeting progresses, but under no circumstance say *anything*. Just bear in mind that, strictly speaking, you should not be here and, if you open your mouth during proceedings, I will turf you out of here … or worse. Is that clear?"

Several come-backs came to mind, but Pete's demeanour suggested responding with any of them would not be wise. I quietly agreed to comply. After all, curiosity had me firmly in its grip. The intrigue was almost unbearable, but it was obvious I was not about to be given advance information on what was about to take place.

A commotion outside sent me scurrying for a chair against a side wall. Pete stood front and centre and squared his shoulders. He was a huge bear of a man and he was not in the best of humour. His was an intimidating presence in the tiny station. I recognised the voice of one of Pete's officers barking orders, and braced myself for what might follow as the door slammed open. I expected Sergeant McClelland would lead the group outside in through the door. Then my next shock for the day arrived.

It wasn't Sergeant McClelland who led them in. It was the other copper attached to the station. I didn't know his name, but he didn't look happy to be surrounded by Pete's blokes. Pete greeted him most affably.

"Good morning, Constable. Please take a seat." He gestured towards a chair he had pulled out from behind the reception desk and placed up against the front of the desk. "Good of you to join us so early in the morning."

"I'm only here because I didn't have a choice. Who the

hell are you anyway? Have you any idea how many laws you have contravened by your takeover of this police station, and for the way your bully-boys have treated a police officer."

"We will get to who we all are shortly but first, I understand you were planning on being elsewhere today. Where might that be?"

"That's none of your business."

"Ah well now, that where the problem lies; it very much is my business … and you would do well to answer my questions honestly and civilly. Now, where were you off to when my lads caught up with you?"

Pete bent down, placed his hand on the chair and leaned in close to the constable as he asked the question. From across on the other side of the room, even I felt intimidated by Pete's action. The constable shrunk down in his chair, and looked up at Pete with eyes the size of saucers. He blinked a couple of times and ran his tongue over his lips before answering.

"I was about to set off on my routine patrol. The same day every week, I spend visiting some of our western area. There are a couple of large properties I call at to see if they have any problems. Then, I visit a couple of small towns out there, spending about three hours at each, before heading back to Cranvale."

"It must make for a long day. What time do you return?"

"Usually around dark; maybe about seven o'clock..."

"Yeah, it is a long day. Do you get paid overtime or how does it work?"

"No, I have tomorrow morning off in lieu of overtime. The arrangement suits both of us, and it works in terms of the station."

"If you are to be out and about today, why isn't Sergeant McClelland here to man the station while you're away?"

"It's as the sign out front says, the station doesn't open today until twelve o'clock. That's when the sergeant comes in and opens up. That's how it's always been – well, for a long time anyway. The community is aware of it and it doesn't seem to create any problems."

"How long have you been stationed out here?"

"It's my first posting out of the academy. Our first postings were to be for twelve months. In a week's time I'll have been here eighteen months. I did apply for a transfer soon after my twelve months were up, but I missed out. I've another application for transfer in now, and should hear about it in the next few days."

"How did you arrive at the arrangement where both of you are away from the station at the same time? Wouldn't it make more sense for your patrols to be on different days rather than both on the same day? That way, the police station wouldn't be closed for one morning every week."

"The officer I replaced had been here for a bit over four years when he retired. Sergeant McClelland has been here for a long time. He said the arrangement was in place for years and the community was used to it that way. Changing things would confuse people. So, we left it as it was."

"I see. So where has Sergeant McClelland's patrol taken him this morning?"

"I don't … I'm not sure where he goes, but it's in a different direction from mine. I think he might go south from here, but I don't know where it takes him."

"You're doing well, son. Now, let's see how you go with the hard stuff. Who has keys to this station?" The question made the young bloke's eyebrows crawl inwards to almost meet across the bridge of his nose. He shook his head as if he didn't understand the question. Pete rephrased it. "Who … How many people have keys to this station, and can let themselves in to come and go as they choose?"

"Nobody… Well, nobody other than the sergeant, myself and the cleaner. Nobody else should have a key and we wouldn't want them to have one."

"I assume you have your key with you. You haven't lost it or anything?" The constable waved his key at Pete. "Good; and I know the cleaning woman was in possession of hers until I took it from her this morning." The young lad's eyebrows shot up almost to his hairline in surprise. "Now, what about the sergeant's key … has he lost it or lent it to anyone lately?"

"Christ no; I imagine that would almost amount to a hanging offence. What's with the questions about keys? All three of us are careful with our station keys."

"Not quite a hanging offence, but certainly a serious one. But, we've no need to concern ourselves about the sergeant's key. I can confirm he was in possession of it earlier this morning. However, you appear to have left someone off your list of key holders."

The young lad shook his head but didn't get a chance to respond. Pete whipped out his phone and flicked through it. Having found what he was looking for, he straightened up, cleared his throat and glared down at the constable, before thrusting his phone almost under the bloke's nose.

"Perhaps you might tell me who this bloke wearing a stiff collar, well-pressed slacks and shiny shoes might be."

More shaking of his head before the young bloke answered. "It's not a good photo; not clear enough. I can't tell who he is. What's he got to do with anything anyway? I thought we were talking about who held keys to the station."

"…We are. That's exactly why I want to know who the bloke in the photo is. Let me tell you a story. Early this morning, the bloke in the photo, whom you can't identify, pulled up out front, got out, and let himself in to the station. He went in carrying a parcel, or a large envelope of some sort. Moments later, he came out empty-handed and drove away."

"That can't be right. Nobody else has a key."

"Obviously, someone else does, but I haven't finished my story yet. Please wait until I do before speaking again."

The constable blinked a couple of times before nodding his agreement.

Pete let the tension run on for a few moments before continuing. He stretched his back, and strode back and forth across the room before taking a few sips from a bottle of water he placed on the desk on our arrival. His phone came out of his pocket again and he studied it for a few moments before returning to stand in front of the young constable.

"Does this place run to coffee of any sort? I've a mind to have a coffee break before continuing with my story."

Lounging against the front wall since their arrival, Pete's men sprang to attention at the mention of coffee. It captured my attention as well. The young constable looked confused but nodded.

"Yes, but it's only instant I'm afraid. The kitchen is back there." He flicked his thumb towards the rear of the building. Pete gestured for him to lead the way.

Constable Pernell (for the first time, I was close enough to read his badge) led us through to a cubicle about the size of a phone box. There was coffee – a cheap brand of instant powder, sugar, and milk that looked like it could be spread rather than poured. The 'kitchen' ran to four chipped and not too clean mugs. I had an instant lack of interest in having coffee. Pernell bustled about filling an electric jug and setting it to boil while we looked on from outside the cubicle. That's when the station's landline rang. Pernell looked at Pete in question. Pete shook his head.

"Lewis, get that phone will you?" Pete called without looking back at his men still waiting out in the front room.

As Lewis was dealing with the phone call, Pete, while standing crammed up against Pernell in the tiny kitchen, clattered a spoon in a mug of coffee. I wanted to shout, *it's instant, Pete. Just pouring the water over it probably dissolved the coffee,* but, in line with my agreement to remain silent, I said nothing. Then Lewis rushed to join me outside the kitchen.

"Sir…!" The urgency in Lewis' voice silenced the clattering spoon. "Could I have a word, please?"

Pernell looked questioningly at me. I shrugged. I didn't know any more than he did, but it was obvious the phone call Lewis answered with significant. A minute or so later Pete summoned Pernell to the front room, where he joined a huddle of Pete and his four officers.

"Pernell, is the property *Coralunga* somewhere along the route you would take today?"

"No, it's in a different direction from my route; in a different part of the area. Why do you ask?"

"I need to know where the hell it is and I haven't got time to mess about trying to find out."

"Sir … I know where it is. What about it?" All members of the group, including Pernell, turned to face Taylor.

"What…? How do you know where it is?" Pete snarled.

"As a kid, I grew up over in that area. While I attended boarding school, I used to work on *Coralunga* whenever I was home for the holidays."

Pete started towards the door while talking over his shoulder. "Right, Taylor, you've got a job to do. Take Bainbridge with you. Come on, catch up. I'll tell you about it on our way out to your car."

Soon after the trio disappeared down the steps, I heard a vehicle start and roar away. Pete bounded up the stairs and in through the door.

"Okay, where were we before all that happened? Oh yes, I was about to have a cup of coffee. Should do that before it goes cold I think."

"By the way, Coralunga is in the area McClelland is visiting today. I take it whatever has sent your men off to Coralunga has something to do with this police station. Since the phone call which triggered it was to this station, I think I'm right in assuming the caller wished to speak to one of the officers stationed here. Is it too much to expect for me to know the details of the call?"

"Not at all; of course you should know. It's interesting McClelland supposedly is out Coralunga way today. Remember the story I was about to tell you? It's just gained an extra chapter or two. Perhaps we should make ourselves comfortable before I continue with the rest of it." Everyone grabbed a chair and placed them in a tight circle around Pete. "No, Pernell, you should sit next to me. There are illustrations that go with the story and you might like to view them as we go along."

Chapter 21

When the scraping of chairs subsided, Pete cleared his throat and cast his eyes around those gathered in front of him. "Okay, let's get on with my story. Now, in the light of new developments, where do I start?"

Pernell piped up, "Well, you could start with the phone call, and why you dispatched two of your blokes in such a hurry."

"You're right. That is a good place to start."

"Hooray…! Then get on with it." Pernell's patience was running out, and my curiosity was killing me.

"Well, as you've probably all worked out, the phone call came from the owner of Coralunga Station. It seems a group of animal rights activists camped out near there for a couple of days have spent their time harassing the local property owners. They've been going on to properties and 'saving' stock by removing animals, by force if necessary. Yesterday they visited Coralunga's neighbour, but left empty-handed. Thanks to the ongoing drought, he has no stock left on the property. It appears the activists weren't happy about wasting their time, and roughed up the owner out of spite."

"I had heard whispers of this sort of thing, but there haven't been any official reports or complaints. I mentioned it to the sergeant. He claimed it was just rumours." Pernell looked genuinely distressed. "I should have investigated the stories instead of dismissing them as rumours."

"Don't beat yourself up about it," Pete said quietly, but I noticed the firm set of his jaw as he spoke. "It wasn't your decision to make. It was up to the officer in charge to decide whether to follow up on the stories or not, and it appears he did."

Murmurs broke out amongst the members of the gathering. I didn't have anything to contribute but, from what I heard, those around me were not impressed with the way the matter was handled. Pete called the group to order before continuing his story.

"Before I progress much further, Pernell, I need an answer from you. This is a closed group. Anything you say here will go no further, but I do need an honest answer to this question: how do you get on with Sergeant McClelland? What's your opinion of him, as a police officer I mean?"

"That's not for me to say. He's my commanding officer, and I do as I'm told. I think you've got a cheek asking that question."

"You can feel that way if you wish, but you are wrong on one aspect. I am your commanding officer." As he spoke, Pete produced his ID and waved it in front of Pernell. "This means I also am Sergeant McClelland's commanding officer. Now, I believe something serious is happening out here, and I intend getting to the bottom of it. I would suggest you think long and hard about what I asked you, if you don't want me to believe you are a part of it. Your career depends on how you answer my questions."

"Okay, okay, I get the message. Since you're asking, I don't think much of McClelland at all. For a while now, I've suspected something was happening out here, and that McClelland was a key player."

"Got any examples to share?"

"The B&S ball was a good example. There are always drunken high jinx and a few minor brawls on the night. Extra officers from surrounding areas were brought in for the occasion. Yet a major incident happened in town in which two people were seriously injured. All of us were stationed around the hall. None of us attended the brawl until the two men were lying injured in the gutter."

"So you didn't know the brawl was happening in another part of town. Why do you think there was something funny about that?"

"I heard a whisper about a brawl in town. I asked McClelland about going to investigate. He bawled me out about obeying orders, and how my orders were to stay close to the hall to monitor behaviour there. I might have accepted it, except I knew he had received two or three phone calls. He chose to ignore them."

"They could have been from anyone about anything. What makes you think they had anything to do with the brawl out front of the council chambers?"

"You need to understand the local situation. A God-bothering old maid lives in a cottage across the street from the pub." Pete jumped in to correct Pernell's descriptors. Pernell tried again. "An elderly single woman with high Christian values lives across the street from the pub." Pete gave him a nod of approval. Pernell continued.

"She calls us regularly during the season when the shearers are in town. Every weekend she complains about the noise, the obscene language, and whatever else emanating from the pub area offends her finer sensibilities. I can't believe she didn't call about a brawl taking place about half a block further along and on the other side of the street from her cottage."

"I agree it was not one of the police's better efforts. Nevertheless, one bad incident doesn't indicate systematic misconduct. Are you suggesting officers were deliberately prevented from attending the incident?"

"It's what I believe happened … and, as a result, two people were seriously injured. Argh, there were other incidents as well; too many little things. Each of them on its own doesn't mean much but, together, they add up to something with a bad smell to it."

"I see. Here's something else to add to your list of things with a bad smell. The owner of Coralunga who called was looking for McClelland. He spoke to the sergeant yesterday and arranged for him to call in early this morning. The owner feared he was next on the animal activists list of properties to attack. He knew what time McClelland usually went past his place on the days he was out that way and, when the sergeant hadn't arrived, he became concerned."

The constable appeared to ponder Pete's statement for a few moments before responding. "Without anything definite to support my theory, I believe McClelland might be sympathetic to the animal activists' cause. In part of a call I overheard, McClelland's comments suggested the drought was working in *their favour.* When landowners had no stock left and no other means of generating a cash flow, CSG wells on their property would become an attractive proposition. Most landowners have destocked to the point of having very few head left. Their future becomes even bleaker if the animal activists further reduce their stock levels by 'rescuing' some of the remaining animals."

"Intriguing isn't it, and perhaps another whiff of that bad smell?"

Pernell shrugged, and then grudgingly nodded. Pete was silent and deep in thought for a while. Then, in a sudden movement, he sat up straight and slapped his hands on his thighs.

"Right, that's the new chapter of my story dealt with. Now let's get back to the original story shall we?"

It was a rhetorical question; no answer required. We straightened up in our chairs in anticipation of what was to follow. Pete pulled out his phone and spent a moment or two flicking through it in search of whatever he required to support his story.

"Earlier, Pernell, I showed you a photo of a smartly dressed bloke letting himself into this police station." He held up his hand to silence Pernell who was about to comment. "You couldn't identify him, and rightly so. It was a blurry shot of the rear of the bloke. Now I want to show you a couple of other shots taken this morning of the same bloke."

Up off my chair, I scarpered around behind Pete to peer over his shoulder at the phone. If Pete sat outside this station photographing people at some ungodly hour this morning, it was for a reason, and he's treating the shots he took as significant. The first shot filled the screen. Pete reached over and held the phone in front of Pernell's face.

"This is the same bloke I showed you earlier; the snappy dresser. See the parcel or whatever it is he's carrying under his arm. Now watch the video for the next few seconds."

The man alighted from a car, mounted the steps to the front door of the station, unlocked it and disappeared inside. No more than a few seconds later, the man reappeared. He closed and locked the door behind him, returned to his vehicle and drove away. At the end of the video, I glanced down at Pernell's face. His mouth hung open. He looked stunned.

"Well, Pernell, what can you tell me about all that? Did you recognise the bloke?"

"Sort of … His name is Connor or Connolly. Something like that I think. He's one of the mining company executives, not at the top of the tree though. More like one of the next level down, and seems something of a trouble shooter for them; does a lot of legwork for the company."

"Notice anything else worth mentioning?"

Pete started the video rolling again. The whole thing lasted only a couple of minutes. As I watched the man come down the steps and head for his car, I caught my breath. It was all I could do not to blurt out what I'd noticed. Pernell didn't need to exercise such restraint, and let out a yelp.

"The parcel…! The parcel or whatever he took inside is missing when he comes out again. He was here to deliver something, went inside, left it somewhere, and went again.

But there was nothing here when I arrived this morning … Nothing except you lot. Did you find the parcel before I arrived? What was in it?”

“No, we did not touch anything after we arrived. I admit we looked around for the parcel but didn't see it anywhere. If I may continue with my story, all will be revealed.”

I wanted to shout *get on with it,* but Pernell beat me to it. Pete's sense of the dramatic was wearing thin with me, and I knew I wasn't alone in that. Pete chuckled at Pernell's impatience and turned his attention to his phone.

“Okay, here's the next chapter of the story. I know nobody checked the time stamp on the previous video, but it doesn't matter. I can tell you this next video was shot about twenty-five minutes after the bloke in the first video drove away from the police station. I'm sure you will have no difficulty with identification this time.”

A vehicle arrived at the station, and a bloke started to emerge from it. Pernell murmured something about it being too early and it couldn't be right. Pete ignored him and kept the video rolling. Even I could identify the man who alighted from the vehicle. His uniform was a dead giveaway for a start. The only incongruous thing about him was a supermarket carry bag bunched up in his left hand.

We watched as the bloke unlocked the door and let himself into the station. He too was only inside for a matter of moments. After locking the door behind him, we watched the target pause for a moment on the top step and visually scan the area before bouncing down the steps to his vehicle and driving off.

“You're right, no problem with identification at all,” Pernell spat out as the video ended. The vitriol in his voice went well beyond his words and matched his clenched fists. “That's McClelland. And yes, I did notice the shopping bag he carried back to his car. It was the scrunched up one he carried inside. Only , when he came out again, it contained something heavy."

Pernell gestured to Pete to rewind the video. "Just go back to where he comes out of the station again. Stop…! Yes, there… See the bag he is carrying?" Pernell reached over and slid his fingers across the screen to enlarge the image. "That's better. If you look at the bag, you can just see a bit of something brown poking out of the top of the bag. I'd wager an important part of my anatomy that what's in the bag is the parcel the first bloke left here."

"Give the young man a prize," Pete chuckled. "Top marks, lad, for your observation and assessment of the situation."

Instead of looking pleased, Pernell sat shaking his head in disbelief. "Are there any more chapters in this story of yours? If they're anything like the ones we've seen so far, I'm going to need another coffee – or something stronger – before we continue."

"Yes, there is one more chapter. You won't need coffee for this one though." Pete again searched his phone, found what he wanted and, with the video rolling, held it up for Pernell.

"That's the cleaner arriving. Argh, don't tell me she is involved too. …What's this bit all about? … Oh, I see. This is your blokes arriving."

"And that ends the story for today," Pete said, and added a theatrical gesture. "On our arrival, we sent the cleaner home again, but took her key before she left. She was reluctant to part with it. We all had to produce our IDs before she handed it over. She then stomped off home again."

I could feel the cogs in my brain working at high speed. It didn't take too much nous to work out what had happened here this morning. The tricky part was working out the bigger picture; the rest of the story. I needed more brain fuel. The coffee Pernell suggested sounded like just the thing. Pete shared our thoughts. After announcing he had a couple of calls to make, he walked to the other end of the room with his phone already attached to his ear. When he returned to the group, he didn't resume his seat, but stood behind it with his hands resting on the chair's back.

"It's time we refuelled in readiness for the rest of the morning. I've arranged with the motel for us to pick over what's left of the breakfast buffet. So, come on, we're off to the motel."

Catering for everything from a continental to a full English, and everything in between, the breakfast buffet in the motel's dining room is a real waistline-wrecker. As we entered the room, Pete went into tour guide mode.

"Those doors down there lead to a small function/meeting room which is at our disposal for as long as we need it today. Help yourselves to whatever is left of the buffet over there, and then bring it through to the meeting room with you."

After rearranging the furniture to suit, we barely had time to taste our coffee before Pete went into meeting mode. The initial period was spent discussing this morning's videos and eliciting comments from everyone around the table. Then, it was time to look beyond the videos; to hypothesise about whether they were indicative of some significant practice. Pete opened the ensuing 'guessing game' with a pertinent question.

"What do we think was in the parcel McClelland collected from the station this morning?"

"Cash…! It had to be cash. What else could it be?" Pernell scanned the faces around the table in search of responses to his question.

His assumption wasn't unrealistic, but I wasn't sure it was correct. When nobody else commented, I decided to share my thoughts.

"Yes, I agree cash is a logical conclusion, but I'm not convinced it's right. It wasn't a large parcel. It was a large envelope. If you're right, and it was cash, how much was it? A bundle of ten one hundred dollar notes amounts to one thousand dollars, and takes up not much space. It would be possible to put several thousand dollars in a standard sized envelope. So, why would someone find it necessary to use such a large envelope?"

"That's the problem. We don't know how many thousands of dollars might have changed hands this morning." Pernell seemed fixated on the idea of cash.

"I'm happy to accept cash might've been involved, but I wonder if something else was in the envelope – along with the cash."

My suggestion of 'something else' brought the predictable raft of questions about what it might be. I didn't have definite thought to offer, but I did have a couple of vague ideas. Best I keep those to myself until there is something positive to back them up. Pernell had gone quiet, and Pete seemed to have run out of prompts to keep the guessing game going. We sat in silence for a minute or so before Pernell refocused our thought processes.

"It's probably not relevant in any way, but I did overhear some gossip. I thought it strange at the time. Now I'm beginning to wonder. It was a while back, when a gang of duffers were active in an area west of here. I went in, sort of undercover, to see if we could catch them in the act. Graziers were making liberal use of the 'long paddock' – the roadside verges – in a bid to keep stock alive. As a member of one of the droving crews, I spent about a week camping out with them and their herds. A couple of the blokes stayed on watch until around midnight when they were relieved by two others from the gang. By the end of the day, I was knackered and crawled into my sleeping bag soon after dinner."

"You would have found the life of bit different from what you used to," Lewis chuckled.

"Yeah, but going to bed early was a good ploy. The two blokes on watch sat around the fire with a rum or two, and yarned to fill in the time. It's amazing what I heard before

I fell asleep. On one occasion, I heard McClelland's name mentioned and pricked up my ears. As I said, I thought it was just gossip, but they were talking about McClelland buying a property somewhere out that way. Their comments suggested it was a good property and only was acquired via 'a deal'."

"I assume you didn't mention this to McClelland," Pete said with a smile.

I noticed Pete's smile only involved his lips. His eyes remained hard. Pernell looked horrified and shook his head in reply.

"No, I thought not. Good lad. Any ideas about what the deal referred to might be? I can accept properties might be going cheap at the moment, but they could be purchased without recourse to any deal."

"There are plenty of properties in trouble as a result of the drought. Stock numbers are down, and trying to keep the remaining flock or herd alive to secure some income is an expensive exercise. The usual situation is for a lack of income to run the property owner deep into debt. At the outset, banks and other financial institutions are sympathetic. Loans are available. When the drought stretches on and conditions become worse even to the point of no income stream at all quite a few property owners opt to walk off their land. Others continue to hang on as long as they can, even when all hope of recovery is gone. Then the bank forecloses, and they lose everything anyway."

Pete sat nodding as Pernell explained the problem local landholders faced. "That's not a unique story though, Pernell. The same situation applies to the whole country at present. It even applies to city dwellers who end up losing everything thanks to low wages and high mortgage repayments … and shonky financial loan arrangements."

"The opportunity for 'deals' comes if the property owner acts before the bank forecloses. When the bank forecloses, it takes everything. Any remaining cash and proceeds from the sale of equipment and other possessions goes directly to reducing the level of debt held by the bank. Then, when the property itself is sold or auctioned off, the proceeds realised are split between all of the landholder's creditors and the bank if there is any remaining bank debt."

"Sounds like the bank comes out of this better than anyone else."

"Yeah, and the Shire Council often loses out big time under the arrangement. Their distributed portion of the funds pool often doesn't cover the amount of the property's outstanding rates. I think I read somewhere about rules or regulations preventing Councils circumventing the system. Regardless, locally, in 'special' cases, they seem to find a way around the problem. It might be one of these 'special deals' the blokes were talking about in regard to McClelland's purchase of a property."

"Okay, but how do these deals work?"

"When outstanding rates on a property are significant, and foreclosure by the bank is imminent, various parties are put in touch with each other. The property owner running the risk of losing everything will settle for whatever he can get. Council wants to recover outstanding rates. A prospective buyer wants the best deal on a property possible. The buyer and the Council negotiate a price which pays the outstanding rates and gives the landowner a small cash package which the bank knows about and can claim, and he also receives another small cash package – which the bank doesn't get to know about – to help with establishing a new life. Unbelievable 'bargains' are available, if the buyer has ready cash."

"If McClelland is buying a property, he might have been lucky enough to negotiate such a deal. Is that what you are suggesting, Pernell?"

"Seems like a strong possibility to me. McClelland and the mayor are good mates. They play golf together regularly, and both belong to the same service club. You work it out."

Chapter 22

None of us questioned the scenario put forward by Pernell. Pete showed particular interest in McClelland's life away from the police station and quizzed Pernell about it.

"Does the sergeant live here in Cranvale?"

"Yeah, he lives in the police house around in the back street."

"Is there a wife and family?"

"I believe there was when he was posted out here. I don't know how long after that she took the kids and shot through. From what I've heard around town, nobody blamed her. Word is he gave her a rough time. The kids would be adults by now and probably living their own lives. I've never heard where they ended up."

"Backhanders for turning a blind eye would come in handy if he were paying maintenance and saving up to capitalise on an opportunity to acquire a cheap property. Of course, we must not jump to conclusions. We don't *know* backhanders are involved." Pete looked around the table as he spoke.

"Your mention of 'wife' brought back something else I overheard on another occasion while camped out under the stars. Gossip had it McClelland was being particularly 'helpful' to a property owner's wife. With their property totally destocked, the husband found work at a mine in Western Australia. He now only comes home for a couple of weeks every two or three months. I don't know any more about that than I do about his buying a property, but McClelland's supposed activities were giving the drovers plenty to talk about."

"Doesn't sound like he is the most popular bloke in town, but I don't suppose coppers are supposed to be popular. What happened to the officer you replaced out here, where did he go after Cranvale?"

"He didn't transfer. He retired – to one of the southern states I think. I never pursued it, but I think he might have left over a bit of bother."

"What sort of 'bother'?"

"As I said, I don't know. I never looked into it; didn't want to know I suppose."

Conversation at the table had been the exclusive domain of Pete and Pernell. Fascinating though it was, the rest of us were becoming restless. For all I was contributing to the discussion, I might be better occupied checking emails in my room. The only thing stopping me leaving was the thought I might miss something important. The sounds of people around the table becoming restless intruded on Pete's consciousness.

"I don't know about anyone else, but I need fresh coffee. It's time we took a short break to stretch our legs and refuel."

After sending Pete a mental thank you, I headed for the coffee set-up in the dining room. Back in the meeting room, everyone was on their feet and stretching various parts of their body to encourage circulation … that is, everyone except Pernell. I hadn't realised he was right on my heels as I returned to the meeting room.

"I can't keep calling you Pernell. Do you have a first name?"

"Only if you promise not to laugh…"

"Wouldn't dream of laughing... With a name like mine, I'm not in a position to laugh."

"It's Cornelius. God knows where it comes from or why they chose it."

"They don't shorten it to 'Corny' do they?" Poor kid, I thought, if he went through school being call Corny.

"No. Everyone calls me Neil."

"Okay Neil; earlier this morning you said you had put in for transfer. Anywhere in particular you applied for?"

"Ralston or Millhaven, but I'd settle for anywhere in a bigger centre than this. Policing out here is limited. I'm not learning anything; not developing as a copper."

"What's your ultimate career ambition?"

"To make detective, I suppose. That's what I want to do, to be involved in solving crimes. I know it will take a while to work my way up, but that's okay if there is a chance I can make it."

"If you will excuse me, Neil, I have a couple of calls to make before we return to the table."

I slipped out into the hallway and called Ben Richards' number. He answered almost on the first ring. "Sonny, good to hear from you again; what's gone wrong now?"

"Sarcasm doesn't become you. Nothing has gone wrong, but I do have something to share with you. A young constable who spent the first eighteen months of his career out here has applied for a transfer to Millhaven. I don't know where you're at with your selection process, but you could do a lot worse than appoint this fellow."

In spite of Ben's scepticism, he listened while I explained why I believed Neil Pernell was excellent future detective material. The call went longer than expected. Ben seemed interested in all I had to say about Pernell. His parting comment took me by surprise.

"I'll take on board what you've said. Thanks for the heads-up about this bloke. He topped our short list of three applicants to interview anyway."

The sod could have told me that at the start of the call and saved us both time. I returned to the meeting room still feeling a bit miffed. Pete had resumed without me. They were revisiting stuff we covered earlier without adding anything new to the mix. Neil's phone chirped. I watched as he went to switch it off. My gut instinct told me he shouldn't do that. For all I knew, it could be his mother calling to ask what he would like for his birthday … but I didn't think so.

"Answer it, Neil. You should answer it. It might be important."

He gave me a confused look before scraping his chair back from the table and striding out into the dining room. He had the phone to his ear and was speaking to his caller by the time he took a couple of strides away from the table. It was some time before he returned to the meeting room. I noticed a renewed spring in his step, and he struggled unsuccessfully to keep his face deadpan. As he regained his seat, he addressed Pete.

"Apologies, Sir. As it turns out, it was an important call. I had to take it. Did I miss anything while I was away?"

"Nothing new..." Pete checked the time. "It's getting close to the 'appointed hour'. Sergeant McClelland should make an appearance at the police station within the next half hour if he is to open the station at twelve o'clock." His comment caused a flurry of wrist movement around the table as everyone followed his example and checked their watch. "I think we need someone in place to let us know when McClelland arrives at the station. We should give him a few minutes to settle in and begin work before we arrive."

Looks were exchanged, but no one questioned the proposal. After a few moments, when Pete asked if anyone had questions or anything to add, no one spoke.

"Right then, Thornton, you take my vehicle and park somewhere close to the station to watch for McClelland's arrival. Call me once he enters the building. We will allow a few minutes before the rest of us join you there."

"But, I'll have your vehicle, Sir. Wouldn't it be better if I walked to the coffee shop and kept watch from there? That way, you would still have your car if things go wrong."

"Ah, good thinking ... I had thought the rest of us might pile into the police vehicle with Pernell, but you are right. It would be better if Lewis went to the station with Pernell, and Sonny and I took my car. Your idea of keeping watch from the coffee shop is good. Give it another five minutes before you head off. If anything out of the ordinary occurs once McClelland arrives, call me straight away."

We spent the next few minutes refining Pete's plans for our assault on the police station. Then Thornton left. Pete walked him out to the street, probably to give him last minute instructions. As Pete and Thornton left the meeting room, Pernell leaned in closer.

"How did you know about that call I took?"

"I didn't. Still don't, and don't need to know. At the time, nothing important was happening here, nothing worth missing a call for anyway."

The look on his face told me he didn't believe a word of it. I smiled sweetly at him, my conscience clear. It was the truth. I didn't know who his caller was … but I had a damned good idea. While it was obvious he continued to doubt me, he decided to share with me anyway.

"One of my applications might be heading in the right direction. I've a phone interview this evening. Wish me luck."

Poor bloke; he must be bursting with excitement, and needed to tell someone about it. I put on my best grave face. "Oh dear, if your interview goes well, it could leave Cranvale district in a tricky position." He tilted his head to one side and drew his eyebrows together as he studied me. "I suspect your sergeant might not be stationed at Cranvale much longer, and if you go too…"

"It might be a good thing. They will have two new officers out here in a flash; be a fresh start for the station. All the old ways will disappear, leaving the place wide open for a new order of things – a new approach to policing in Cranvale."

I gave myself a mental pat on the back for my call to Ben Richards. Pernell was one astute lad. As I told Ben, he had the making of a good detective one day. I was excited for him. I hoped he would tell me how tonight's interview went, if I can engineer somehow to run into him tomorrow. Any chance to discuss things further was lost when Pete strode back into the room.

"That's phase one of the plan initiated. Now all we have to do is sit and wait for the good sergeant to arrive at the station. If no one has anything they want to discuss, I suggest we relocate to the dining room for an early lunch. Life might be a bit busy for the remainder of the day."

Twelve o'clock came and went with still no word from Thornton. Just before one o'clock, Pete's phone came to life. The rest of us sprung upright in our chairs as Pete's contribution to the call was a string of one-word responses. He didn't immediately return to his seat when the call ended, opting instead to prowl through the dining room and out to the reception area. It was the aimless wandering of someone deep in thought.

When he returned, he slumped in his chair, placed his phone on the table and sat studying it for a few heartbeats before speaking.

"It appears the sergeant is delayed. Is he often late returning from his tour of the properties?"

"I wouldn't know, Sir. I don't return to Cranvale after my jaunt around the countryside until nearly dark. He's always gone home by the time I'm back here."

"So, as a rule, you wouldn't expect to see him again until tomorrow morning. Was there ever any evidence he was in the station after returning from being out in the sticks?"

"Er, I don't think so, but it would be hard to tell. At the end of the day, all paperwork and anything else we worked on during the day is locked away. If you broke into the place at night, you might be forgiven for thinking no one had been in the place for ages."

The waiting could last the rest of the day, I warned myself. Rather than sitting around bored witless, I took myself off to my room to check emails and messages. That occupied me for half an hour. By then I felt guilty about abandoning the others. I returned to the meeting room to find the scene there much as it was when I left.

A quick check assured me I hadn't missed anything. Seated at the table again, I wondered how I might prevent dying of boredom while we waited for something to happen. About twenty minutes later, Pete's phone shattered the silence. The call was brief. Pete beamed as he ended the call.

"Well folks, attend to anything you need to during the next few minutes. We are about to drive to the police station. Our person-of-interest has returned. It's possible we will be busy for the remainder of the afternoon."

As Pete announced what we'd been waiting to hear for the last however many hours, I saw Pernell flick over his wrist for a quick check on the time, before giving Pete a hard look.

"Christ, the afternoon is more than half gone. He must've run into trouble out there somewhere to return this late. Maybe, before we do anything else, I should check if there's been an incident of some sort."

"Oh, I don't think there's any need for that, lad. We'll all go together and ask the man to tell us where he has been. I can understand if you're a bit nervous about being a part of what happens in the next while. So, if you would prefer to distance yourself from the exercise, now would be the time to say so. It won't cause a problem. The only difference will be that the three of us will drive to the station in my car, while you take your police vehicle and disappear somewhere. Take a snack with you though, and don't return to town until about your normal time."

Pernell appeared to give the suggestion some thought before responding. "No, that's not necessary. I expect life might be difficult at the station after this afternoon's events, but I'll manage it. I need to be a part of what happens next."

"Good lad; I knew you had it in you, but it takes guts to take down the lion in its den. Okay, I think that's enough time. Pick up your gear and head for my car. Today is about to get interesting."

Pete left none of us in any doubt the 'next stage of the plan', as we were calling it, was unlikely to be amongst the more pleasant experiences of life. It's a short drive from the motel to the police station. From the moment we climbed into the vehicle, I could feel my stomach tightening. It had developed into a heavy lead ball by the time we reached our destination.

In accordance with Pete's instructions, Pete strode into the station alone. Pernell, Lewis and I remained on the narrow front porch. Thornton joined us. For a few frustrating seconds, we heard nothing. Then the voices inside became raised. It was the cue for our grand entrance. Without any preliminary discussion, we automatically fell into line in the order of our relevance to proceedings. Lewis led the way, followed by Thornton and then Pernell. I tacked onto the end, and hung back near the door once we were inside.

McClelland looked as though he was about to burst a blood vessel. His face was bright red as he screamed obscenities at Pete. Pete appeared unruffled, his voice calm and quiet. From experience, I knew it wouldn't last long. When he finally snapped, it would not be a pretty thing. It seemed only moments later proceedings reached that breaking point.

The shocked look on McClelland's face was priceless when Pete reached across and shoved his ID almost on the end of McClelland's nose. "Sergeant McClelland, I would advise you to amend your tone. Already, your rant in front of several people – who would attest to the content of such rant – is enough to have you up on several charges of insubordination. Oh, don't worry too much. It's only of minor importance … so far."

While his voice remained calm and quiet, Pete's words had the desired effect. McClelland slumped back onto his chair. His red face slowly blanched. More than a hint of fear crossed his features, and one foot tap danced under the desk.

"That's better. Now we can discuss our problems in a civilised manner." McClelland went to speak, but Pete continued, preventing him from getting a word out. "Let's start with where you've been today. I don't want to know in general terms, I want to know exactly where you went, who you visited, and about anything that happened. Don't omit any details. They could prove important to you."

"I was on my usual run visiting properties south of here. It's a weekly thing. On the same morning every week, I do much the same run. The only thing different is, I vary the properties I call into. So, unless there is a problem at one of them, I tend not to visit the same properties as last week."

"Good approach. Were there any incidents out there today; anything you needed to investigate?"

McClelland shook his head. "No, there weren't any problems; nothing to investigate. There rarely is. The weekly trip is more about PR and maintaining a police presence across the area. It keeps us in touch with the property owners and what's going on around the place."

"That's well and good, but the sign outside says the station opens at twelve o'clock today. I want to know where you were until three o'clock, and what prevented you from opening up at twelve o'clock."

"You know how it is, some of those properties don't get many visitors. When someone calls in, they're up for a chat, a cup of tea, and maybe a piece of cake if you're lucky. You can't just say g'day and drive off. It would defeat the purpose of the exercise, if I didn't take the time to establish a good relationship with them."

"Yes, I know. But, I need you to tell me which properties you visited, who you spoke to, what you did or talked about while you were there – and, how long it took at each place."

McClelland hunched further down in his chair. He kept licking his lips, the stress was getting to him, not surprising I suppose with his hulking commanding officer leaning over him. Pete stared hard at him for a moment before suddenly standing up straight.

"Pernell, see if you can bring some water out here, and some glasses or mugs or something, so we can keep ourselves hydrated. Why don't we all relax until Pernell returns?" McClelland blinked a few times but didn't move. There was a danger, if he hunched down any further, he would slide under the desk and disappear from sight.

In no time Pernell was back carrying a blue and white cooler jug similar to those used by campers. He made a return trip to the kitchen to fetch a mismatched collection of glasses and coffee mugs. During the pause in activities while Pernell did his *Gunga Din* impersonation, I had a quiet word to Pete.

"I'll hang around as long as it's likely to be of relevance to my investigation. I doubt it will take long for your questioning to move into the area of police business only. When the time is right, I'll slope off and go back to the motel. Just ignore me if I leave, I don't want to interrupt proceedings." Pete nodded but made no comment.

There was something else I wanted to tell Pete, but I wasn't sure how to do it without breaking a confidence. Time was of the essence so, instead of trying to find the right words, I just launched into it.

"How long do you think this might continue for?" Pete shrugged. "Call me when you're free if you're interested in having dinner together. What will you do with McClelland? There is little doubt you want him charged but, in the meantime, you can hardly lock him up in one of his own cells. And, that would require someone on guard duty all night –probably Pernell. He's had a long day, and it's been a rough one for him. At the moment, I'm sure he's feeling both guilty and conflicted by everything that's happening."

"We won't make things any worse for him. What to do with McClelland won't be a problem either. He will have a nice flight back to Ralston at the government's expense. I've arranged for a light plane. It should be on the airstrip by five o'clock. In which case, I better get a move on if I am to achieve anything before the plane arrives."

As soon as everyone had a drink, Pete resumed his questioning. I stuck to my plan. When questioning moved into the area of police misconduct, I took my leave without as much as a nod to anyone. I was at the bottom of the steps when Pernell called my name softly before racing down the steps to join me.

"Has something happened, Sonny?" I was confused by the question. Pernell rushed on to explain. "I saw you sneak out, and wondered whether something was wrong, or if you were sent off to do something in relation to McClelland's questioning. Cranvale is a safe place, but it might not be so safe if you start digging around on your own."

"Neil, is that some sort of warning? If it is, perhaps you should explain yourself and why you felt it necessary to make the comment."

"What? No, of course not... Argh, I'm just a bit edgy after today's events. I was concerned about you going off to do something on your own."

"I'm going back to the motel. My involvement in this is finished. I didn't tell you this, but the inquisition happening in there has to be finished in time to have McClelland at the airstrip by five o'clock. He is being flown back to Ralston."

"Thank God for that. I was terrified I might have to stand guard over him in one of the cells tonight."

"No, no; you can't be doing that tonight. You have something much more important to attend to after you leave here. Good luck with the interview. Perhaps we'll catch up again tomorrow – and you can tell me how it went."

I watched Pernell go into the station before setting off on foot for the motel. The heat radiating off the street had me in a lather of sweat long before I reached my room. My first priority was a shower, followed soon after by a long cold drink. Between the shower and the drink, I had plenty of me-time to think about my investigation. My most important decision was whether to stay in Cranvale a little longer, or head to Ralston as soon as tomorrow.

It was too hard to decide. I'll leave the decision until I talk to Pete later tonight for an update on anything arising from his questioning. If his focus now is on investigating the activities of a bent copper, there's no reason for me to stay. Nevertheless, I'm dying to know exactly how 'bent' the copper is, and in what way.

Chapter 23

Dinner with Pete was late last night. He didn't return to the motel until well after seven o'clock. On his way back, he called room service and ordered dinner in my room for both of us. We both were tired, so it wasn't a late-night but, by talking 'shop' as we ate, I managed to gain everything I needed to know to decide about tomorrow.

"It looks like McClelland was setting himself up for a comfortable future retirement. Maybe it will come sooner than he expected. I assume his days in the Police Service are over as a result of his activities. I doubt I'll gain anything more out here. I'll check out in the morning and head for Ralston. I'll need to be back in Millhaven soon, but I could spend at least a couple of days in Ralston if I had access to Callum."

Callum's condition had improved according to Pete's latest information. I allowed myself to feel confident about being able to speak to him. Pete said he would arrange for the hospital and the police guards to allow me access as soon as possible. Neither of us felt much like talking. With nothing more to say about today's exercise, Pete returned to his own room before nine o'clock. I was thinking of climbing into bed when the phone rang.

"Sonny, I hope I didn't wake you." I assured Neil Pernell he did not wake me. "Good, I know it's late, but I wanted to tell you about my interview. I think the interview went well. I think it ended on a positive note … at least, I felt it did. Superintendent Richards thinks I'll receive a definite answer about the position sometime tomorrow."

After explaining my plans for the next two days, I gave him my mobile number and told him to call me regardless of the outcome of his interview. By the time the call ended, I didn't feel so tired. I packed most of my things in readiness for an early morning checkout. But, today must've been more tiring than I thought. From the moment my head hit the pillow, I was asleep.

*****

The dining room was deserted this morning. I didn't linger long before returning to my room to complete my packing, and then checking out. The drone pilot was on reception duty. My day received a boost when he expressed his disappointment at my leaving Cranvale. I promised, if I had time, I would drop by the drone flying competition. I didn't expect to see him there, but I was keen to see how good the other pilots were.

Then I was on the road for the long drive to Ralston. I stopped on the outskirts of town for a quick lunch at a coffee shop before heading into the hospital to check on Callum's condition. He was all but weaned off sedation. They reported he had a few lucid moments during the day, but he wasn't up to visitors yet. We agreed, if his progress continued, I might be able to talk to him after ten o'clock tomorrow morning.

A call at about seven o'clock took me by surprise. I splashed water on my face to freshen up, grabbed my bag and headed for the hospital. They called to say Callum was fully awake and, when he learned I was waiting in Ralston to see him, he demanded they call me. Rather than upset him by refusing, they waived the usual rules about visitors and asked me to come as soon as I could.

Pale and drawn and propped up in bed with pillows, Callum looked a whole lot better than when we found him in the vehicle on the track through the scrub. Aware he might be in a fragile psychological state, I eased into our meeting with the usual platitudes. In response to my enquiry, he admitted he felt weak and a bit detached from the world ... but he needed to talk to me. After all the usual warnings about not tiring him out and ending the meeting if it became too much for him, we got down to business. His opening gambit took me by surprise.

"What happened to Sherry? How is she? Nobody here will tell me anything about her."

I didn't know who Sherry was, but I guessed she was the woman in the vehicle with him. Last night Pete shared the update on her condition and, on my earlier visit to the hospital today, I asked after her. Callum's concern for her was a bit disconcerting. While I thought she had some part in his being held in the hut on the property, he seemed genuinely concerned about her condition.

The news wasn't good, but withholding it might cause stress. Choosing my words carefully, I tried putting a positive spin on a situation that was anything but positive. With the bad news delivered, I began a gentle exploration of the nature of his relationship with the young woman. I needed to know how things were between them before I started asking questions. It was too easy to say the wrong thing in ignorance, and perhaps hamper or reverse his recovery.

He took the news well enough and, for a fleeting moment, I wondered if, in my attempt to soften the blow, I had obscured the reality of her situation. His next comment reassured me I hadn't.

"I knew she was in a bad way. Of course I knew she was in a bad way. I caused it. What do the police know so far?"

"We'll come back to what the police do or don't know. For the moment, let's concentrate on why you think you caused Sherry's condition."

"It's a long story. If I only tell you how she became so badly injured, it won't make much sense. But, if I start at the beginning, it might take all night to get to the part about what happened to her."

He was becoming agitated, wringing his hands and swinging his head from side to side. I thought I detected a slight slur in his speech. It was time to bring this interview to an end, but without upsetting him further.

"You're right. To understand, I probably do need to know the story from start to finish. I would hate to be halfway through the story and have the hospital staff chuck me out because they were concerned I'd been in here too long and might be tiring you. Here's my suggestion: we leave the story until I come back in the morning. I'll try for an update on Sherry's condition before I see you. By then, they should be more relaxed about allowing me a longer visit with you."

While some persuasion was required, he agreed, on the proviso I came as early as possible. As I drove back to my hotel, I didn't know whether to feel excited or disappointed. Part of me was excited he wanted to tell me what happened. But, there was a tinge of disappointment. I had expected – hoped – to know more after my first meeting with him. I came away with what amounted to nothing about his disappearance or what happened afterwards.

As I sat sipping a drink before bed, I knew I was in for a long restless night. I also knew I would be at the hospital first thing tomorrow, regardless of their visiting rules.

*****

On my way to the hospital this morning, I remembered something Pete told me a couple of days ago. He approved for the hospital to let Emily know when Callum recovered sufficiently to receive visitors. First thing, I needed to know whether Emily had been advised of Callum's improved condition. She and I worked closely on a number of cases in the past but, with her so close to this one, I needed to handle it on my own … at least until I knew all of Callum's story.

The hospital wasn't overjoyed to see me, and went to great pains to explain it was far too early for visitors. I wasn't having much success persuading them this was different when one of the police officers on guard duty wandered up to the desk to see what all the fuss was about. It only took a few words from him to flatten ruffled feathers. I took a risk on pushing my luck too far and asked about Sherry's condition. The nurse was about to fob me off, but a hard look from the police officer changed her mind.

"There is no change in the young woman's condition. It remains critical and, at this stage, it seems unlikely she will improve."

Her news wasn't something I looked forward to passing on to Callum. I still didn't know about his relationship to Sherry, but I suspected the news her injuries were likely to prove fatal wouldn't sit well with him. As I made my way along the corridor to his room, I secretly hoped he already had that information.

Propped up in bed again and still connected to various tubes and machines much as he had been last night, Callum's colour was better this morning. I opened with platitudes again. Anxious to begin his story, he dismissed my attempt at small talk. The nurse on duty didn't know if anyone had contacted Emily since he regained consciousness. It meant I didn't know how long I might have before she arrived. I invited him to tell me his story in his own words, and in his own way, and promised not to interrupt until he finished.

"The whole thing started at the B&S ball. It had been a boring weekend, and the ball was no better. I suppose I was a bit put out when Emily agreed to have a dance with some bloke just as we were about to leave the hall. The bar looked inviting, so I took a drink and sat by myself on one of the hay bales spread out around the bar for that purpose. A young woman wandered over and we started chatting. Things became increasingly rowdy around the bar. We were shouting to make ourselves heard. She suggested we finish our drinks at her camp where it was quieter."

"I know I said I wouldn't interrupt until you finished, but I need to clarify one thing before we proceed: is the young woman you mentioned Sherry?"

"Yeah. She had a tent rigged up off the side of her SUV like an annex. We made ourselves comfortable on a couple of camp chairs, introduced ourselves, and I asked her if she was from one of the properties in the area. She laughed: *God, no. I'm from the other side – one of the enemy.* I asked her to explain. She said she was involved with the mining company. That was all I needed to hear. I adopted my dumb city slicker routine, and told her how I'd heard the mining company mentioned in unsavoury terms since my arrival, and persuaded her to help me understand what all the fuss was about."

There was a short break in the story when a nurse came in to attend to routine observations and generally fuss around her patient. It wasn't the same nurse I'd spoken to earlier. She gave me a filthy look on her way out. It was clear she disapproved of my presence. Callum craned his neck to watch her leave the room and disappear from view before resuming his story.

"I think I overplayed my hand. I thought I might gather some good material for an article, but I misjudged Sherry. She waxed lyrical about how the mining company was going to be the salvation of the community, a community on the bones of its backside as a result of the long drought. And, she criticised and dismissed as ludicrous all those in the community who opposed fracking.

It was when she was on about fracking, I made my mistake. I couldn't help it; probably thanks to the grog. I told her: *Then, the mining company hasn't a clue what it's doing. Why are they considering it? It's a ridiculous proposal. This area isn't suitable for fracking. CSG extraction should be a simple matter out here, and won't require fracking.*

She defended the mining company: *Shows how much you know. You sound just like one of the ill-informed locals. It's all about the modern technology that makes it possible to extract CSG out here.* I argued with her, and flexed my ego. The debate went on for a bit until she demanded to know why I thought I was an authority on such matters. I told her I was a geologist and it was my business to know. I should have shut up. It was obvious to me, even in my drunken state, she was totally pro-mining company. For a few moments, she seemed to take my comments as a personal affront before calming down and suggesting another drink."

"What could I do? I knew I'd blown it with her. The best I could do was to have another drink and hopefully calm her down. I don't know what was in the drink, but I don't remember anything more of that night. When I woke up again in totally unfamiliar surroundings, I had no idea what day it was. It took me a few moments to realise I was locked in a building. It was dark, there were no windows, and the door looked as though it might be a challenge for a bulldozer to knock it down. How long I had been out to it remains a mystery."

"Have you any idea how long they kept you there?"

"No, there was no way of knowing. I cursed myself for not having a watch which showed the date. But, it would have been useless anyway. It was so dark in there, I wouldn't be able read it. The only time any light entered the room was when someone brought me food and water. I had no toilet, but I tripped over a bucket in the dark and decided to use that. No one was too interested in emptying it."

His story continued in much the same way: locked in the dark with no way of knowing what day it was. He knew others were around. Vehicles came and went, and he heard snippets of conversation when people were close by. At first he thought he was gathering valuable information for the expose he planned to write. Then the reality of his situation dawned on him. They didn't care what he overheard because he wouldn't be writing anything. He wouldn't be around to write anything ever again. His story moved on to early the morning of our first visit to the property.

"Then, one morning there was a sudden change." He shook his head as if to clear it of bad memories before again starting to tell me about the change. "Nothing changed until the other morning. I knew it was morning because it was half way to sun up when they took me outside. Sherry and a bloke dragged me out of my cell. I had a brief glimpse of the world outside before they pulled a bag of some sort over my head. After they tied me up, they bundled me into the back of their vehicle and took me somewhere. I know don't know where they took me, but it was not too far from where I had been held. My new prison wasn't much better, but it was larger than the previous one. A few hours later, I thought I heard people outside. Whatever it was Sherry injected me with before they left me there, it knocked me out straight away. It was as I was coming out of it, I thought I heard the people outside, but I passed out again. The next time I came to, every-thing was quiet. In the meantime, someone had left bread and a small bottle of water. I think it was night by then."

"This is useful information, Callum, but we should take a break if you start feeling stressed or tired."

"I'm fine and I want to tell the whole story while it is fresh in my mind … or as fresh as it can be under the circumstances."

I nodded and gestured for him to continue. After a couple of sips of water, he began again.

"It might have been the next day, but I think it was two days later … the sequence of events is a bit foggy. Anyway, it was before sun up, when Sherry arrived. She seemed in a hurry and jabbed me with something again before dragging me out and loading me into a vehicle. The same vehicle I crashed. I don't know if it was because she was in a hurry, but she didn't give me enough of that stuff. It didn't knock me out, just made me groggy; drowsy.

"Being injected with unknown substances concerns me. Have you mentioned it to the doctors? They will need to run some tests. I'm sure the police will require them as well."

"No, not yet; there hasn't been opportunity. Shall I continue?" I gestured for him to proceed. "It was still dark outside when Sherry came that last time. She was on her own , but I was half knocked out, so she was able to jam me into the cargo area of the SUV. Then she drove like a maniac across some pretty rough country. I was almost car sick. During the last part of the trip, I could hear what I thought were tree branches bashing against the vehicle. And then we had arrived."

"Okay, but where were you? Were you able to see where you were this time?"

"When we first pulled up, I pretended I was a lot more out of it than I was. Sprawled in the cargo area, I couldn't see much. I know Sherry looked over at me. She must've decided I was out to it and not going to give her any trouble, so she just left me there while she got out of the car and went somewhere. It was my chance to have a look around. Without moving too much, I lifted my head a little to look out through the windows. There was scrub around us, but we seemed to be in a clearing of some sort, a clearing with a number of shipping containers."

"You took a risk. Sherry might only be gone briefly."

"Yep, she was gone only a few moments, but I had to do something. I had to work out how to get away. My chance to work out where we were came to an end when I heard a door slam. Then she was back in the car. We drove a short distance before stopping again. She got out of the car, and I heard rattling and clanking, before she came to the rear of the vehicle and dragged me out. I flopped over her as if I was so groggy I couldn't stand up. She had to half carry me into an open shipping container."

"I appreciate the time between car and shipping container was brief, but did you see any more of where you were?"

"You're right. I had no chance to look at my surroundings, and I was busy putting on a show of mounting some resistance. It wasn't all show. I would have scarpered if I could. After belting me one to quieten me down, she dragged me into the shipping container and dumped me on the floor at the far end. She threw a bottle of water onto the floor beside me, and turned to leave. I knew she was going to lock me in, and she confirmed it as she turned to walk away. I'll remember her words forever: *I'm off now. Be a good boy and don't make too much noise. She stopped and laughed. On second thoughts, make as much noise as you like. No one is going to hear you out here. If you're lucky, I'll be back in a day or two. Don't do anything silly while I'm gone.*

"What changed her mind? It's obvious she had second thoughts about leaving you there. We found both of you in the vehicle after the accident."

"I don't think she had second thoughts … but I did. She was facing the door; didn't look at me while she spoke. I didn't like the picture she painted of my future, so I lashed out with an almighty kick. It took the legs out from under her. She crashed backwards onto the floor, almost landing on top of me. It's as well she didn't, but that's when the damage occurred. As she fell, she hit the back of her head on a steel reinforcing column on the side of the container. It opened the back of her skull up pretty badly. She just lay there. A pool of blood spread across the floor. I knew her injury was bad, but I also knew it was my one chance for freedom."

"You're lucky she was operating on her own and nobody else was around. Things might have ended quite differently if some of the others were there."

"I thought about that, but I hadn't heard or seen anyone after we arrived. Nevertheless, I half expected some big lump to rush in to see what was going on. I just lay there – I don't know how long – straining my ears for any sound to suggest others were around. Nothing happened … No one showed up … It was my chance to get away. But I knew she was badly injured. Her eyes had rolled back in her head. I didn't like the look of her condition, and I knew I was responsible for it. I had to get us both away from there and find help."

Isn't it always the way? Just as you're getting to the dénouement, something happens to interrupt the story. In this case, a doctor and some other medical staff arrived. I headed for the door. The doctor called after me. He suggested I get a coffee or something as they probably would be with Callum for about twenty minutes. The nearest vending machine was on the floor below, but so was the cafeteria. If I was going down to that floor, I might as well go to the cafeteria and have a decent coffee in comfort. I wasn't keeping an eye on the time. When I checked my watch, half an hour had elapsed.

The medical staff took longer than expected. They were exiting Callum's room when I arrived back on his floor. I felt my stomach tightened when the doctor took me aside. He reminded me about not tiring Callum, and then added that he was very pleased with the lad's progress. I asked him if Emily had been notified. He shook his head and said the police had advised waiting a day or two before contacting her. After I explained my relationship with Emily, he agreed to my request to let me update her on Callum's situation, but suggested I leave it until tomorrow – in accordance with the police's request.

After the medical team moved on, I didn't immediately return to Callum's room. I flopped into a chair in a small waiting area near the nurse's station and spent a few minutes going over in my mind everything he told this morning.

Chapter 24

We reached what I thought must be the final chapter of his story, and I was keen to get on with it. Callum had other ideas.

"Do you know how Sherry is? I asked the doctor, but he wouldn't tell me anything. He just asked if I was family. He knows I'm not, but he still went through the performance of telling me if I wasn't a family member he couldn't discuss another patient. Surely he at least could tell me how she is in general terms, without going into any of the details."

"Callum, you know her information is confidential. Apart from a breach of patient confidentiality, it would be illegal for him to discuss her in any way with you."

"Argh, I know, but her condition is important to me. Sonny, can't you find out something for me?" I opened my mouth to explain my situation was no different from his, but he continued before I got a word out. "Look, I'm not a fool. I know she was in a critical condition. It doesn't matter what her condition is now, I can handle it. I caused it, and not knowing is eating at me. Please try to find out something for me; maybe ask one of your police mates to find out for you."

"Are you sure you want the truth?"

"Christ, yes. Haven't I just explained how important it is to me?"

"Okay, don't go getting yourself all excited. I'm sure it would not do you any good at all. I did enquire about Sherry's condition, both last night and again this morning. There's been no change; no improvement. If you want the truth, they don't expect there will be any improvement."

"Are you saying she is going to remain… Oh, I see that's not what you're saying. You're telling me she is not going to make it, aren't you? Her injury will prove fatal?"

Nervous about how he might handle the news, I only nodded in response and sat silently watching him for a few moments. He appeared to digest the information while I watched for any adverse reaction. Without looking up at me, he murmured 'good to know' a couple of times. Then, he slid his eyes up to meet mine, took a deep breath and launched back into the story.

"Well, when her injury happened, I knew it was bad. And, I knew I had to get away from them. She had the car keys in her hand when she went down and they skated some distance across the floor. I was still groggy but somehow I seemed to be more in control. Maybe an adrenaline rush had me thinking more clearly. I scrambled up, grabbed the keys and raced out to the vehicle. It wasn't locked. I put the key in the ignition, opened the cargo area, and went back into the container for her. I didn't have the strength to lift and carry her out to the car. So, with the rear of the car still open, I reversed it up to the container until the car's open hatch and the container doorway were level. I suspect she picked up a few bruises as I hauled her up off the floor and shoved her into the rear of the vehicle."

"I doubt any bruises she received from that are of any consequence in the long run. So, once you loaded her into the car, you attempted to drive to freedom?"

"Yeah… No … I don't think I thought about freedom so much as getting away from wherever we were and making it safely into Cranvale. My thoughts were more about police and hospitals, but freedom was in the mix as well. I had no idea where I was going. With only one track out of the clearing, no decision on where to go was required. It all gets a bit blurry after that. I remember driving along the track through the scrub. It looked like it was deliberately cleared. After a while, up ahead, I spotted another track leading off to the left. I don't remember it as a deliberate decision, but I might have turned off onto the side track. Whether due to the adrenaline wearing off, or the stuff she jabbed me with earlier in the morning taking over again, I became groggy and struggled to focus. Tree branches slapped the side of the vehicle. I struggled to keep it on the track."

That must be the point at which the accident happened, I thought as he lapsed into silence. I let the silence drag for the best part of a minute. It was important for him to be the one to tell the end of the story. At last, he gave me a wry smile, and apologised.

"Sorry; I was churning through my memory bank in the hope of finding something more. There's nothing, nothing at all beyond that point until I woke up here in the hospital. How about filling in the end of my story for me?"

It didn't take long to tell him how we found him and Sherry in the crashed vehicle on the track through the scrub after I spotted the car when I flew the drone. He didn't react. I told myself it might be a good sign. But, the story had ended. It's the reason I was there: to hear his story. But there was one more important question I felt needed to be asked.

"I don't want to make this into an inquisition of mammoth proportions, so I am going to call time on this interview for now. I will come back to talk further with you later this afternoon. In the meantime, I'd like you to do something for me: think about anything and everything you heard while you were being held … not just overhead snippets of conversation, but sounds, smells … anything at all you remember. There is a proviso, you must think about it only if it doesn't bother you. If you start feeling tense or upset, forget about it. Have a sleep or do something to take your mind off it again. Don't be concerned if nothing more than you've already mentioned comes to mind."

As I stood and dragged my bag up off the floor beside my chair, I said, "Get some rest now." I had taken only a couple of steps towards the door when he spoke.

"How is Emily? I mean, how is she coping with all this? More important than that, what does she think of me after all that's happened?"

"That's something you will have to ask her. As I'm not a mind reader, I've no way of knowing what she thinks about anything. I can tell you she phoned me in the wee small hours of the morning shortly after you disappeared from the ball. She was upset and worried and remained that way. She refused to leave Cranvale until she knew you'd been found and were being treated here in Ralston. As soon as she knew, she left for Ralston and tried to see you. When they told her it might be a while before she could, she went back to Millhaven to wait for word you had regained consciousness."

"So, what happens now? I doubt she'll want to see me after all that's happened. She is entitled to an apology, and I need to try to explain what happened. I know what happened doesn't excuse my behaviour. Is she likely to call me, or maybe come to see me when she learns I'm okay again?"

"I can't answer that but, after I leave here, I will call her to update her on your situation. Then, it's up to her what happens. That's enough for now. I'll see you again later."

Callum must feel drained after this morning's session. It left me feeling exhausted. Rather than go up to my room, after parking my car at the hotel, I opted for a long stroll along the Esplanade. A cool breeze was coming off the river, and the trees provided welcome shade. The stroll gave me a chance to organise my thoughts and plan what to say to Emily when I called. At certain intervals along the Esplanade, in the densest areas of shade, the Council had provided bench seats for people to sit and contemplate the river. I parked myself on one of them with the clear intention of calling Emily.

As I scrabbled around in my bag for my phone, my hand found my tape recorder. Callum's story had ended none too soon this morning. The recording had almost reached capacity and would have stopped within a few minutes. I listened to a few random excerpts to check the quality of the recording. With the machine operating from in my bag on the floor of Callum's room, I couldn't be sure how much was recorded and whether any of it was recoverable. It was perfect, even recording the rattle of my spoon as I stirred my coffee in the cafeteria. A major transcription task lay ahead of me. While it was pleasant watching the pelicans working the river, it wasn't dealing with the call to Emily I needed to make.

She wasn't available, but returned my call about ten minutes later. There was obvious relief and lots of questions; not such a difficult call after all. Then, she dropped a bombshell.

"I'm attending a conference in Ralston on Monday and Tuesday, and booked into my hotel for three nights. I planned to drive to Ralston on Sunday afternoon, but I could arrive earlier and call in to see Callum if it's possible. I have been concerned about him, but visiting him in hospital would be more like a courtesy visit than anything else. I don't feel anything – nothing at all, one way or the other – for him anymore, but I feel an obligation to at least talk to him. Apart from anything else, I think such a visit might put the whole episode to rest for me. Afterwards, I should be able to move on without giving it another thought."

I knew where she was coming from, and was inclined to agree that talking to Callum might put an end to the whole thing for her. Before we finished the call, she made me promise to share Callum's story with her once life settled back to normal in Millhaven. By the time life was normal again, I might even have my head around the whole story and all its implications. In the meantime, my gut was telling me I should call Pete to find out what he's discovered today.

While it was quite pleasant when I availed myself of this bench, the heat of the day had intruded. An air-conditioned room in the hotel waited for me. I could pick up something for a late lunch on the way back there. Sometime afterwards, I'll call Pete, and maybe Sam Keller, to see if there's anything new today.

Pete's phone was engaged. While I didn't expect her to answer, I tried my luck and called Sam. She answered almost straight away. We arranged to have dinner at a little Italian place she knows in a quiet part of the city. My call wasn't wasted though. She gave me an outline of the information extracted earlier from one of the mining mob, and promised to share full details tonight.

It was almost six o'clock when Pete discovered his missed call and rang me. He said he was busy, and it sounded like he was in a meeting.

"I don't have much time now, but I'd like to catch up with you first thing tomorrow morning. I'm leaving here early, and should be in Ralston by about nine o'clock."

He arranged to meet me at the hotel as soon as he was back in town. The other information I gained from his call was that Lewis wouldn't be returning with him. Lewis was to stay on in Cranvale to fill the gap created by McClelland's departure. Once the call ended, I returned to transcribing this morning's session with Callum. It would take about another hour to complete. I wanted it finished and out of the way before I met Sam for dinner. Failing that, even if it meant a late-night, I was determined to have it finished before I met with Pete tomorrow.

Dinner with Sam was fabulous: good authentic food, nice wine and, best of all, it was enlightening. The mining mob member who decided to tell all had provided tantalising clues about Cranvale's mayor, Roland Garnham. They were tantalising enough to have Sam and her crew of detectives working flat out all afternoon. It seems Mr Garnham has been busy, and might be playing a dangerous game.

"I haven't had a chance to give Pete all this information yet, so keep quiet about it," Sam warned me. "It seems Garnham held power of attorney and the health directive for Edna Newman, his adoptive mother. The woman has been quite ill, and a few days ago took a turn for the worse. Garnham rushed to the nursing home where she was being cared for only to be told Mrs Newman probably wouldn't last more than twenty-four hours. She passed away yesterday. Unless there is another will nobody knows anything about, Garnham is about to score well from her death. Of course, he won't be able to do much until probate is granted, but there is some suggestion he's been exercising his power of attorney to his own advantage for some time now. Apart from a considerable amount of cash, his inheritance includes at least two large parcels of land."

"It doesn't sound like it's criminal activity, so why are the police interested in the situation?"

"Ah well, that's what we are not sure about yet, and it's why dinner is not going to drag on for long tonight. My bloodhounds are still sifting through information. We'll probably be doing so for most of the night. It's imperative we have everything tied up tight as soon as possible. From my point of view, I'd prefer the majority of it was done before Pete is back in Ralston tomorrow."

"You might have a little extra time in the morning. I've arranged to meet with Pete at the hotel as soon as he's back in town. Don't know how long that might last, but it might give you some time if you're still trying to tie up loose ends."

"Did he mention he was leaving Lewis behind in Cranvale. Proceedings have started against McClelland. No doubt, the *Police Gazette* will soon be advertising a vacancy there."

Maybe more than one vacancy, I thought. If Pernell's interview went as well as he believed, there might be a complete turnover of officers at Cranvale police station. By eight o'clock I was back in my room and had finished transcribing this morning's interview by a little after nine o'clock. I took my drink and sat by the window to take in the lights and sounds of the city below. It was a quiet time for gathering thoughts and trying to make sense of events since that fateful B&S ball.

By the time I climbed into bed around midnight, I had decided to go to the hospital first thing in the morning to spend maybe an hour or so with Callum before meeting Pete here at the hotel. That's the trouble with sitting and thinking, you come up with a whole lot of questions to which no one has given you answers. I would like some of those answers before catching up with Pete.

*****

The nurse on duty made no secret of her reluctance to allow me to see Callum so early in the morning. I was feeling sufficiently belligerent to threaten to call one of the police officers on guard duty to sort her out. Having made my threat, I didn't wait for a reaction, but simply flounced off to Callum's room and marched in.

"I hadn't expected visitors quite so early this morning but, now you're here, what shall we discuss today?" he said with a grin.

"Yesterday, in the early stages of your story about your disappearance, you mentioned asking Sherry about why the mining company planned using fracking to extract the coal seam gas. You went on to say the geology of this area wasn't suitable for the use of fracking. It struck me as odd such a big mining company wouldn't know that."

"Ah, it seems I left a vital piece of information out of my story. Their threat to use fracking is all a ploy. The company knew it would stir everyone up, resulting in protests and divisions within the community. I suppose it's a case of 'what unites us, divides us'. The drought has been hard on everyone out there. Many have gone to the wall. Businesses have closed. Some have been forced to walk off their land with nothing. But the drought served to unite the community in a common cause.

It strengthened the bonds within the community. Then along came the mining company with its talk of fracking. While in better times, there would have been unanimous opposition to any such suggestion, in the present environment, some were prepared to put their true feelings aside in the interest of securing an income and protecting their families."

"Yes, I understand what you're saying, but it doesn't answer the question of why the company would employ fracking when there are contra indications for its use."

"I was coming to that. The company's intention was to rile the community and create as much opposition and civil unrest as it could before appearing to stage a back-down. Such a back-down would appear to be the company's acquiescing to the community's wishes. They would announce scrapping their plans for fracking in favour of more conventional means of extraction. While the community would remain unhappy with the prospect of any method of CSG extraction, the company gambled on their about-face winning over a considerable portion of the dissenters."

"Let me get this straight. You are telling me there never was any intention to employ fracking in the area?"

"Yes, that's exactly what I'm telling you, Sonny ... And a number of the town's leading lights were aware of the ruse from the outset. The mayor was an ardent supporter of the company, and facilitated much of what was happening in town. Some of the comments I heard also pointed the finger at the local police sergeant, who it seems was doing quite nicely out of turning a blind eye to whatever went on around the place."

Time had run out. I needed to return to the hotel. Without elaborating, I told Callum I had a meeting to attend and might return again later in the day. Pete didn't arrive until almost ten o'clock, so I had a little time to put a few more pieces of the puzzle together. By the time he arrived, I was sure there was nothing else I needed to know about Cranvale or Callum's disappearance, and I could happily return to Millhaven as early as tomorrow.

Chapter 25

The rest of the day became something of a blur. My meeting with Pete turned into a sort of hybrid cross between morning coffee and brunch. While providing a few of the finer details, most of his information only served to confirm what I already knew. I gave him a printout of the transcript of yesterday's session with Callum, and told him I probably would head back to Millhaven in the morning. As he was leaving, I also remembered to tell him Emily was arriving sometime this afternoon.

Then, Pete was hurrying off to a meeting with Sam, and I was happy to retreat to my room. I was adding Callum's comments from this morning to yesterday's transcript when Neil Pernell called. I heard the excitement in his voice the moment he said hello. Ben Richards had not long called to offer him a position at the Millhaven precinct. They arranged for Neil to take up his new post at the end of the month. He already had submitted an application for leave for the week prior to relocating to Millhaven.

Emily knocked on my door at about two o'clock. She was keen for me to accompany her to the hospital. I wasn't sure it was the right thing to do. We eventually agreed I would accompany her when she first went in to see Callum, but would leave immediately to allow them to say whatever needed to be said to each other. I hoped to hear how the meeting went over dinner with Emily in the hotel's restaurant tonight.

In accordance with our agreement, at the hospital, I went in with Emily to meet with Callum, and then left. As I pulled out of the hospital's parking lot, I remembered the drone flying competition and Melvin, the young drone pilot from the Cranvale motel. Instead of returning to the hotel, I detoured to an area on the outskirts of town where the competition was being held. My timing was perfect.

The semi-finals of the competition were in progress. I heard Melvin's name announced, and was barely able to watch as he put his drone through its paces. He won his heat. About an hour later, I was trying to control the frisson of excitement racing through me as he launched his drone in the championship final. The other finals competitor appeared more confident than Melvin. I heard someone in the crowd say the other bloke flew drones as part of his job with some agricultural systems company. My heart sank. I was sure he would take out the championship.

Melvin's performance stunned me. I knew he was competent, but his performance was every bit deserving of his win. His grin was so wide when they presented him with the trophy, I feared his face would split. As soon as the presentation was over I rushed to congratulate him. He seemed genuinely moved I bothered to come to watch him perform. From the outset, I thought he was a nice lad. Today confirmed it.

I went down to the restaurant a little earlier than arranged with the intention of sitting quietly with a drink while I waited for Emily to join me. She was already there with drink in hand. My initial reaction was concern. Had things gone badly at the hospital, and so badly she needed a drink?

"No, it was fine. It was all quite civilised, and I'm pleased I went to see him. I suspect we won't be friends in the future – probably more like casual acquaintances. While I have to admit to being nervous about how the meeting would go, it ended on a pleasant, friendly note. Sonny, in future, please step in and protect me from myself if I look like doing something stupid."

"Something stupid … like what?"

"Like becoming involved with people with whom I'm definitely not suited; people like Callum. If I'm honest, I knew what he was like from the outset. I just didn't want to accept the truth. He told me you had the whole story of his disappearance, and I should talk to you rather than have him tell me about it. By the way, do you know anything more about the woman who was in the vehicle with him?"

"Her name is Sherry. I don't know anything more about her other than I think she has a police record. Nothing major I don't think; just petty stuff. She probably got in with the wrong crowd somewhere along the line."

"What's she like?"

"What do you mean? What do you want to know?"

"Argh, come on, Sonny. You know what I mean: how old is she, what does she look like? A girl needs to know about the competition she lost out to. So, come on, tell me about her."

"Ooh, I think I see a little green monster lurking about. You've nothing to feel jealous about. I'd be guessing if I tried to put an age to her. I suspect she is quite young – probably in her early twenties. She's probably had a hard life and it's taken its toll. I can't tell you much about what she looks like. She didn't look too flash when we found her in the back of the car after the accident, and she doesn't look great now with her head in bandages and tubes running in and out of her every-where. She has quite a few tattoos, and she is about as skinny as a brolga's leg … and about as attractive."

"Depends on whether you're a brolga, I suppose…"

"Very funny…! Anyway, she wasn't competition. Outside the hall on the night of the ball, Callum only thought he was going to have a drink with her."

"Yes, I suppose you're right, but it's hard to accept he wasn't attracted to her before everything turned sour for him."

"As I said, she was not your competition. No, don't interrupt. There's more you should know. You had competition, plenty of it – but Sherry wasn't part of it. I think Callum was a serial collector of scalps before all this happened. I doubt he'll be foolish enough to have a stable of women on the go at the same time in future."

Dinner wasn't late again tonight. Emily needed some time alone to come to terms with everything she learned today. I was happy to retreat to my room to pack in readiness to leave first thing in the morning. There was a certain excitement about the prospect of being at home in my own bed tomorrow night.

*****

After driving to Millhaven in the cool of the morning, I spent the afternoon in my office in the city. Ben Richards' appearance late in the afternoon came as a surprise. I hadn't let him know I was returning today.

"Good to see you're back and in one piece. Anything special you'd like me to bring for dinner tonight? I should be free and able to be at your place by seven o'clock. And, I don't want to waste too much time on eating. I want all the juicy details of your jaunt in the country. I know my mate, Pete, will be 'judicious' about what he shares with me. You'd think two old friends holding the same positions in two adjoining precincts would share information freely and openly with each other. Funny how it doesn't seem to happen that way."

I just about managed not to laugh. Ben, Pete and I go back a long way. Our friendship is as solid as any. It's because of that friendship we can work together so well when situations call for it. I know, the next time they talk, Pete will share with Ben every last detail of what went on out west. Ben's problem is impatience. He wants to know all about it now, and hence I haven't even managed to unpack before he has reinstated our usual arrangement of having dinner together. It is not because he missed my riveting company. It's because he wants to know tonight everything he would have to wait to hear from Pete.

Aaah … It is good to be home and to have everything back to normal. The only thing bothering me at the moment is this strange tingle of excitement I'm experiencing at the thought of having a quiet dinner with Ben. Can't imagine what that's all about. Dinner at my house with Ben Richards is a fairly regular event when we are both in town.

The End.

Thanks

Thank you for reading my book. I hope you enjoyed it. If you did, please consider taking a moment to leave a review at your favourite retailer.

Thanks

Neive Denis